Aka

Aka

TRISTAN JONES

SHERIDAN HOUSE

First paperback edition
published 1998 by
Sheridan House Inc.
145 Palisade Street
Dobbs Ferry, New York 10522

First published 1981 by Macmillan Publishing Co., Inc.

Library of Congress Cataloging-in Publication Data

Jones, Tristan, 1924-1995
   Aka.

   I. Title.
PR6060.059A77   823'.914   81-7279
                                    AACR2

Printed in the United States of America

ISBN 1-57409-026-7

To *Dagon,* for the dolphins, that they may be spared
further slaughter by man.

Da cael ynys mor mawr.
(It is good to find an island in an ocean.)
Cyrys ar Yale (Welsh bard) *The Red Book of*
Talgarth (A.D. 1400).

Antigua, Guadaloupe,
Santo Domingo, Copenhagen,
and Manhattan, January–
December 1980.

(Dagon was the main god of the Philistines, and later
of the Phoenicians. He was represented with the upper part of a man and the tail of a dolphin.)

Contents

Foreword

THIS STORY is not told only for ocean-yacht-racing enthusiasts, nor only for experts, nor only for perfectionists in any field.

My tale is told also for those who have never stepped on board an ocean-sailing vessel, who have never known the elation of running free before the wind under a star-laden sky, who have rarely seen our wonderful relatives, the mammals of the sea, except in captivity.

If my tale can bring to people ashore a little of the joy, a little of the elation and wonder, and even a mite of the pain and suffering that voyagers and other mammals know at sea, then any carping of pierhead critics will be to this book as the squeaks of an unoiled sheet-block are to a vessel safely at anchor in her own quiet haven.

Acknowledgments

TO Professor Charles H. Hapgood, author of *Maps of the Ancient Sea Kings* (E. P. Dutton)

To Surgeon Commander F. St. C. Golden, Royal Navy, senior medical officer (survival medicine), Institute of Naval Medicine, Alverstoke, England, for valuable information on the effects of immersion of a human in seawater for a prolonged period

To Lieutenant Colonel Peter Thomas, Royal Marines (Ret.), Secretary, Royal Naval Sailing Association, Portsmouth, England, for his patience and assistance in making valuable contacts.

To International Marine Paint Company, New Jersey, for information on cupreous traces in seawater.

To the members of the Atlantic Society, for their faith in the past and hope for the future.

To the survivors of the last warship of the World War II Polish navy, who lent me the hallowed name of their ship, *Blytskwtska*; for their superb examples in gallantry.

Part 1: Departure

Tursiops truncatus, a subspecies of the family Delphinidae, of the order Ceteacea, is known to sailors as the bottle-nosed dolphin. In North America some landsmen call them the "common porpoise."

Chapter 1

THE LONGEST AKA'S DOLPHIN TRIBE ever stays in one area is when the females give birth. All through their history, as long as the legends of their Wise Ones reached back, their calves had been born in the warm waters that wash the two lonely rocks in the equatorial mid-Atlantic.

Aka and the Wise Ones, in the tale-telling times, transmit holographic images to the rest of the 143 bottle-nosed dolphins in the tribe of how their home had once been, before the seas rose and covered all but the two tiny islets, the very top of the highest peak of the beautiful land that had been Atlantis, the home-island of the Sea Kings. The Atlanteans had been different from modern Man, "say" the Wise Ones. True, they had fished, but they had never harmed or purposely murdered the dolphins. On the contrary, the Sea Kings had learned to communicate with them, and had included the dolphins in their pantheon of gods, and in return the dolphins had herded the fish for the Atlanteans and accompanied the Sea Kings on their voyages of trade and exploration.

Eventually, after eons of time, the waters had swiftly risen and it had been time for the last of the Sea Kings to leave once-lovely Atlantis in the warm seas. On their long graceful ships with purple sails the Sea Kings had figureheads of dolphins cast in gold, and as they hauled their anchors for the last time their high priest had made a vow that when they reached their new home in the inland sea, they would raise a temple which would be the new center of the world and they would name it in honor of their sea gods. *Eh-ee*, the name of the temple, had come down in the dolphin legends through twelve thousand years and twelve thousand treks around the North Atlantic Ocean. It was the closest the dolphins could come to pronouncing the human word *Delphi*.

Each August, when the calves are two to three months old, the dolphins of Aka's tribe leave the lonely rocks, now known to humans as St. Paul's, and make their way, by taste and their guiding stars, into the west-flowing Guinea Current, warm after its long traipse up the west African coast. They do not hurry. The fish scouts and the shoal herders range up to a hundred miles either side of the main body of 112 dolphins. After two months in the warm Guinea Current, they join the North Equatorial Current, which flows down the coast of Africa from the north and swings west across the ocean to the West Indies. The tribe roams around the West Indies Islands for three months; there the fish abound from October to December. Then it is time to move northeast, into the Gulf Stream. It takes the tribe four months to make its way east across the North Atlantic, ranging north almost as far as Iceland, to their traditional landfall of Cape Finisterre, the northwest tip of Spain. From then on, as they continue south, is their mating time, from Finisterre to the Moroccan coast.

From Finisterre, the dolphins steadily make their way south during March and April, south in the cool Portugal current, in a vast area which extends right down the coast of Portugal, across the herring, cod, and pilchard-teeming Straits of Gibraltar, right down to the coast of Mauritania, where the shoals of mullet darken the oceans like undersea clouds. They do not swim along in a direct route, but range as far west as Madeira and the Canary Islands, and sometimes they even visit into the Mediterranean as far east as the Balearic Islands and Corsica; but, by their ancient law, no further.

By mid-April each year the tribe has plowed its way through the Cape Verde Islands and, always with several females heavy with calf from the previous year's mating, heads southwest by south, right across the Guinea Current again, in a line as straight as an arrow, guided as always by their taste and the stars, back to the two lonely warm islets and the safe inlet, which is all that remains of Atlantis, which has always been their ancestral home, ever since the dawning of their recorded history twenty million years ago.

Conan reread the telegram, picked up the phone, and as he dialed, reminded himself not to mention the name *Josephine*. Outside, the New York traffic roared.

"Ruth," he said in a slight Scottish burr, "I want to see you urgently . . . no, I don't want to discuss it on the phone . . . I have to go away for a while . . ."

He listened for a moment, then he said, "Okay, Formelli's then, at seven." He waited for another minute, listening. Then he smiled and murmured, "I love you, too," and hung up the phone.

Conan picked up the cable again and scanned it. His hand shook as he read it, then he groaned quietly to himself and let the cable fall onto his desk. He was in corduroy pants and shirt sleeves. He was of medium build, sinewy yet not thin, with thinning dark hair and trimly shaped graying beard. He held his head slightly thrust forward, as if he were sniffing the air. His gray eyes were now half-closed in shock and sorrow.

For a few minutes he stared out of his fifth-floor apartment window at the Seventh Avenue traffic rumbling below. As Conan stood at the window he held both feet planted apart, as if he were on the deck of a ship at sea. Every move he made, even as he turned his head to look along the avenue, was as decisive as if it had been considered beforehand. He had the look of a man who is accustomed to making up his mind and acting upon his decision—the kind of man whose obvious inner strength is, when all is well, resented by weaker beings. He was the rare kind of person who was disbelieved in by those who had no inkling of the furnace in which Conan's strength had been forged.

In his mind's eye, Conan saw *Josephine* and Shaughnessy again as he had two years previously: *Josephine* shapely and trim, sleek as ever; Shaughnessy, a grinning, bald wiry leprechaun, burned by the ocean sun. It had been at Annapolis, at the town quay. Shaughnessy had just anchored the forty-four-foot sloop after a four-thousand-mile passage from England, cleared U.S. Customs, and had rowed ashore to meet Conan again for the first time in six years.

He and Shaughnessy had drunk the afternoon away together at a crowded bar on the waterfront. On principle neither of them drank at sea and Shaughnessy had been thirty-two days dry, Conan remembered. He picked up the cable again, read it, sighed, and looked around his tiny, grubby, too expensive apartment, at the tatty furniture, most of it salvaged from the street. His gaze wandered over the piles of books on the floor and he glared for a few seconds at the half-finished book-typescript, which, like a greedy, insatiable stepchild, sat accusingly on his desk. Conan took another quick glance at the cable:

SHAUGHNESSY KILLED ACCIDENT STOP QUERY CAN YOU SKIP-
PER SLOOP JOSEPHINE LISBON GLOBE AROUND WORLD RACE
COMMENCES SECOND APRIL REPLY URGENTEST STOP MIKE
HOUGHTON.

Conan picked up the phone.

"Western Union," he said after a few seconds. "Yes, a cable . . . international . . . to England . . . Mike Houghton, Southern Counties Ocean
Cruising Club, Sandleston . . ." Conan spelled out the name of the town
for the operator. "England . . . the text of the message is 'yes stop arrive
Lisbon Friday twenty-seventh March stop Bill Conan.' "

Then he headed for his travel agent's office.

When Conan arrived at Formelli's restaurant it was six-forty. The
place was not yet packed. He ordered a Watney's Red Barrel beer—Formelli's stocked brews from several different countries. Conan looked
around the restaurant. Most of the customers were young people who,
Conan guessed, were students, but there were a few older people, mostly
men, regulars, who always seemed to be either reading or writing as
they ate. Conan supposed that they, too, were writers, though there was
no way he could know for sure. Most people tended to keep to themselves in Manhattan, even in Greenwich Village.

While he waited for his beer, Conan looked around the restaurant and
noted a couple of good-looking girls. He delved into his inside jacket
pocket, brought out the airline tickets, and inspected them. He started
to make mental notes on the clothes and other gear he would need to
take with him. Suddenly, as if startled, he looked up, his head turned toward the restaurant doorway.

There are magic moments in the lives of lovers. For some they are
rare, for others not. Suddenly, for no obvious reason, there is an awareness, a private certainty, that the *other* is close by, no matter what the
time or place, nor how many other people may be present. There is a
quickening of the senses; colors brighten, noises soften, shapes sharpen,
life is kinder, strangers tend to fade into an amorphous background that
is all their own. Suddenly, almost involuntarily, and yet perhaps not,
one's head turns, one's pulse quickens, one's eyes focus, and there is
one's beloved. So it was, at precisely three minutes to seven in the evening, in the crowded restaurant, between Bill Conan and Ruth Fleming,
he sitting at a wall table at the far inner end of the room, and she peering over the shoulders of recent arrivals waiting around the doorway for
a table.

Conan smiled as Ruth edged her way past the coterie at the entrance, her eyes fixed on Conan all the while, and made her way to him. He started to rise, she shook her head.

Conan glanced at his wristwatch. "Early," he said. It was a private joke between them. He reached for the parcel she was carrying and put it beside his chair.

"Don't drop my skates, Conan," she said. Her voice was husky and low. She leaned over the corner of the table and lightly brushed his beard with her lips.

She was three inches shorter than Conan, about five feet eight, but her slenderness made her appear taller. She looked to be in her middle twenties, and only the self-assured grace with which she opened her gray coat and shucked it over her shoulders for Conan to take from her gave any indication of her true age of thirty-four.

She wore her natural ash-blond hair shoulder length. Her face was peculiarly American—middle American. It was a mite too long to be considered classical. Her cheekbones were high enough to be German, yet her green eyes and brow were purely Irish, while her nose, very slightly patrician, and her complexion, were straight out of the English Home Counties. As her head moved and the light touched and defined the planes and angles of her facial structure, so, to Conan's eyes, she seemed to change into, and back from, and yet again into, three different women, while always remaining the same person. Both the roaming sailor and the writer in Conan were well aware of the quicksilver alchemy of Ruth's appearance. As he watched her sit, he remembered how sometimes, in the companionable moments after they had made love, he told her long, rambling, fanciful tales about her ancestry, and she laughed softly and held him closer to her. Those were the rare moments when the hard veneer which her ten years in New York City had imposed on her dissolved and her almost-naive middle-western innocence—openness might be a better way to think of it, Conan thought—was exposed.

"So what's happening?" Ruth asked quietly. She placed a hand on Conan's arm. She wore a tailored suit, gray with green trimmings, for work at the bank office during the week.

Conan reached into his pocket, extracted the cable, and passed it to her.

Ruth quickly donned a pair of fashionably oversized glasses, and read it, twice. She tried to stop herself from saying, "And you've accepted." It was a flat statement.

"There really wasn't time to discuss—I had to get a cable away fast, so that Houghton would get it in time . . ." He trailed off meekly. His accent had the soft brogue of a northern Briton who has been most of his life at sea, but after four years in the States, Conan's vowels were beginning to flatten out American style.

"How long's the race?" Ruth asked in a small voice, as she replaced the glasses in her purse.

"It's the Sunday Globe race.... There's a fifty-thousand-pound prize—"

Ruth broke in, as a waitress, a young "resting" actress, arrived to take their orders. "What's that in real money?" She was smiling.

By the time the waitress had left, Conan had done the calculation. "A hundred and eighteen thousand dollars ... that's the prize," he said, as he lifted his beer glass. He thought of the other prizes—the visions, the obscurities, the revelations; the profundity, the finality of the sea, the way in which the sea renders remote the cares and wastes of the land. That, to Conan, was the greatest of her prizes—the one worth all the discomforts, the perils and dangers the sea so slyly hid from the unwary.

Ruth was silent. For a moment she drummed her fingers on the table and stared at Conan. She reflected on the way his soul seemed to stir in his eyes when he looked at her, and how they changed to granite when he did not; how the light and warmth left when he looked around him, away from her.

She said, "But what about your writing, Bill? You've written four books since you came to New York.... You're becoming better known.... Why do you have to go on this stupid race? How long is it for, anyhow?"

Conan finished his beer. He firmly placed the glass on the table and looked directly into Ruth's eyes. "It's round the world, nonstop, Lisbon to Lisbon," he said. His tone was boyishly defensive.

There was dead silence between them for a full minute. Ruth opened her mouth slightly as she stared at Conan. She winced and said, "Say that again, Conan ... slowly. My adrenaline is getting in my ears."

Conan regarded her without expression for a moment. He started to say, "Round the—" His voice was hoarse. He cleared his throat.

"Yes, come on, Bill."

"It's a tremendous chance for me to ...." He hesitated.

"Prove yourself?" Ruth asked quietly, sharply. "Jesus Christ, Conan, you're fifty-six years old. You've just about done everything. You've proved yourself time and again. All your life you've been proving yourself. What was it ... ordinary seaman to lieutenant, Royal bloody Navy...?"

"Please, Ruth," Conan murmured as the waitress set their plates on the table. There was a silence until the waitress left. Ruth picked up her fork. She left her knife on the table, as Americans do, until she needed it.

Quietly she said, "All that time at sea . . . in small sailing boats . . . how many years was it?"

"Twenty-two . . . and fourteen in the service . . ."

"And you still haven't had enough?"

"That was mostly delivery trips," he said. "This race is something really special . . ." Again his voice trailed off.

There was another painful silence between them.

Ruth thought of how, after almost two decades of disappointment, she had at last found a man whom she could respect as well as truly love. She envisioned, vaguely, the faces of her ex-husband and some of her previous lovers, but they were mere blurs in her consciousness. For the most they had been either childish, vain, or jealous. To her, Bill Conan had more personality, more intelligence, and certainly more good humor and affection in his little finger than the rest had among them.

Conan felt again the hopelessness of the years he had been alone; a creeping inner coldness, the old orphaning. As he looked at Ruth he wished to God he could take her with him. That was impossible. That he loved her—well and truly loved her, to the depths of his soul—there was not, in his whole being, a shard of doubt. That he needed her was self-evident, the stirring of his mind and groin informed him as he looked at her. Besides, she was his friend.

"What about us, Conan?" Ruth finally asked.

Conan laid down his knife and fork and took a swig of beer, his eyes fixed all the while on hers. He wiped his lips with his napkin and leaned slightly toward her. "It's only for a few short months, Ruth. . . . Just this one last time. . . . I'm drying up . . . I'm writing less and less every day. They don't want to know about real people in real situations. They want . . ." he hesitated, then almost breathed the quotes around the word " 'romance' and they don't see that the real romance is in reality . . . the way things really are."

He looked briefly away from her around the restaurant. He stared for a moment at two males, both, he guessed, in their mid-thirties, one bearded, the other heavily mustachioed, both dressed in black leather caps and jackets, both heavily festooned with chains, both with eyes like lost children. She followed his gaze, then their eyes met again. She smiled. Conan looked away from her again, to where three blank-eyed youths, two of them with their hair longer than Ruth's were making their way to a table.

Suddenly, one of the youths, big and heavy and, thought Conan, fed for most of his few years on prime Texas beef, noticed Conan watching him. The boy glared at him in sullen hostility, a look that swiftly took in Conan's graying beard and glared in the arrogance that is a common intuitive reaction of much American youth toward older people. Conan, for a split second, thought of some of the lads he had sailed with over the years; then, just as fast as the remembrances had come, so, as he turned back to Ruth, they dissolved.

Ruth said, "Is it the danger, Conan?"

He looked at her steadily for a moment. Then he said, "Partly . . . there's that, too. But I have to be independent, Ruth. I suppose it's the way I was brought up. It may be considered old-fashioned here and now, but I just don't ever want to have to be in the situation of having possibly to ask you"—or any woman, he thought—"for anything. . . ."

"How long is this race, anyway?" she asked him.

Conan's face brightened. He took out his small notebook and consulted it. "Well, let's see," he said. He leafed through the pages. "Yes, here we are. Chichester did it in nine months back in sixty-six and sixty-seven . . . and Alex Rose did it in a year . . . Knox-Johnston in almost eleven months . . ." Conan grinned at Ruth. ". . . and Chay Blythe did it the wrong way round in just over nine months in seventy-one."

"Well, bully for Captain Blythe," said Ruth.

"Looks like it'll be around ten months," observed Conan.

There was a silence between them for what seemed to Conan to be an eternity. Then Ruth said, "You're mad, Conan. You know that?" She put her hand on his arm. "But I love you, you crazy, off-the-wall limey!"

"Then it's all right with you, Ruth? Okay with you? You can get away from the office and come to Lisbon with me?"

"No, it's not all right, Conan, and you goddamwell know it, and yes, I'll come . . ." She withdrew her hand from his arm. ". . . and I might *just* be here when you get back, *if* you get back to New York." There was a pause for a few seconds, then she said, "A year, a whole goddam year!" Quickly she finished her coffee. "Why do you do it, Conan? Don't you know, can't you get it into that stupid Scottish head of yours that the time for heroes is long gone? Why the hell couldn't you be a—an advertising agent, for God's sake, or—or—a—a taxi driver?"

Conan glanced momentarily at the old half-model hulls on the wall, their varnish now dulled with years of exposure to the steam and smoke of the restaurant. Phrases flashed through his head (the subtlety, the flexibility, the *mystery* of sail—the infinite variety and the incalculable complexity of the forces that are harnessed to serve the sailor's purpose: the wayward wind that resists all mastery, the would-be bitch sea, the frail, fierce phantom which is the ship herself, and which is always something more than the sum of her myriad parts. Her power, at the same time restraining and urgent—the sleek, reluctant beauty of her hull under the dominion of the mute sails she wears. . .).

Conan looked at Ruth. He smiled at her. "It'll keep me off the booze," he said. "Come on, let's get out of here." He picked up her parcel.

"Just don't make up for it when you get back," she admonished, as he took her elbow and guided her with courtliness through the passage between the tables, toward the doorway. He opened the door for her. "For you," he offered, as he took her arm, "only a glass of wine at mealtimes."

Out in the street, she pressed his arm under her breast. "Eight meals a day, huh?" she tested, smiling at him.

Ruth had the free-swinging stride of the middle-American woman. As she strode along, with her free hand she swung her pocketbook alongside her. It was a pace that sang of open spaces and horizons that never ended. Her hair, as she paced along, bobbed from side to side, like Nebraskan wheat, thought Conan, and as always when he walked with her, he made a conscious effort not to compare her presence to the mousy cling of many European women.

Conan, with no more recognition than Ruth, held up a hand in dubious greeting to an individual resembling a painter, who rushed past them in the street declaiming to himself in a loud voice. He carried two large cans of paint and threw, almost barked, a laughing word at Conan that sounded like *"amigo!"*

"Friend?" asked Ruth.

"I'm not sure. . . . I may have met him in one of the bars."

Silently then, they reached the front door of Conan's apartment house. They neither of them saw a pile of black plastic garbage bags on the sidewalk outside the door, nor did they hear the roaring and grinding of the trucks on Seventh Avenue; they were both only aware that soon they would be again in each other's arms, and that she had already forgiven him, even though she did not quite perfectly understand yet why he was going away from her. He was her man, she was his woman, that they both knew, and that, for the time being, was enough for them.

Later, much later, in the quiet dark, Ruth said sleepily, "If you sail a boat like you sail a woman, Conan, you're gonna win that stupid race."

"Hmmm?" he murmured. "Making up for lost time. . . ."

"What do you do alone at sea?" she asked drowsily, as she gently caressed him.

"Wha—?"

"Whaddaya do at sea all on your own for months at a time?"

"Tie a knot in it," Conan replied. They both slept then, locked together, with the pain of the coming parting held at quiet bay.

Chapter 2

FROM THE PLANE, as it descended to land, central Lisbon looked as quaint and colorful as Ruth's dreams and Conan's remembrances of it— a central valley of crowded, narrow streets and spacious plazas surrounded by seven hills built over with ancient pastel-painted dwellings, most of them topped with rust-colored tiles, and one of the hills crowned by the child's picture-book castle of San Jorge, its brave flags whipped by the breeze atop its biscuit-hued ramparts.

The TAP airliner had departed from New York crowded, except for Ruth and Conan, with Portuguese-Americans heading for the old country. They mostly spoke English in the broad vowels of New England. Somewhere over mid-Atlantic a transformation had come over them. After dinner had been served, they—the men, mostly—started to move around the aisles, greeting each other, and as groups catalyzed and dissolved and others formed, so the language changed from English to Portuguese, so the gestures intensified, the smiles broadened, and the laughter rang, and the men, most of them past middle age, seemed younger, and sturdier, and stronger, and less anxious and careworn.

"It's a sea change," Conan had observed.

Conan had thought better than to cable ahead to book a hotel. "If we stay at one of those American-operated chain hotels, we might just as well be in Denver or Chicago, and everything will cost at least a third more," he had explained. Instead, they had been driven at breakneck speed to the main square of Lisbon, the Rossio. Then, after the ancient green taxi took yet another sharp corner on what seemed to Ruth to be two wheels, they halted in yet another broad square, less crowded than the Rossio. Ruth got the impression that except for a few buses and a fountain in the middle, the square was deserted and empty.

"Praca de Figueras, Pension Coimbra-Madrid, senhor," cried the rotund cab driver, a red-faced man of fifty or so, who had sung out of tune, ostensibly to himself, most of the way from the airport.

"*Muito bom,*" enunciated Conan, exhausting two of his dozen words in Portuguese. Ruth looked at him, surprise on her face. Conan explained quietly, "I don't know it; I use French or Spanish here."

With the cab driver's help, they carried their luggage up three flights of wide, dingy stairs crowded with men and women, most with fistfuls of paper money, who sat on the steps or leaned against the peeling walls of the stairway. They all chatted away in subdued tones and stared at Ruth and Conan as they passed.

"Wow, I can just imagine that in New York," murmured Ruth.

"They're lottery vendors. This is their sort of office," Conan said, puffing slightly.

"There must be a few thousand bucks among them," observed Ruth as they arrived at the ornate, iron-grilled main door of the pension. The cab driver tugged the bell cord.

"More like a million at a guess," declared Conan.

Inside the door the pension was clean, bright, and well-furnished in the graceful Portuguese way, stark and pure and well-proportioned. The pension owner's eldest son, on desk duty, immediately recognized Conan from his previous stay five years before. He stared for a second at Conan, gasped, and ran into the family living room to return to the desk followed by his whole family—father, mother, grandfather, six brothers, three sisters, an aunt, and a male cousin on a visit from Oporto, as he rapidly explained in a mixture of Portuguese, Spanish, broken French, and fractured English.

"She con here, Senhor Conan, fron Oporto, on faire le plus bueno vino alli, Engleez likee ver mucho, no?" Eldest son turned from Conan to Ruth, whom all the girls and women were inspecting minutely, from the top of her head to her toes, shod in gray suede boots. "La senhora es Engleeze tambien?"

Everyone in the crowded office, except for two small girls who shyly smiled, stared seriously at Ruth.

"No—Americana," explained Conan, grinning at Ruth's embarrassment. Everyone broke into wide smiles.

"Ah, America, ver bueno, muitos Portuguesas alli. . . ." There was a general applause of approving murmurs from all the assembled family.

"Con zees way, I har very bueno room—only ten dollar . . ." Eldest Son invited them, as he gently made way through the throng.

Their room, long, wide, high, airy, and bright, overlooked the Praca de Figueras, across to the steep, villa-covered hill a mile away, on top of which, like a castellated pie crust atop a heaped fruit salad, lay the long walls of the fortress of San Jorge. Ruth quickly glanced around the room and took in the large dark-wooded bedstead with its quilted covers, the small desk, the ebonylike chest of drawers, the two chairs, and the curtain of the shower stall. Lightly, she moved across to one of the windows and leaned out. Below, the townsfolk, having finished their siesta, milled about on their business, much of which, in Lisbon, is carried out on the street. Above, the fat cumulus clouds, fresh from the ocean, scurried across the breezy March sky toward the castle ramparts in the distance.

"Noisy," Ruth called to Conan over her shoulder, "but the view is . . . magnifico!"

Conan joined her at the window. He reached out past her to both sides, took hold of the two massive window shutters which were swung back against the outside wall, and closed them. "I wrote half a book in this room," he confided, as if to himself, "there." He turned, in the now silent room, reached for Ruth, and urgently kissed her on the lips.

An hour and a century later she lazily murmured to him, "I still think you're crazy, Conan." Her voice was small and low and she spoke as if in her sleep.

Conan reached over to her and gently fondled her breast. She did not stir. He lightly stroked the sweeping line below her breast to her thigh. Still she did not stir. He let his hand rest delicately on the mound of her belly. Lying thus, Conan shut the thoughts of the coming meetings, the hard effort, the struggles, and the possible triumph ahead, out of his consciousness. "Houghton's not due here until Sunday, and the race doesn't start until Thursday. Let's try to forget it, Ruth; we've two nights together here before the thing starts. Let's just make the most of it, hmm?"

Ruth showed no sign that she had heard what he had murmured. Conan, as he dozed off, felt glad, although he could not fathom why.

When they rose and readied and left the pension, dusk was falling.

"It's like some kind of surrealistic vision," exclaimed Ruth, as they emerged from the street door onto the crowded sidewalk. "To be surrounded by all these people in modern clothes . . . well, most of them . . ." Her eyes followed four gypsy women with nut brown faces, dressed in long skirts of bright, clashing colors, with bright, flashing eyes, who talked loudly and laughed as they lithely sidled past. ". . . and all the traffic honking, and then to look up there,"—she raised her chin in the direction of the castled hill—"it's something out of this world . . . like Disneyland . . . only it's real."

The long castle walls glowed amber in the last rays of the sun dying in the western sky. All around and below the glowing walls, the houses, seemingly piled on top of one another in their thousands, reflected the light in azure, lavender, rose, salmon, lemon, and apricot blazes and the blood-red roofs appeared to pulsate and breathe in the warmth of the evening, as if they were bursting with the emotions they held under them.

"It's the most beautiful city in Europe," claimed Conan, "at least to me. Sure, Paris and Venice are all very well, but there's all that damned Parisian arrogance and those smelly canals. . . ." They turned the corner, wended their way along a short, crowded street, and emerged into the great Rossio square. "Here the air is fresh and the natives are friendly and . . ." Conan gazed up at the gold-edged clouds passing overhead "the ocean breezes blow right in over the city." Ruth could taste the iodine in the breeze.

Aka's dolphin tribe was now passing through the waters where Kweela's calf, Om, had been conceived two years before. Kweela felt pleasure. She knew the place by the set of the sea, the look of the clouds, and the stars. In her mind the memory-vision of that time was as clear as if it had happened only moments ago. Aka, the scarred leader of the tribe, had made his intentions quite clear. He had signalled to her—1,200 clicks in that one second—and although she had not yet seen him on that day, two years ago, she had received the hologram he had sent to her . . . of the two rocky exposed peaks of the undersea mountain, and the warm waters swirling about the fish-abounding shallows . . . far away in the south, where the tribal females gave birth. The vision-image had focused on a shallow inlet in the rocky islets safe from the threat of the stupid but vicious sharks, and the most terrifying of all—Man, who did not seem to kill because he was hungry, but merely because he wanted to. Huk, the dreamer, one of Aka's male companions, had even signalled that Man did not eat, but Aka had refuted those ideas, and so had Kweela.

Now, Kweela's school of mothers with their offspring, all together, rose to the surface to breathe through their blowholes. Some of the thirty-four mothers pushed their calves up ahead of them with one flipper. As they ascended, the school "agreed" to leap. Up to the sea surface they went, each of the mothers eight to twelve feet long, sleek, gleaming, blue, black, white, and powerful. In a hundred watery eruptions and explosions, fountains of spray shone in the sun, green, orange, blue, and silver. The mothers and calves, together, within a split second of each other, broke the surface and leapt and rolled and somersaulted in the air, eight, ten, twelve feet. One mother, Kweela's close friend Sheena, shot into the sky higher than all the others—sixteen feet—and as she did so she twisted herself over and over five times. Then, as they all crashed back into the sea, their speed and weight sent great sheets of sparkling white spray in all directions. As they fell, their quick eyes enjoyed the rainbow colors as the sunshine caught the spray and mist, and they revelled in the delighted grunts, clicks, and squeals of the youngsters as they leapfrogged each other, crisscross, and tumbled back into the sea. Below again, all was cool and calm and blue. Although there were 142 signal groups, each of four separate transmissions, coming at her from the 142 other dolphins in the tribe, Kweela, with Om close to her side, could sense no urgency in them, no alarms. Down into the depths they all went, Om almost touching Kweela's sensitive skin, at a rush. Their tails pushed up and down, up and down, 120 strokes a minute, until at 250 feet depth they levelled out and slowed down, all still grouped together, ready to rise again to the surface of the sea, all revelling in life and their dreams.

As he and Ruth crossed the wide Rossio, Conan thought of the first time he had visited Lisbon. The memory was dimming, but he knew it must have been in late 1941. He had been an able seaman at the time, one of a hastily gathered mob of semiamateurs gotten together somehow by the Admiralty to commission an ancient three-funnelled cruiser, which some genius in Whitehall had imagined would be fit consort for a convoy out to Malta past the iron Axis gauntlet of U-boats and dive-bombers. The ship had been forced to call at Lisbon for repairs.

Of the fifteen merchant ships that left England, only two had gotten through to Malta. They themselves, in the three-funnelled wonder, had received Kesselring's coup de grace, in a welter of flying iron and burning fuel oil, only a hundred miles short of the beleaguered island. Conan thought better than to talk to Ruth of the sea and the hazards of the sea, so he pointed out to her the Pastilleria Suisse, an outside pavement cafe.

"That was the espionage stamping grounds of Europe in the war," he told Ruth. There was no need to explain to her which war. The other conflicts he had been engaged in, Greece, Cyprus, Malaya, Korea, he referred to as "fracases" or "affairs."

For fun, they sat at a table at the north end of the parade of tables, which had been the Axis end of the promenade, and Ruth giggled while Conan, his eyes sparkling, in an impossibly thick German accent, made up hilarious signals about casual passersby "to be sent back to Abwehr headquarters in Berlin."

Then Conan was silent. Now and then he looked briefly at the sky and the passing clouds overhead. Ruth knew that he was anticipating the race, longing to go down to the waterfront, to the yacht *Josephine*, to look over its lines, to touch it and fondle it and take command of the thing—a collection of nuts and bolts and bits of wire. In brief glances she watched him and wondered how long he could stand to be away · from the boat. In a moment of pain she was filled with a sense of impending loss, but she determined not to spoil this perfect day. Conan looked at her and smiled and they rose to cross the square, still in silence.

Ahead of them, across the wide Rossio, beyond the Dom Enrique column, another hill, adorned with villas and mansions and palaces and alive with gardens and bursts of flowers, rose steeply up to golden shafts of sunlight shining on the bases of the clouds. As they crossed the square, startled flights of pigeons wheeled and swooped around them. They stood for a few minutes by the statue and drank in the scene all around them. There were hawkers, little old men dressed in black, who lugged huge straw baskets heaped with oranges and green peas and cabbages. Women, some young, some middle-aged, with bare feet and strong limbs and gold chains around their necks, balanced wooden trays of fish on their heads as they passed gracefully across the plaza. Sitting on the base of the statue and standing around on the mosaic-patterned paving, a dozen lottery ticket sellers displayed hundreds of *bilhetes* which fluttered and flapped on rickety wooden frames like blackboard easels. All around the square, on the sidewalks, dozens more hucksters had set up their wooden trays crammed with cheap notions, while others strolled around, their necks festooned with a score and more of gaudy ties, or with a dozen shining, lumpy wristwatches on each arm.

Arm in arm, silently trying to take in the seemingly chaotic scenes around them, Ruth and Conan passed by the central station, "which looks like an opera house," she observed, and the opera house, "ought to be a station," he rejoined, and led her onto the wide, noisy Avenida da Liberdade, a parade of *fin de siècle* buildings, grassy parkways, pavement cafes, and gaudy umbrellas. Even here, on the Champs Elysées of Lisbon, multicolored lines of washed clothing, baskets of flowers, and birdcages decorated the upper stories of some of the buildings. All along the sidewalk, groups of people, some all male, some mixed, old and young, moved slowly, hesitantly, and stopped frequently while one of their number gesticulated and stressed a point in the debate to the gathering, laughing or serious.

"It's a bit like being in a stage show . . . you know, like the scene at Ascot in *My Fair Lady*," Ruth exclaimed. "Everyone is inspecting everyone else, the way they stare—"

"No harm in it; it's the custom," explained Conan. "They expect you to stare back. It's all hands in, here; a sort of togetherness, as you say. The men consider that they're paying you a compliment and the women . . . well, I suppose they're warning you off."

All the tables near the serving booth were crowded. They eventually found one a hundred yards away from it, and from there watched the passing scene for twenty minutes.

"Life is slower here than in New York," observed Ruth, just as a waiter arrived at their table. He was a white-haired little man of about sixty-five. About him was an air of sad courtesy. He wore heavy glasses and a white apron down to the ankles of his boots, which were shiny and new and squeaked as he moved.

Conan ordered ginger beer for Ruth ("You must try it. Lisbon is the only place on the Continent where they make real ginger beer") and coffee and Drambuie for himself as Ruth grinned and shook her head slightly.

"Sim, senhor," acknowledged the waiter. He bobbed his ancient head and creaked off. Five minutes later he was back with a paper tablecloth and two napkins, which he silently laid on the table and weighted down with an ashtray. He then creaked off again, the hundred yards back to the booth. Another five minutes passed and again the waiter appeared at their table. "Would the senhora and senhor care for a snack . . . ? We have mussels and clams and prawns in cream sauce and ham rolls and steak sandwich . . ."

Conan ordered two small steak sandwiches to tide them over until dinner.

"Sim, senhor." The waiter creaked off another hundred yards, to return in five minutes with knives and forks, which he gravely laid on the table. On his next passage to the booth and back he bore the drinks. They waited another ten minutes for him to return with the food. By the time Conan paid the check—all of three dollars—the waiter had creaked and squeaked to the booth five times.

"That makes roughly a thousand yards," estimated Conan. "And they grossed three dollars, and the waiter practically kissed my hand for the fifty-cent tip," he observed to a vastly amused Ruth.

They crossed the road again and made their way through the throng on the sidewalk up the slight incline of the Avenida. They passed a dozen women dressed in black with armsful of straw hats and a score of men with hands full of dark glasses, and they stopped and watched four laborers crouched on the roadside. The men tapped at large gray stones, which they deftly split into tiny cubes. These they methodically, patiently, set in intricate patterns in the newly cemented area of the sidewalk. Then they watched as other men, with wooden pestles as tall as themselves, pounded the stones with rhythmic swings until they were firmly imbedded in the cement, evenly and good for another hundred years.

They waited with a small crowd at the bottom of a steep incline which gives out onto the Avenida. Conan passed a coin to a legless beggar who rushed himself along on a tiny cart.

Ruth peered up the narrow alleyway which faded away up in dim light. She read aloud the street sign, as a question. "Calcada de Gloria?—Something to Glory?"

"Rise of Glory," translated Conan.

"What a lovely name for such a crummy street."

"Wait—this is really something, Ruth."

Even as Conan spoke a dark shape made its quiet way down the hill toward them in the twilight, at first black, then gray, it finally revealed itself as a trolley car—but the most oddly shaped trolley car Ruth had ever seen. The downhill end of the heavily scrolled Edwardian passenger compartment was a good six feet above the street level, perched on a spindly iron chassis which conformed to the steepness of the hill at an angle of thirty degrees, while the uphill end of the passenger compartment almost scraped the ground. It reminded Ruth of some kind of insect she had once surprised in a hotel bathtub in Bermuda.

They silently pushed their way on board the trolley among a jostling crowd which included three women with baskets of flowers and one with a cage of four live hens. Ruth made to sit, but Conan firmly led her to the downhill end of the cabin to stand at the window. "Don't miss this," he said as, with a jerk, the trolley started to move silently up the hill.

After a few moments, when she could see over the roofs of the near building, the city, strings, necklaces, and diadems of twinkling lights below seemed to drop away from them as the car rose up the incline, and then, like a theatrical backdrop, the Castle of San Jorge, its ramparts and towers flooded with golden light, hove into view, leaving Ruth, for a few moments, speechless with wonder. Even Conan, although he had seen it a dozen times, was still moved by the drama of the scene.

As the trolley reached the top of the mile-long hill with a slight bump, Conan grabbed Ruth's arm to steady her. "How's that?" he asked with a grin. "Welcome to the Bairro Alto!"

"Makes the view of Manhattan look . . . mundane," she declared as they alighted.

"Only two other views like it," he said. "Rio de Janeiro at dawn, from the ocean . . ." They heard the sound of plaintive music coming from a small tavern. They started across the road, heading toward it.

"And the other?"

"Princess Street, Edinburgh, on a cold winter's night when a mist lies near the ground in the valley below the castle."

Ruth laughed, low, and grabbed Conan's arm. "What a contrast," she exclaimed, "Rio and Edinburgh! What would Freud make of that?"

"Coffee and Drambuie."

She shook her head, smiling the while, as they passed a handsome youth idling in front of an iron-grilled window. Inside the window but in front of a curtain, in the shadow, a young woman sat. Both were gazing at each other in absolute silence.

"Courting," explained Conan laconically.

Ruth was taken aback, almost unable to believe what she had seen. "I thought that went out with crinolines," she exclaimed quietly.

"In Portugal, nothing that's worthwhile goes out," he replied, "and sometimes silence is worthwhile."

Before Ruth had time to take him up on the matter, they reached the door of the tavern, which was piled around with green plant fronds.

Inside the tavern half the tables were unoccupied. At first Ruth wondered if they should stay, but Conan reassured her that they were early. The headwaiter led them to a table inside an alcove let into the plain whitewashed walls. On the opposite side of the tavern, behind an ornate mahogany bar, varnished hogsheads of wine were stacked, four rows of them, all the way up to the great rafters of the wooden ceiling, from which hung hams and sides of bacon, as well as wire flower baskets brilliant with blooms.

The other customers in the tavern were mainly either family groups or couples, most of them, Ruth felt instinctively, very accustomed to each others' company. Ruth let Conan order for her. A *vichyssoise*, a delicious light white wine, *bacalhau*—cod cooked as only the Portuguese can cook it—and a *Serra*—goat cheese. For the finale Conan chose finely sugared oranges *à la maltaise*. They had just started to eat the dessert when suddenly the lights in the tavern all dimmed and a hush descended. Even the noise from the kitchen ceased. In the gloom Ruth could see that the tavern was now crowded, at almost full capacity. The waiters stopped serving and stood against the walls, their silver trays held down in front of them. A noisy German tourist at one of the tables was hissed into silence. A spotlight lit up one of the tables, which was adorned simply with a white cloth, the same as all the other tables. At it sat two men, one middle-aged, the other young. The older man strummed a Portuguese guitar, which reminded Ruth of an oversized banjo, but had a more fluid, delicate tone. He carried the melody. The younger man filled in the chords, heavy and plaintive, on a Spanish guitar.

A woman emerged out of the shadows behind the musicians. She was dressed all in black, with a black shawl thrown around her shoulders. She was not young, nor was she beautiful, yet when she leaned her head back and closed her eyes, trancelike, and surrendered to the sadness of pain and parting, there was something, it seemed to Conan, very beautiful in her acceptance of fate.

As the music of the *fado* rose and fell, slowed and quickened, it became a wild cry of pain, of parting, of jealousy, of loss and ashes and fire and guilt and despair and longing and hopeless desolation. It was a moan from the depth of the singer's soul and into it she heaped and she shovelled all her past tribulations and cast them at everyone sitting in the tavern. Ruth, after one song, almost overcome by the anguish of the *fado* music, begged Conan to take her out.

They moved out through the silent, serious crowd at the door and crossed the road again to the small, dark tree-overhung park atop the cliff that overlooks the city center. There they stood, side by side, for half an hour or more, and gazed at the carpet of twinkling diamonds a thousand feet below them, from the pulsing loom of Campo Grande in the north, down past the magic glow of the Castle of San Jorge, past the leave-taking lamps of Lisbon docks and beyond, to an ocean steamer, her lights all ablaze as she moved slowly out into the blackness of the Tagus River.

Trying to hold back the tears she felt, Ruth clung to Conan's arm as she watched the steamer pass out of sight toward the ocean. She thought of his coming departure. She looked at his face. He, too, was gazing toward the darkened river. He turned and looked into her eyes, calm and unsmiling. She reached up and brought his mouth down to hers and kissed him and pressed her body close to him. She kissed him passionately and long and after the first bittersweet taste of her kiss, as she tightened his hold around her, Conan knew again the stir at his loins. She sensed it and pressed herself to him. He thought of the time long ago when he had been a jaunty young sailor and had imagined that by the time he reached fifty all this would be but a memory. Now, he thought, as Ruth eased herself away from him, it was even worse—better?—worse?—it certainly was deeper. So deep inside him, the insatiable longing, the wanting of her, as to cause him physical pain. He held her away from him and looked at her. There were tears in her eyes, yet she was smiling for him.

"Come on, Ruth." He took her elbow gently. "Let's go and have a nightcap," he said, as he led her away from the railings, out of the little park, back toward the cockeyed trolley and the Rise of Glory.

Chapter 3

NEXT MORNING, Saturday, they set out to visit the Castle of San Jorge. The day was sunny and fine, an early spring day in Lisbon. Conan wore the same corduroys he had worn in New York—he would wear them ashore until they dropped off him, Ruth thought with amusement. It was strange, for a man so impetuous, so ready to pick up stakes and voyage the world at the drop of a hat, how he was also a man of certain idiosyncrasies, how he wore the same clothes and used the same restaurant, the same bar (when he wasn't writing), until they almost seemed to be a part of him, and he of them. When they had gone to the Pastilleria Suisse for breakfast that morning, Conan had insisted that they wait a few minutes. Gruffly, he had made the excuse of buying a newspaper across the square, until the table they had occupied the previous evening was vacant; they had even sat on the same chairs.

Ruth wore a white peasant blouse and a flowered cotton skirt, with white shoes she had hurriedly picked up at Macy's in New York on their way to the airport as Conan sat impatiently in a cab outside. Now, as they strolled arm in arm down the Rua Agosta toward Black Horse Square, Conan told her of how Lisbon was reputed to have been founded by Ulysses and he spoke of kings and queens—Don Afonso, Queen Leonora, King Manuel—and explained to her as they passed ancient churches and palaces who had built what. Ruth, half-listening to him, reflected that the panic over the shoes had been completely unnecessary. Here, there were shoe shops galore, their windows proud with elegant creations at only half the prices of New York.

They came to a narrow street, as straight as a die and as long as a rifle shot—"Rua dos Bacalhoeiros" Ruth read the sign aloud.

"Cod-Fisherman's Street," explained Conan. They stared at the House of Pointed Stones, its facade covered with strange, pointed granite blocks facing outward. The play of sun and shadow on the sharp angles was a triumph of natural decoration. It reminded Ruth of a rhinoceros or an armadillo. They visited the *Se*, the Cathedral, the oldest church in Lisbon, with its rose windows half as big as a basketball court "Built in 1147," Conan read from a guide pamphlet. Ruth calculated quickly. "Well, let's see, 1147 from 1981 . . . that's 834 years."

Ruth tied a gauze scarf loosely over her head and they, both feeling awed, walked slowly through the chancel, a silent treasury of intricately worked plaster and marble and on through the ambulatory, a vast, domed hall from which radiated chapels in which sunlight streamed through the stained glass of centuries-old windows. Solid-seeming oblique shafts of blue and gold and scarlet and silver pierced the still gloom and shone on the tombs of kings and saints and knights and martyrs, and played on the carved emblematic shields of love and respect and remembrance. "And fear, too," observed Conan, as their muted footsteps echoed into the cloister, where a magnificent Romanesque grill of black iron curleycues—thousands of them—and draped behind it a great blood red curtain, almost a thousand feet square, guarded what they guarded from prying eyes.

Out in the spring sunshine again, a sultry wind blew. They strolled slowly under newly blossoming trees, still arm in arm, up the hill past the little platform-park of Santa Luzia and the imposing silhouette of the church of Saint Vincent-outside-the-walls. Conan pointed out to Ruth the crumbled remains of the twelve-hundred-year-old Moorish city wall. They sat for a while on the stones and Conan brought to life for her visions of splendor and love and terror and triumph as she, turning one of the small stones over and over in her hands, listened to him recount some of the history of the wall.

They wandered, almost nonchalantly, by an old house which leaned drunkenly against the Moorish wall. They found it was a museum of decorative arts. They entered. It was a mansion full of rooms from all the ages back to the twelfth century, and actually seemed to be still inhabited. All the rooms were crammed full of precious artifacts—furniture, gold, and silver tablewear, richly shot brocades, carpets, clocks, chandeliers, paintings, carvings and statuettes, suits of armor (there was even one "tailored" for a child of six!), painted ceilings, ornate gilt-framed mirrors, spinning wheels, strange-looking kitchen utensils, and heart-wrenching little paint boxes and combs and ladies' looking glasses used long, long ago for vanity which has gone the way of all vanity, except for that which, in the height of its beauty, had been depicted in the dark portraits on the walls. The bequest of the artist only is not vanity.

They passed two urchins, shaven-headed, elf-faced, and barefoot, of about six years old who were sitting on a house doorstep. They were eating with their fingers from tin cans. Ruth smiled at them.

"*E servido, senhora,*" they both greeted her in piping voices.

Conan grinned.

"What did they say?" she asked him.

"*It is served.* They meant the food, of course. They're offering to share it with you. It's the common thing here."

She turned and smiled at the two boys. They shaded their eyes with sticky hands from the sun's glare and grinned at her. Both had their front teeth missing. For a moment she hesitated, then called to them, "*Bom dia!*"

Both lads saluted, fingers to foreheads. "*Bom dia, senhor e senhora! Que vais com Dios!*"

Ruth turned and bent her head. "Well, well," she said softly. "Where've I been this past ten years!"

They passed through the archway of the main entrance to the Castle of San Jorge, "There to commune with the ghosts of randy Romans, vicious Visigoths, and sensuous Saracens," he told her, as they made their way over the rough cobbled street and onto a gravel walk between lush grass lawns, which covered most of the area of the castle grounds.

Ruth stopped and gasped in astonishment as soon as they had covered the rise just inside the castle. Typically, Conan watched her face as, at first in wonder, then in delight, she gaped at the stupendous view.

Twenty yards in front of her, down a gentle slope, a low, biscuit-colored wall, only three feet high but ten feet thick, contained the acres of grassy forecourt on the rise of which she stood. At intervals along the wall, olive trees, gnarled and twisted with age, their green oily leaves glistening, gave shade. Between the trees a score of great bronze cannons mutely, quaintly now, glowered over miles and miles of tiled roofs and steeples and church towers, gables and mansards, chimneys and windows, streets, avenues, and facades which stretched out below the castle into the distance, all crowded, hemmed in between the house-covered heights of the six other hills of Lisbon on three sides, and on the other side the azure blue Tagus River.

Conan pointed out to her the Salazar Bridge, which reminded Ruth of the Golden Gate and which led over the bluffs on the south bank of the Tagus, past the immense monument of Christ, seven hundred feet high. His arms were, she could see, outstretched in white benefaction under a sky blue and clear and ocean clean.

"Belém's over there, beyond the bridge, on this side of the river," Conan told her, pointing it out. "That's where the boat is," he said. *From whence blew the wind,* he thought. *Southwest, six knots, the way those olive tree leaves twinkle and shiver. The wind should veer around to the northwest by Thursday, with any luck. Just the job for getting the hell south down past Cape Saint Vincent . . .*

She looked at his face. He was staring intently, eyes almost closed into slits, at a point just somewhere near the city end of the bridge. Suddenly he turned and caught her look, and wished he had not yet mentioned the boat. He took her arm and led her down to the wall, where they sat for an hour looking at the houses and gardens and trees and flowered walks far below them, all laid out like a child's toy town, but Ruth was sadly aware every time Conan's eyes strayed to a sail on the river, or back to the spot by the bridge. She knew it was unreasonable to feel this way. She wondered to herself if it was jealousy she felt whenever she thought of *Josephine,* or whether it was merely the knowledge that the boat was the instrument of his leaving her for the bleak months ahead.

She determined not to let him know how she felt about their parting. It was strange. She was caught between two stools. If she ranted and raved and cried and threatened she would be playing the role of the scorned woman. If she suffered in silence she would be playing the (to her) ridiculous role of the loyal little woman. She made up her mind to play herself, to put love to one side, no matter how much she loved him. She would be herself. She had her work, she had her friends, she would live her own life until he returned. What they'd had between them had been good—very, very good, the best she would ever have.

Nothing would or could, she was sure, ever change that. She looked at Conan again. Strange, she thought, how he shed his age at times— when he was with her—in bed especially. He had told her it was because he'd been at sea most of his life, and while that aged a man's head beyond the ken of landsmen, it preserved his body. He had told her it was because of all the activity, all the isolation, all the peace of mind, all the comparative freedom from outside pressures and commercial stress.

She smiled to herself as she remembered the time they had discussed a cigarette advertisement that had featured a rugged-faced cowboy. She had admired the craggy-visaged model. "Symbol of freedom?" he had scoffed. "Cowboys? Christ, the ocean sailors make them look like office runners! Free? Those saddle pounders, compared to small-craft ocean roamers, are about as free as bus drivers!" True, he had been a little drunk at the time, but she had to admit there was probably something in what he said; the man in the ad looked a little *too* handsome . . . a mite *too* rugged.

Nothing could ever change what had passed between them. For her it had been the happiest period in her life. His gruff bluntness, his down to earth disdain of pretensions and shallowness had, at first, put her off, but to her he had always been honest. He had never, as her ex-husband and her previous lovers had done, put her anywhere near a pedestal. He treated her as a dear friend, as an equal being on the face of the earth, whose hand and heart and mind and body he loved and whose passage, alone, through the maze of experience called life, he eased and made more gentle. Colors were more brilliant when he was near her. Besides, she told herself, if anyone could make her laugh, Conan could.

Suddenly, from a small arched doorway in the castle keep, six all-white peacocks strutted out, like little ships in line ahead. Both Ruth and Conan watched them, bemused, as one by one they spread out their tails into magnificent ivory fans dotted with blue and red commas. Slowly, they strolled over toward the birds.

"Engleez?" a high voice said. He was small and skinny. At first Conan thought it was a boy. He turned and saw that it was a little old man. He had a red face, slightly pockmarked, and a three-day growth of white whiskers which framed, like snow in a roof gutter, his long face. He wore a shiny blue frock coat which was too big for him and gray trousers too short for him, and on his chest dangled a brass medallion about four inches across. "I am zhe keeper of zhe birds," he explained. A clock nearby struck eleven.

Conan grinned at him and nodded. "Yes, English," he said. No sense in complicating matters, he thought.

"Ah, Engleez. Many Engleez pippel con here," said the old man, smiling at Ruth.

"What beautiful peacocks," she exclaimed. "Do you breed them?"

"Ah yes, I brid zhem," the keeper replied.

"I don't think I've ever seen white peacocks before," she said. "Why are they white?"

"You see, senhora," the old man smiled, "we do not have any snow in Lisbon, and zhe cheeldren do not know what zhe snow look like, so we brid zhe birds to look like zhe snow."

Conan laughed and slapped his hand on his pocket. He took Ruth's arm.

"Come on, time for lunch," he said. "Good-bye, senhor." He shook the little old man's hand and they moved away. Ruth still stared at the birds.

"What a lovely story," she said, laughing softly.

"Yes," said Conan, "I'll bet he tells it to all the girls," he said and laughed again, "but bless him all the same. It's a good line."

They walked back down the hilly streets to the Cais de Sodre, the tenderloin district near the docks. It is a district of narrow streets lined with flower- and birdcage-bedecked bars, cafes, restaurants, ship chandler's and sailor's clothing stores with windows full of canvas and cotton, blazes of blue and red. Unbelievable sunburned nautical characters of all ages, who, to Ruth, looked as if they had just stepped out of a stage show of *Treasure Island,* wandered, clothed in red-and-white and blue-and-white striped shirts, wide-sleeved smocks and white bell-bottomed pants, bandanas around their heads, some barefoot, in and out of the bars, or played dice for drinks inside the shady doorways.

Conan, as they ate a plain, cheap meal, *caldo verde* of sausage, potatoes, and cabbage with seafood and good rose wine, all for three dollars, remembered that the Arizona and Texas bars, each with a hundred or so girls, had been, years before, in this same street. Perhaps they were still there. He didn't need them now as he had then, he thought gratefully, as he discussed with Ruth how she would handle the subletting of his apartment.

"Someone steady, not someone who's promiscuous, or likely to just take off into the blue," he said.

"Someone like you," she rejoined, smiling at him.

"Yes," he said seriously, as he signed a power of attorney for her.

"At approximately five cents, this must be one of the great travel bargains of Europe," said Conan, as he and Ruth boarded the train at Cais de Sodre station, bound five miles along the shoreline for Belém. The train was crowded. They stood, clinging to roof-straps. All around them peasants, sailors, and factory workers talked loudly and merrily.

The first couple of miles was mainly vistas of slums—yet still colorful—and dreary factory walls bedaubed with Communist slogans. "Relics of the gentle revolution of 1974," explained Conan. "It was all very sedate—the soldiers stuck flowers in their rifles. God knows, after thirty-odd years of Salazar's dictatorship, they deserved a bit of a binge."

"I can't imagine communism attracting these people," said Ruth, looking around the crowded open train carriage. "They seem to be far too individualistic."

"That's why it never took," Conan explained. "Look." He ducked his head and pointed his beard at a wall mural. It was a huge painting, almost a hundred yards long, executed in the "socialist reality" technique—dozens of "heroic" workers, men and women, all striding toward the Marxist Utopia, which evidently was somewhere on the vacant lot between the railroad line and the factory wall.

"Dramatic," she said.

"I've seen them all over the world, from Mexico to Lithuania," said Conan. "But there's a difference here . . . see, all the faces are distinctly different from one another. What they depict here is not a mass of people, but a group of individuals . . . any one of whom looks as if he's about to take off on his own road any minute."

As the train stopped, a working man in light blue coveralls offered Ruth his seat. No sooner had she sat down than a chubby old lady on the seat opposite her, dressed all in black, offered Ruth an apple almost as red and shiny as her own cheeks. Ruth, embarrassed and a little confused, shook her head, smiling. The old lady then, wordlessly, reached up and offered the apple to Conan, who, with a wide smile and courteous *"Obrigado, senhora,"* accepted it, rubbed it on the sleeve of his corduroy jacket, and bit into it, winking at Ruth as he did so. The old lady, seeing him wink, laughed softly. When they alighted at Belém, minutes later, Conan, with the half-eaten apple in hand, blew the old lady a kiss. She replied by rolling her merry blue eyes at him as she threw her head back and jiggled her basket against the gold crucifix on her black-vested breasts.

"What a marvelous old dear!" said Conan on the platform.

Ruth jogged his arm. "Watch it, Conan," she murmured jocosely, pretending jealousy. "The old crone probably poisoned it."

In the bright afternoon sunshine they ambled through a tree-lined park and watched swans swimming under genteel fountains in ornate pools, fended off a half-dozen incredibly tiny shoeshine boys and tie hucksters, then made their way to the coach museum. There, under meticulously painted, scrolled plaster ceilings, they wondered at a score of golden royal coaches, each one different, and at the handiwork of their precious red-plush and silver interiors. As they stood alone in the vast hall—they were the only visitors—it was as if they could hear the carriages whispering of the scenes of past pomp and glory they had witnessed.

They inspected, awed by the workmanship displayed, the finest of pride from past centuries—chaises, litters, berlins, pleasure carts, calashes, saddles, horse trappings decorated in silver, riding accessories, boots, spurs, uniforms, livery, court arrays and dress for the royal hunts, and the sinister armories and trappings of horse warfare.

They passed along the main street of Belém, old houses with colonnaded ground floors cluttered with shops full of chrome chairs and plastic-topped tables and Japanese radios, and then, suddenly, as if in a fairy tale, Ruth saw before her eyes a miracle in stone. It was as if the rocks of earth had burst out of the ground in a hymn of praise, a poem in living stone rising up to heaven.

"The Monastery of Jerónimos," explained Conan. "Sacred to all mariners . . . or it ought to be. From here the Portuguese sent out the first of the Renaissance ships of discovery, up to 150 years before your Columbus sailed—Diaz, Da Gama, Magellan—they all sailed out from here."

As she listened to Conan, Ruth stared at the intricately detailed sculpture on the great west portal—saints with features so alive, so human, that they seemed to breathe, and a lacework of finely carved granite all around them and over them, all the way up to the roof, where Christ surveyed all calmly, His eyes fixed on the far horizon.

Listening to Conan, Ruth's eyes followed the straw-colored highlights and deep shadows of sun-warmed stone filled with saintly angels, angelic saints, mitred bishops, martyred disciples, and a repentant Mary Magdalene, who crouched below and stared in wonder at the horizon-searching Virgin.

"It all seems so clean and brand new," she exclaimed.

"Clean air—straight from the ocean," he replied.

"What made them do all this, where does it all come from?"

"They sailed in crazy, frail vessels we wouldn't cross the Hudson in," he murmured. "They knew next to nothing about nutrition or medicine, or even what the world looked like and they sailed into the terror of the unknown. They had only their courage and their faith . . ." Conan looked at Ruth. "And that's what all this tries to express . . ." He hesitated for a moment, thinking. "Guts and God," he finally said. "That's all they had—and in the end it's all that counts, and that's where it came from, I reckon."

And love, Ruth thought, but she remained silent, because perhaps that was what he meant. They were silent for a moment. She knew—understood—his mind was on the waiting boat.

"When are we going to see *Josephine?*" she found herself saying.

"What? . . . Oh, she's over there, back through the park," he replied casually, as if it were the last thing on his mind. "But I thought you might want to go inside the monastery. There's a wonderful Renaissance high chapel . . ."

Ruth slowly turned and looked at him for a few seconds. Conan looked down and kicked a pebble with one foot. "You're a terrible kidder, Conan. You know damn well you don't want to go inside. All you want to do is get to the damned boat." She seized his arm and pulled him, grinning, away from the monastery doorway. "All right," she said, "let's go."

They walked through the waterfront park and across the busy Avenida de Brasilia and soon came within the smell of low-tide seaweed and the sound of the wire rigging from a hundred sailing vessels frapping on metal masts. The three-acre square yacht basin was full of boats tied up stern to the high surrounding jetties. Along the seaward side of the basin were the race boats—Ruth knew they were the race boats. There was, to her, a sinister animal-like crouch to their appearance. Conan's pace quickened as they passed by the line of sleek hulls cluttered with chrome fittings. Conan read the names on the hulls out loud as he strode along. "*Ocean Pacer, Sir John Falstaff, Ocean Viking*—the Swedes are in, eh? *Flagrante Delicto* . . ." He looked around, craning his neck. "No one around at all. They must all be in town. *Etoile du Sud*—I wonder who's sailing her? Surely not Terlain?" Conan's voice suddenly was lower. "Ah, there she is!" He turned to Ruth. "Pretty as a picture, eh?"

Ruth saw a long, low dark blue hull. She glanced at the silver steering wheel and the massive chrome sheet windlasses, and up at the arrogant-looking anodized golden mainmast.

"She's all locked up—I suppose until Houghton gets here in the morning," Conan said. "No sense in going aboard."

"Then let's go back to Lisbon, Conan. My feet are getting tired," said Ruth, and then she wished she hadn't.

"Okay, but I'd like to look over the others." He nodded toward the other race craft. To Ruth they seemed only a jumble of very expensive playthings. "Look, you rest your feet here a minute, I won't be more than a jiffy." He strode off, his attention focused on the other craft along the basin.

Ruth sat on a low bollard and waited for him. She stared down at *Josephine* and hated it as she had never hated any other inanimate object in her life. She hated *Josephine* so much that she could taste the hatred welling up inside her. She glared at the boat and wished with all her heart that it would sink in its moorings right then and there. With a grimace she pulled herself together and decided that she would ignore the boat, walk further away from it, pretend it was not there, waiting to take Conan away from her. She had resented, much of the time, being a woman at all until Conan had come along. Just to know him, the man in him, made it all worthwhile. Anyway, she asked herself, what fool ever promised that love necessarily meant endless happiness? For a moment she wished that she had not meant her love for Conan, that she could have been ... frivolous about it all; but then she knew that if she had been frivolous it would not have been love. "So the hell with it," she told herself aloud. She was leaving for New York and her work and her friends and her own life in the morning. There was no stopping—no sense in stopping—a man like Conan once he had made up his mind.

Conan caught up with her. Wordlessly he smiled. She, also wordlessly, reached up for him and kissed him hard. Still silent, they made their way back to the railway station, where, as they waited, Conan amused her with fanciful tales about the other skippers, most of whom he had not yet met, and whom he only imagined and brought to life for her hilariously.

The rest of the day and night was for Ruth bliss, passion, and rapture, until the sweet sorrow of their bodies parting at daybreak.

Chapter 4

NEITHER RUTH NOR CONAN were fond of leave-taking at any time. When the time came for their own parting they liked it even less. At breakfast, at their accustomed table in front of the Pastilleria Suisse, in the taxi out to the airport, and during an interminable wait for a plane which was a mere fifteen minutes late, they made small talk, mainly of the arrangements for Conan's New York apartment and the retention of mail. Ruth agreed to forward any letters from publishers or editors to Conan's agent and to keep the rest herself until his return.

"He's got a copy of my will, too," said Conan, doing his best to sound casual about it. "It's only a formality, of course," he said, embarrassed. "There isn't really much in the kitty."

Ruth hugged his arm. She looked into his eyes directly. "Look after yourself, Conan." His love—her love for him was all that mattered.

He looked at her. "Will you come away with me then? I've a book in my head about the Philippines, a sort of Conradian saga, as well as a thing about this voyage, of course. We could go there to live for a couple of years. . . . It's cool in the mountains. . . . Since I've loved you . . . my love for you makes me love everything and everyone . . . more than . . . I've never felt like it before." He stammered as he recognized himself in her, as over all the airport loudspeakers ordered passengers to board for New York. Ruth took the small case which Conan handed her. She

[34]

put it down again on the floor, reached up, and kissed him.

"Look after yourself, Conan. Try to win—for both of us," she murmured. She quickly picked up the case and walked through the doorway onto the tarmac. Conan watched her swing her way firmly to the plane steps, watched her climb the steps, and watched her disappear inside the great jet plane without once looking back.

In a way Conan was glad there were not many people about in the airport, it somehow made the parting easier. He glanced at his watch and, slowly, made his way up the wide stairway to the coffee lounge. He would be able to see Ruth's plane take off from there, through the wide windows, and he could wait there for Mike Houghton's plane from London to arrive in two hour's time. He bought the previous Sunday's *London Globe* newspaper on the way to the coffee lounge, found an empty table, sat down, and leafed through the pages. The paper was last week's edition, but there it was on the front page of the sports section—"Globe Round the World Sailing Race—the Lineup." Below the headline were pictures of most of the boats taking part in the race, with brief details of the boat and skipper.

Ruth's plane started to move out across the tarmac to its take-off station. He watched until it snootily cocked its nose up and confidently, nonchalantly, zoomed off out of sight. He felt numb and relieved at the same time. He turned again to the newspaper. There was a rather fuzzy picture of *Josephine*. "Built," he read, "1973 at Struther's, Southampton. Designers Lightman and Reevers, U.S.A., length overall, 44 feet, length waterline, 38 feet, sloop, sail area 980 square feet (working rig). Placed in Round Britain race, 1978." Pretty good, thought Conan. He read on— "Participant in disastrous Fastnet race, 1979. *Josephine*, with Sean Shaughnessy as skipper and four crew, abandoned the race at midstage and arrived safely back in Falmouth. Fifteen crewmen died in the 1979 Fastnet race, 24 yachts were abandoned, and 138 racing sailors"—Conan whistled softly as he read the numbers—"were rescued by search and rescue services from three NATO countries."

There they go again, thought Conan. Trust the press to play up death and disaster. They must have had a ball with hostages languishing all over the place under threats of death.... Funny how the Yanks still hadn't learned that some others were not as they ...

He focused his eyes back onto *Josephine*'s details. "Skipper Shaughnessy, slated for the Globe £50,000 single-handed round-the-world race, lost his life in a car crash outside London last week. He was returning to London airport from an inquiry, held in Portsmouth, into the Fastnet race debacle. Mike Houghton, *Josephine*'s manager, states that Shaughnessy's place is being taken by Bill Conan, though this has not yet been confirmed. Conan, who skippered the 24-foot *Hobson's Choice* in the Observer single-handed transatlantic race of 1976, was involved in a collision with a power boat six miles from the finishing line in Newport, U.S.A., and, although first in his handicap class, was disqualified."

Conan laid the paper down and stared out of the window. He remembered how the power boat had charged into *Hobson's Choice*. One minute he'd been anxiously dressed for arrival, in a clean jersey and blue jeans and best deck shoes, standing at the helm, excitedly anticipating the end of three weeks of rough going, mainly on cold food, and the next minute he'd been floundering around holding on grimly to a capsized, shattered hull.

As Conan stared through the window, his frown changed to a grin. He recalled his first words when the power boat owner, in a frenetic panic, had hove to. Conan had slowly swum over to the power boat. When the crew had dragged him on board, the owner, a Pickwickian little man in an impossibly immaculate white suit, moaned over him, "Gee, feller, I'm really sorry about this ..." At that moment a U.S. Coast Guard launch had arrived close by and was hailing for Conan to be passed on board it. Conan, dripping wet through and deeply angry, had grabbed the boat owner by the shoulder, shaken him like a terrier, and shouted into his face, "You clumsy bastard!" Then, to the consternation of the power boat crew he had jumped back in the sea and swum the few yards over to the Coast Guard launch, whose ratings hauled him on board their vessel boatless, penniless, and hopping mad. Thus his arrival in America.

Conan turned back to the newspaper account. "As Bill Conan has not been active in ocean racing," he read, "nor, according to reports, even in sailing, for the past four years, his chances in the Globe £50,000 round-the-world race are considered by most experts to be slim, although in an event of this nature, of course, anything can happen. Conan, if he joins *Josephine* in Lisbon early this week, will have his work cut out to accustom himself to the boat in time to make a good showing on the first leg down to a point off the coast of Brazil. Conan was renowned as a hard skipper, a first-class driver; it will be interesting to see what the effect of four years of soft shore life in America have had on his performance in the initial stages of the race."

Conan snorted quietly and turned to the form of the other eight entrants in the race.

"*Sir John Falstaff,*" he read. "British, sloop, 55 foot length overall ... skipper Lieutenant Commander Joseph Morgan, forty-two, sponsored by major British yacht clubs . . . considered the favorite . . . *Ocean Pacer*, British, yawl, 53 feet overall . . . skipper John Tyler, forty, this will be his third solo circumnavigation, which will set a new record. Tyler is considered the second favorite . . . *Southern Star*, Australian, sloop, 53 feet overall, Paddy Hunt, thirty-five, winner of four single-handed ocean races . . . *Flagrante Delicto*, New Zealand, ketch, 46 feet overall, skipper Mary Chatterton, twenty-eight, the only woman entrant, her third single-handed ocean race . . . *Etoile du Sud*, French, yawl, 48 feet overall, skipper Jaques Duplessis, forty-four, winner three single-handed ocean races . . . *Sundance Kid*, U.S.A., a yawl, 48 feet overall, skipper Jack Hanson, twenty-three, sponsored by an international conglomerate. She is the most extensively equipped vessel in the fleet. Hanson, from California, is a surfing and dinghy-racing champion, but apart from his qualifying thousand-mile passage to Lisbon from U.K., he has had no other single-handed ocean experience. However, because of the sophisticated radio weather-report receiving system, and the radio navigational system, both via satellite, Hanson shares the third favorite place with . . . *Ocean Viking*, Swedish, yawl, 47 feet overall, skipper Sven Larsen, forty, winner of five single-handed ocean races, shares third favorite place with Jack Hanson. Here, it will be a case of youthful exuberance and modern technology being pitted against seamanship and hard-earned experience."

Conan shook his head as he read the last name on the list. "*Blytskwtska*." At first he thought it was a printer's error, then he tried to pronounce it a couple of times, moving his lips silently, and finally he gave up and read on. "Poland, yawl, 44 feet overall, skipper Petr Bartusok, thirty-eight, sponsored by the Polish Railway Worker's Sailing Association. This will be Bartusok's second circumnavigation, but apart from the qualifying passage from Gdynia to Lisbon, his first single-handed ocean event . . ." Conan waded through the words until he came across a passage that he read twice. "Of the fifteen yachts on the original entry list that left Weymouth for the passage to Lisbon, the starting line, six dropped out before their arrival in Lisbon. This seems to have been due as much to equipment failure as to the bad weather that was encountered in the Bay of Biscay. General Sir Hubert Alwys-Botheringham, who at seventy-two years of age set out for the race in his 45-foot yawl *Able*, not only lost his mainmast, but also suffered a heart attack. He died shortly after being picked up by a Royal Navy minesweeper when only three hundred miles out. 'Bobby' Gantry, twenty-two, who set out in the 25-foot folkboat *Rolling Stone*, gave up after the first night, and radioed for a rescue helicopter. Gantry now says that he is opening a disco as he feels it is more suitable to his personality. Gantry, former member of a pop group, stated that he found solo sailing 'very boring, being on my own and going up and down and all that.' "

Conan grinned wryly. The reporter, himself probably bored stiff in the Fleet Street office, must have enjoyed writing that, he thought.

At one o'clock the BOAC plane from London landed. As the line of passengers traipsed across the tarmac Conan caught sight of Mike Houghton bringing up the rear, behind early vacationers and prosperous-looking wine merchants and their families. Conan studied Mike as he approached the wide open entry doors. He was as jaunty as ever, though he was slightly older looking than when Conan had last set eyes on him five years before—Conan reckoned he must be fifty now. He was a thin as a rail. As usual, he was dressed in a good quality blue blazer and gray slacks. As Houghton drew closer to the door Conan saw that he was wearing the gold badge of the Southern Counties Ocean Cruising Club on the breast pocket of the blazer. Houghton's wavy brown hair was, he saw, now graying over the ears. His skin was pallid. He wore dark sunglasses. Conan wondered if Houghton's eyesight was any worse. Houghton had lost one eye and damaged the other when a mainsail boom had smashed him. It had been during a transatlantic solo race. Houghton had been damned lucky to be sighted by a freighter which, seeing his sails flapping wildly, had rescued him after he had been two days unconscious on deck, prevented from falling overboard only by the fallen, loose mainsail. He was pleased that he had not mentioned Houghton's half-blindness to Ruth. It would have only made her worry the more . . .

Houghton was shaking his hand. He was taller than Conan by two inches. His voice was high, and his accent was pure Cambridge. To Conan, after four years' sojourn among New York accents, Houghton's voice sounded, at first, a little effusive but he dismissed that thought quickly from his mind. There had never been a tougher nut than Houghton in his sailing days. Never, anywhere.

The fact that it was rumored that Houghton preferred men to women was neither here nor there, Conan reflected. There had never been a breath of scandal about him where his crews were concerned and for Conan, as for most ocean roamers, what Houghton did ashore was his own concern. His semiblindness must be cramping his style, poor devil, was Conan's only thought about it.

Houghton greeted him, "Bill Conan! Hul*lo* old chap! How *are* you?" He glanced at the newspaper Conan had tucked under his arm. "Ah, see you've been weighing up the competition, eh?"

"Mike, good to see you. Yes, it's quite a lineup, isn't it?" Conan took one of the club race-coordinator's small cases from him, held his elbow, and guided him toward the taxi rank. "Do you mind if we call at my pension? I want to collect my things. We can have a spot of lunch there, too, before we go over to *Josephine*," he explained.

They reached the cab rank and stood waiting for the line of passengers to slowly move along. It was the only place in Portugal that Conan had ever seen a queue. Usually it was everyone for himself and the devil take the hindmost. He turned to Houghton. "Bad luck about poor old Shaughnessy."

Houghton peered at him through his dark glasses. "Yes, an awful shame. Julia—did you meet his wife?"

Conan shook his head. Then remembering that Houghton might not be able to see him clearly, he said, "No."

"She took it very badly . . . still in hospital for shock . . ."

"I can't recall, did he have any children?" Conan asked.

"Yes, two. One of school age. The Royal Air Force—he used to be in the air force you know."

Conan hesitated, then said, "No, I didn't, he never mentioned it to me . . . oh, yes, he—I remember seeing the R.A.F. ensign on *Josephine* in Annapolis."

Houghton continued, "The Air Force Benevolent Association are taking care of the school expenses, at least for this year."

There was silence between them until Conan said quietly, "What a stupid way for a man like Shaughnessy to go—in a car accident, of all things."

"Yes, he flew back from here for yet another inquiry into the Fastnet fiasco. He was on his way back to Heathrow Airport. . . . I rather think he would have been happier going some other—" Houghton stopped himself, leaving the sentence unfinished. They both could end it themselves. They both, in the brilliant Lisbon sunshine, had momentary visions of fierce, angry, black seas overwhelming them. Conan mentally shook himself free of the nightmarish image. They had both stared death in the face more times than they cared to remember, yet they both knew that under the threat of imminent death is the closest a man gets to absolute freedom. They also both knew how, when death is surveyed at close quarters, a little too close, the imagination can come into its own, and that if a man yields to it his emotions can take on an intensity, a depth, that while clarifying the reasons for life, tend to obscure the means of staying alive. They were terribly British about it; they pragmatically stowed the thoughts of death away in the nethermost lockers of their minds. Death and taxes are always with the Americans—to these eternal banes the British customarily add a third, all their own, the weather.

"Looks like we'll have fine weather, anyway," Conan observed, "for the start."

Houghton inspected the sky briefly. "Beautiful, gorgeous day," he agreed.

It was their turn for a cab. Managing to look officious and servile at the same time, the airport cab-regulator ordered up a car with an imperious bark, and bowed and scraped as Conan pressed a five escudo note into his hand for justifying his existence.

As the cab accelerated Houghton said, "Aw'fly glad to get your telegram. We were worried stiff. No one else, at least no one we could get hold of in time, was qualified by the thousand-mile solo trip, you see. If we'd found anyone who stood a chance it would have meant they'd have had to take *Josephine* out immediately—last week d'you see—and sail around like the dickens for a week or so to get the thousand miles under their belt, then come back into Lisbon and immediately depart for the race. What with all the stores and last minute checkups it would have been absolutely impossible, d'you see, Bill?"

"What about Tim Sharples? I heard he sailed back from Capetown months ago."

"He did, but he's delivering a sixty-footer for some Continental bigwig—Holland to Rio. Took off three weeks ago."

"Who's sponsoring *Josephine*, anyway?" asked Conan.

"The British Paper Industries."

"God, don't tell me she's made of reinforced papier-mâché!"

Houghton laughed and slapped his knee. "Same old Conan," he guffawed. "No, regular Fiberglas, all built under Lloyd's supervision, of course, three inch by the keel and all that. She's an aw'fly good vessel, Bill, take anything thrown her. She took quite a beating in the Round Britain race and in the Fastnet last year . . . came through with hardly a scratch . . . solid as the Rock of Gibraltar . . . but you know her . . ."

A vision flashed through Conan's mind of the miles of tunnel which honeycomb Gibraltar, but all he said was yes.

Houghton continued, speaking softly as he stared through the cab window at the scenery they were passing. "We stored her for fourteen months. There's everything . . . oodles of food cans, labels all stripped off and the contents marked with paint, of course . . . and freeze-dried foods . . . the food companies did us proud."

"Side band radio?" asked Conan. "Auxiliary generator?"

"The best—I can't recall the details, but you'll see when we get aboard." Houghton lit a cigarette. "Shaughnessy stripped just about everything from the accommodation, of course. He was a ruthless devil when it came to saving weight, but you'll see for yourself. And by the way . . ." Houghton tapped his knee "you'd better check as much as you can as soon as possible—we've only three working days until the start of the race. I'm sorry, I'm afraid it's something of a pierhead jump for you, Bill." They were silent as the cab stopped at a light. Then, as they shot forward again Houghton said, "But anyway, if I know—knew Shaughnessy, he left everything shipshape, in apple-pie order."

Conan thought that would make an odd epitaph. He envisaged the legend carved into a stone cross set into the green sward atop a sea-beaten cliff in Donegal: *"Sean Shaughnessy—1930–1980—he left everything shipshape and in apple-pie order."* He dismissed the sacrilegious image from his mind as the cab came to a halt outside the Pension Coimbra-Madrid.

They sat down to lunch at Conan's regular table on the pavement outside the Pastilleria Suisse. Houghton offered to treat Conan, who, taking advantage of a rare occasion, ordered sauerkraut with apples and beer, *bife a Portuguesa*—an eight-ounce steak, sautéed in garlic with a thick slice of ham on top—and a *Barriga de Freira*, a chocolate pudding. "Might as well fill up now," he said to Houghton, as the waiter took his order. Houghton ordered *Carne de Porco com Ameijoas*—pork with clams, on Conan's recommendation. "I'd have it myself if seafood agreed with my stomach," he told the race coordinator. For wine, Conan, at Houghton's invitation, chose a fine *vinho verde* which the coordinator, who had a sensitive palate, acclaimed. They ate leisurely, discussing at first the many British influences in Lisbon. Houghton remarked on the green double-decker buses and the red British-style free-standing, upright cylindrical mailboxes. "Yes, you can get genuine ginger beer and a good cup of tea here, too," commented Conan, half-sarcastically. "And the London papers, of course," he added.

As the waiter brought after-lunch coffees, Conan leaned across to Houghton, who sat pensively watching the passersby on the sidewalk. "Mike," he said, "this Fastnet race disaster—what was it all about? I've been rather shut away in New York and only heard and saw a few obviously garbled reports on the radio and TV."

Houghton looked at him in surprise. "I should have thought that you, of all people, would have found out as much as possible about it," he said. He could be unctuous when he wanted to be. "I believe the *New York Times* reported it, and the American yachting magazines." He flicked some cigarette ash from his blazer. "But I suppose that now you're a *writer*—" Houghton pressed his chin into his neck and pursed his lips.

Conan did not let him finish. "I was writing my first novel," he said. "It took me eight months. I live like a bloody hermit when I'm writing, Mike—all I do is write, eat, keep off booze, and sleep. I had a deadline on *The Flying Dutchman,* and, well, I just didn't see anything about the Fastnet."

"Of course, old man, I understand," said Houghton. He lit a cigarette. "What happened, very briefly, is this. It wasn't exactly a fiasco; more aw'fly bad luck. Just over three hundred yachts—three hundred and three, to be precise—left Falmouth, the starting point, in August, for the usual course: out across the Irish Sea, around Fastnet rock, and back to Falmouth. They were mostly well into the middle of the Celtic Sea, as you know a roughish spot at the best of times, when suddenly, virtually without warning, gale force winds generated, it turned out, by a rapidly deepening low pressure area, struck the fleet. The wind rose to Force Eleven and the seas steepened until they were forty to forty-four feet high; quite a dusting, you see, Bill."

"Mmm," said Conan. "Quite a dusting." He inwardly smiled at the understatement. Force Eleven is just under hurricane strength.

"There was the devil to pay. One hundred and twelve boats were knocked over on their beam ends to the horizontal..." Houghton's brow knitted as he recalled the figures "and seventy-seven of those were blown over *beyond* the horizontal. Five of the boats reported that they spent between thirty seconds and five minutes totally inverted—upside down in the sea. Fifty-one vessels reported that one or more crew members were washed overboard. Of these, several went overboard more than once. Twenty-six boats reported a safety harness failure. Of the fifteen men in all who died during or as a result of the storm, six died after their safety harness, or a safety harness attachment point, failed. Seven more of the dead were lost in incidents involving life rafts..." A pained look crossed Houghton's face. "You can guess what happened. . . ."

Conan nodded slowly. "I think so. The yachts they abandoned were afterward found safely afloat."

"Exactly, each and every yacht was recovered. If those people had only stayed on board their yachts they would have very probably, all of them, been still alive today."

"The old story," commented Conan. "It sounds like a massacre. Tell me, Mike, were there many inexperienced skippers out there? I suppose there must have been. There's not much of a qualification requirement for the Fastnet, is there?"

A sudden gust of wind blew along the Rossio, sending a peasant woman's wide straw hat flying. There was a honk of horns and squeals of brakes as cars swerved to avoid the half-dozen men, idlers and hucksters, who ran and scrambled to retrieve the hat as it rolled away across the wide square. The woman, a basket of tomatoes at her feet, stood, arms angled, hands on her wide hips, her face red with the sun and the excitement of the city. Conan and Houghton watched, intrigued, as a one-armed bootblack, with grave courtesy, handed the woman back her headgear.

Houghton returned to the subject of the disaster. "That's a moot point. The main board of inquiry did not think that experience or lack of it had a great deal of bearing on the number of knockdowns, the amount of severe damage, abandonments, or loss of life. I personally disagree with them on the latter two, the desertions and deaths, and I think you'll agree with me, Bill, that few experienced skippers would allow their crew to abandon a vessel that is still watertight to a degree, still afloat?"

"Bloody right. They should have stuck to their vessels. If she'll float for an hour she'll float for a day, as the old saying has it, and God knows, even a vessel hull down and leaking like a sieve is safer than any life raft in seas that big."

"Quite," said Houghton.

"What happened to the BBC, I mean the weather forecasts?"

"Those who listened-in got three hours' warning of the gale. Most of the boats could not receive the VHF and Coast Radio forecasts. You know the Western Approaches, Bill, how rapidly a storm can brew up with hardly any warning."

"How many did you say were lost through safety harness failure?" asked Conan.

"Six," Houghton sighed. "I'm glad you brought that up, because the RORC recommended that double harness be worn in severe conditions, so I've brought you an extra harness along—you already have two on board, of course."

"I appreciate it," said Conan.

"They also pointed out the danger of clipping the harness line onto the vessel's standing lifelines, and they recommend an adequte deck line from the cockpit to points forward in the boat, to clip the harness line to."

"I do that anyway."

"I'll discuss the life raft, life jacket, and pyrotechnics with you tomorrow, Bill. I know you'll ask what's the point when your course will mainly be over such empty spaces of the ocean, but there might be a chance of collision in a shipping lane, that kind of thing—"

"Cheerful today, Mike," Conan murmured.

"Well, you never know, nice to be on the safe side . . ." As he paid the check, Houghton left the rest unsaid.

Houghton, at this moment, actually envied Conan because he knew that the more one lives life the less one fears death. It was only when drumming away on a close reach or winging on a dead run out in the ocean that he had ever really lived life and forgotten the shadow of eventual death. His continual disappointments in love had been so many that now Houghton accepted it as a rather unpleasant necessity. He no longer looked for a meaning to life in that direction, and as a poor substitute (he could no longer skipper a boat), threw himself into his work with an intensity that amazed everyone who knew him. It was sad, but true, Houghton reflected, if we don't love we don't live fully—and if we don't live fully then we fear death all the more. He knew the paradox that it is only by loving that we come to realize the full import of death. Houghton envied the Scot, too, because death must now be always with Conan, near the surface of his consciousness, bringing stark contrast to the brilliant colors of life in all their glory, enabling him to savor every breath, every drop, every morsel, every sight, every sound, every emotion; more than anyone who has not lived with death could ever know.

For Conan it was different. He always lived life—really lived life—even in his writing, fully, *all stops out and damn the torpedoes!*

Conan collected his duffel bag from the floor and strode to the edge of the sidewalk to hail a cab. Houghton joined him. Conan studied him for a minute, then grinned widely. Houghton looked at him quizzically. Conan, his eyes briefly following the motion of a passing woman, said, "Yes, like you say, Mike, it really is nice to be on the safe side."

As a taxi drew up, they both piled inside, chuckling softly at the subtlety of the allusion.

"Club Nautico de Belém," Conan ordered the driver, as the cab, horn honking, shot off into the traffic.

They were silent on the way to Belém, but both of them knew what the other was thinking of . . . the thirty thousand miles of wind-swept, heaving, empty ocean and the months of effort and struggle that lay between Bill Conan and victory.

As they overtook the Lisbon-Belém train, Conan remembered being with Ruth the day before. He was still thinking of Ruth when they arrived on the jetty. He felt deprived. Her leaving had left a void in part of him. He was aware of his own conceits, his own egotism, but he knew that loving Ruth, missing her, was his own salvation.

"She's a beauty!" Houghton exclaimed, looking down at *Josephine*, as if it were not the fiftieth time he had gazed on the boat.

"She surely is," Conan said, as he clambered out lugging his duffel bag, not thinking at all, yet, of *Josephine*. "She surely is!"

Chapter 5

"THANK GOD SHAUGHNESSY had good musical taste, anyway," Conan remarked to Houghton who, with the ship's checklist held close to his failing eye under the main cabin lamp, was marking off items as Conan called them out. The list was thirty-five pages long. There were a total of 1,754 items on the list. This was apart from the engine and generator spares lists.

"Tape cassettes—thirty-five in all." Conan called out. "Debussy—Vivaldi—Ravel—Brahms—Mendelssohn—*The Hebrides Overture*—Beethoven—Chopin—Bach—Tchaikovsky, 1812—great stuff in dirty weather." Conan crouched to read labels on the plastic boxes under the coach roof. "*Tannhäuser, Ride of the Valkyries*, and here's Gilbert and Sullivan—*The Mikado, The Pirates of Penzance*, and . . . well, well, good old Sean, I never knew he was a jazz buff—Bix Beiderbecke, Fats Waller—Jelly Roll Morton . . . and . . . hello, what's this? . . . Noel Coward . . . 'Selection including "Don't put your daughter on the stage Mrs. . . . Worthington" '?"

"I gave that to Julia . . . his wife . . . to present to him. Thought it might amuse him," asserted Houghton sadly.

"Well, that's about it for today," declared Conan. They had started the inventory—checking the manifest, they called it—as soon as they had boarded *Josephine* and stowed their gear below. In the bright afternoon sunlight, Conan had carefully checked all the rigging, the cables, and the turnbuckles. They had rigged the bosun's chair and he had gone up to the masthead and worked his way down, carefully examining the radar reflector, every block, the spreaders, every tang, every toggle, every clevis pin, every inch of the mast and the standing and running rigging. Then, working his way forward from the stern, Conan had inspected the self-steering gear, the backstay adjusters and insulators, the booms, the bales, the claws, the vangs, the goosenecks on the mainmast, the lifelines, their stanchions and their fixings, above deck and below, the sheet and halyard winches—great, self-tailing beauties from Barlow—all the cleats, fairleads, sail tracks, sheet stoppers, sail slides, the reefing gear on the main, every shackle, the navigation lights; in short he went over the deck and sailing gear as carefully as would any skipper worth his salt, who held his life in his own hands.

As he made the topside inspection, and gazed over the sleek deck, the smooth lines, and *Josephine*'s heavy chrome fittings, Conan wryly thought to himself what a change had been wrought in small craft over the past three decades. He remembered some of the craft he had picked up and commissioned years ago. They were mostly wood. Some of them fifty or sixty years old, fastened with iron. Headed for the tropics they were the prospective feeding grounds of the teredo worm, an unpleasant creature that inhabits tropical waters and that can reduce a wooden vessel to the watertight integrity of Gruyère within months. The teredo, he remembered, has a head shaped like a metal drill, and about as hard. The teredo would make a pinhole in a plank, work its way in, then, still a tiny animal, it would turn at right angles and attack the length of the plank, eating its way through the wood until the plank was, in a few weeks, riddled right through, but treacherously; outside the plank there would be no sign of the teredo worm's depredations. To repel the teredo worm, boat's bottoms had been sheathed in copper. But nothing was easy or as simple as it looked on wooden ships. If the bottom was copper covered and the fastenings of the vessel were of iron, then galvanic action would set up, the iron would be eaten away, and in a year or two the boat's planks would be falling apart.

On arrival in the tropics, he, sometimes alone, sometimes with a crew, would careen the boat, that is, lay her over at low tide on a beach or in a mosquito-infested mangrove swamp, and inspect the bottom for minute holes. Nine out of ten times they found, after hot and heavy work scraping the bottom clean, it would be holed in a hundred places. They used to burn the bottom planks with a blowtorch to bring the worms, long now and fat, squirming out of their holes. Then they left the hull heeled over for a few days. This was, by tradition, supposed to kill what worms were left. Then they keeled the boat over on her other side and started three days' work on that. *Josephine* was Fiberglas. There would be no teredos in her, ever; blood, tears, anxiety, and sweat maybe—but no teredo.

Down below again, as the sun eased its way over the spreader, Conan checked the two full sets of spare sails and the three storm jibs and the three trysails—again carefully, for the heavy weather sails must be the best on board, "like a whorehouse madam, a vessel only wears her best clothes when the going gets rough," as Conan put it to Houghton, who wrinkled his nose slightly, then snorted a short laugh of agreement.

Next Conan, working his way back through what Houghton called "the rather Spartan" main cabin—the table had been stripped out by Shaughnessy—he checked the mast step in the bilge and the bilges themselves. As he did so, he wondered what Houghton would have thought of the Arab dhow he had once taken over in Egypt and delivered to a mad British army colonel in Malta. It was twenty-one years before—in 1960. When Conan had first boarded the dhow the two Arab crew had been hauling up clear water from her bilge well. They had bailed her out all the five days they had waited for permission from the authorities to leave port, and all the two weeks' sail to Malta. Of all the dhows that had been in Alexandria she was the smallest, dirtiest, and smelliest. She had no accommodation at all and there was always short rations. The only thing that kept the sea from swamping her, once they were on passage, was a loosely woven palm-leaf matting which they had lashed to her bulwarks. She was fast, graceful, with good lines, but she was one of the most God-awful craft he had ever sailed in. Her high mainmast, riggingless and raked sharply forward, seemed to have sprouted out of the hull. The lateen yards, all of fifty feet long, were made of two tree branches tied together, her cordage was homemade from coconut fiber and her sails had been run up by the ex-owner's wife, patiently, from cheap number six Egyptian cotton.

They had worn into Valetta thin, thirsty, and half-dead from bailing continuously, and the mad colonel had accused them of malingering. They were a day later than Conan had estimated in his letter to the colonel.

Conan smiled as he lit the alcohol pressure stove and oven in the galley. "Might as well make hay while the sun shines," he said as he made tea for Houghton and himself.

The engine was a straightforward Perkins 41 horsepower diesel. He browsed through the operator's manual, checked the engine's holding down bolts and oil level, saw that it was charging the batteries and that the ahead and astern gear were functioning, then stopped the main engine—it would be used little, if at all, on the race—and turned his attention to the auxiliary generator, another Perkins, a 15-kw diesel. With this he would charge his four batteries daily with enough electricity to operate the radio twice daily, and give him the small amount of light he would need for navigation and domestic purposes.

"I'll go over the side in the morning and check the through-hull fittings and propellor, and give her a bit of a scrub," Conan told Houghton, after he had checked the fuel and the water tanks. All full.

Next Conan checked the navigational gear, the two sextants, the walnut-boxed chronometer, the navigational tables and nautical almanac, and a hundred charts—a few ocean charts and one for every major port near the race route, in case *Josephine* might have to abandon the race and make for safe haven. "One hundred and five pencils," Conan called out, as he completed the navigational stock-taking.

He recalled the time he had sighted a little twenty-foot sloop way out in mid-Atlantic, between the Canary Islands and Barbados. The small, scruffy boat had hailed his thirty-footer, and he had gone close to her and heaved to. The lone sailor was a young Swiss, anxious to know his whereabouts. Conan had told him, and then asked if he needed anything else, and how was he navigating? The Swiss youth, Ronnie by name, had waved an ordinary household atlas at him, then opened to the page showing the Atlantic Ocean and indicated to him a red pencil line scratched out on the map. As far as he could find out, Ronnie never did reach Barbados. It had been late June. There had been a hurricane only a few days later. . . . Conan frowned and turned back to the job in hand.

By the time the electronics—the anemometer, wind direction indicator, wind speed indicator, knot meter, depth-sounder, the Loran, and radio transmitter-receiver (the finest, from Denmark)—had been checked out, it was well past suppertime. Wearily, they made their way up the companionway to the cockpit. They were aware of movement and voices on the other race vessels each side of *Josephine*.

"Well, what do you think of her, Bill?" asked Houghton.

"She'll do."

"We'll go through the food list tomorrow afternoon. Sean took in fourteen months' supply—a lot of freeze-dried stuff well sealed up, steaks and all that." Houghton handed Conan the keys to *Josephine*. It was a very British ceremony. It was now official; Conan was now skipper of *Josephine*.

"Cheers, Mike," Conan acknowledged, and bent to lock the hatch door. As he straightened up again Conan said, "Sad, that last entry in the log by Shaughnessy before he left the boat."

"Oh?"

"Yes, he wrote 'a very fine, sea-kindly vessel and I have every confidence in making a good show in the coming months.' "

"Poor old—" Houghton did not finish the sentence. A voice calling from the jetty high above them interrupted.

"Ahoy, *Josephine!*"

"Be right up, we're coming ashore!" Conan shouted. He looked up and saw a figure silhouetted in one of the yellow-orange pools of light that streamed from the dockside lamps. Holding on to the boat's mooring lines, they made their way up the sea-moss covered sloping jetty wall, Houghton first, with Conan close behind him. They pulled themselves onto the quay. In the clear, star-laden sky a three-quarter moon was suspended over the gigantic granite memorial to Prince Henry the Navigator which overlooks the Tagus River close by the yacht basin.

The figure on the quay approached them. Soon Conan saw that it was that of a tall, slim young man wearing a baseball cap. The young man smiled, showing a perfect set of teeth in the lamplight, and stretched out his hand. "Jack Hanson, *Sundance Kid,*" he drawled in a loud voice. "Real pleased to meet you dudes. Which one of you is Bill Conan?"

"The man himself," replied Conan, putting out his hand.

"Wow," shouted Hanson, "this's really something . . . there was a rumor goin' around you were here . . . I'm an avid reader of your stuff . . . you really laid a trip on me, man!" He was dressed casually, in an old brown sweater and blue jeans and running shoes. Under his long-peaked baseball cap his hair was dirty blond and so long it was almost down to his shoulders. He wore a pair of rimless half-glasses low down on his short nose, and a beard so stringy and fair that at first Conan did not see it.

"This is Mike Houghton. He's race-coordinator of the Southern Counties Ocean Cruising—"

Hanson didn't let Conan finish. He grabbed Houghton's hand. "Say, you're not the Mike Houghton that won the Capetown-Perth 71?" he shouted.

"Actually, yes," murmured Houghton, somewhat abashed.

"Yeah . . . read the account in . . . some magazine. Say, that was some tough trip, huh, Mike?" Hanson's voice reminded Conan of a foghorn.

"Quite boisterous." Houghton peered at Hanson, trying to see him in the dim lamplight. Three of the five boats that had competed in the race had disappeared without trace in the angry Southern Ocean.

"Were you in the last Fastnet race?" Hanson shouted at Houghton. Then, without waiting for a reply, in a rush of words he addressed Conan. "I know *you* weren't . . . I saw you on the Geoff Muffin show last August . . . hell, I wish I'd known you'd be out in California, I live only a few blocks away from Geoff's studio . . ."

Houghton said, his voice cutting softly through the shadows, "We're just off to eat. Have you—?"

"Hell no, I been out joggin' . . . I run ten miles a day . . . ashore."

"Why don't you come with us?" Houghton offered. "We're only going for something simple at one of the local places over in the village."

"Can I? Wow, ain't that somethin'? Me going to dinner with Bill Conan and Mike Houghton." Hanson nodded over his shoulder at the other racing boats. "The others . . . well, the two Brits keep pretty much to themselves. The Aussie's taken up with the chick from New Zealand, and the Frenchman Duplessis and the Swede, Larsen, both have their wives here. There's only the Polish guy left on his own, and his English is . . . zip." He grinned. "Pete, that's the Polish guy, he's real cool, though. Ballin' a chick from the harbor master's office."

"Good bloke, eh?" Conan interpreted for Houghton, whose brow was furrowing in puzzlement at Hanson's brand of English.

"Really," murmured Hanson, his voice, for the first time, low and normal. "First foreign commie I ever met . . . but maybe he isn't . . . but if they let him go like this . . . ? "

They walked through the park, past the swan pool now bathed in moonlight. Conan recalled being there with Ruth only yesterday afternoon in the sunshine. He quickened his pace to escape from the recollection. It was too painful, too soon after her leaving.

The cafe on Belém's main street was plain and garishly lit with fluorescent lamps, which cast a cold, pallid glare over the table. They were served a simple meal of local ham—rather tough, bitter, and dry to their tastes—eggs, and beans, which they eased down with a good bottle of *vinho verde*.

While Houghton silently listened, Conan and the young American discussed various aspects of their respective vessels and the coming race.

"*Sundance Kid* sounds like a first-class boat," concluded Conan, after Hanson had enumerated her equipment, all the latest, up-to-date, "state-of-the-art" gear.

"I ain't sweatin'. It's going to take some real downers for me to cop out. It—she was cool in the Bay of Biscay, and that was rough weather, man."

"How did you get into this, Jack?" Houghton asked Hanson quietly.

Hanson's voice echoed around the room. "Oh . . . I was doin' my thing . . . surfin' an' dinghy racin' and all that stuff, out in Long Beach, and this dude Cooley comes out from nowhere and like socks it to me . . . I'm tellin' you, he just zonked me down flat . . . it was *far out* . . . he just comes up to me an' asks like if I could get into it. He's gotten the A.C.H. and the I.P.P. and three other of those fat-cat companies puttin' up the green. When I asked him why he was layin' this on me he said"—Hanson grinned hugely—"it was 'cos they wanted like an all-out all-American boy out there. So I said okay, but whattam I gonna do in the meanwhile—this was the beginnin' of last year, see?—I was like at college an' stuff an' he got them to lay five hundred bucks a month on me as a retainer, see?" Hanson had a way of leaning back, his eyebrows raised, his pale blue eyes wide open, staring to see the effect of his words on whomever he talked at.

"Good deal," remarked Conan, smiling at the American.

"Astonishingly good," agreed Houghton.

Hanson continued, "If I win I pay 'em back, but if not I'm like still on the five hundred charlies a month until the end of the race, see?" He leaned back again, eyes wide open, looking over his half-glasses at Conan.

"How will they cover the expenditures?" asked Houghton.

"I've already filmed eight commercials for stuff supplied to the boat, like each one was filmed twice, one version for if I win and one for if not. Cooley's a real hotshot manager."

"That's what we used to call covering your yardarm," Conan asserted.

Hanson turned to him and beamed over his half-glasses. His light blue eyes twinkled. "Hey, I dig that," he said.

"What does Cooley get out of it?" Houghton asked Hanson.

"The sponsors, Cooley, and me split three ways if I win."

"Fair enough," observed Houghton, "but Conan's on a better deal. If he wins he keeps the lot, lucky devil."

They drank their coffees in silence until Hanson demanded, "Say, you guys been to the Maritime Museum just up the road? The Aussie— what's he called?—Hunt . . . yeah, Paddy Hunt, was telling me like it's quite a trip . . . really something. He says it's like one of the best in the world."

"It is, I know it well," agreed Conan. "I'll show you round, if you'd like to come, on . . . let's see, we're going to be bloody busy tomorrow and Tuesday scrubbing the bottom, checking out the last items in the boat, and the Yacht Club reception in the evening . . . make it Wednesday, in the afternoon, eh, Jack? We should be all on top line for the off by then."

Houghton interjected, "Make it Thursday morning, Bill, my flight is in the early afternoon and I would like to come with you. There are some portalanos I want to see . . ." He saw Hanson's brow knit. "They are ancient sea charts. I've been reading Charles Hapgood—he's one of your people, you know, American professor. He's written a book, *Maps of the Ancient Sea Kings.* You really ought to read it some time. Very intriguing. He postulates that the earth's coasts and oceans were mapped—charted—thousands of years before Christ ... and the Piri Re'is map"—Houghton tapped a cup with a spoon to stress his point—"... dated 1512, mark you, was the direct descendant of charts made by the ancient sea-peoples of Atlantis."

"Atlantis, wow!" exclaimed Hanson. His voice rocked the room.

"Quite," said Houghton, as Conan, grinning, watched him and listened intently. "The Turkish Admiral Piri Re'is must have had something to work from when he drew quite accurate maps of the coasts of western South America and Africa and—and this is the strangest thing—of the coasts of Greenland and Antarctica before they were covered by ice ... and now, using modern detection instruments, which can measure under the ice, we've found that the coast of Queen Maud Land, Antarctica, is pretty near as it's depicted by Piri Re'is. Very strange indeed. Perhaps there's something in it ..."

"Atlantis—what about Atlantis?" Hanson eagerly asked.

"Hapgood suggests that it was in the central, equatorial Atlantic," Houghton replied, "between the closest parts of Africa and South America, somewhere around where St. Paul's Rocks now are. He also suggests that the ancient Sea Kings of Atlantis colonized Crete and Cyprus and Egypt ... and even this area around Lisbon, before the great disaster, whatever it was, which destroyed Atlantis."

"Wow, like race memories of the Flood," exclaimed Hanson.

"Quite," Houghton agreed. "But look here"—he signalled the cafe owner for the check—"I don't know about you chaps, but I'm bone weary. Got up at five A.M. to catch my plane. I think we ought to ..." He turned to Hanson and smiled as he hesitated. "What is it you fellows say? Hit the sack?"

"Crash, flake out," replied the American.

Conan asked, "Do you use those terms now?"

"Yeah."

"That's funny. We used to use exactly the same expressions in the Andrew years ago."

Hanson looked puzzled. "The *what?*"

"Bill means the Royal Navy," explained Houghton, as they left the cafe to walk back to the boats.

Hanson turned to Houghton and looked at him for a long moment. Then he exclaimed, quietly, in an awed tone, "Atlantis ... wow?" and, grinning, shook his head and hair for a minute in semidisbelief.

Conan said jocosely, "Mike's got a bee in his bonnet about ancient voyages. He believes that the world, the oceans, rather, were once ruled by a great race of mariners who were based on the legendary island-continent of Atlantis. That's the theory, right, Mike?"

They were passing again through the waterfront park. The moon hung silver over the black-shining estuary of the Tagus, away in the west. The stars in their constellations trailed after her.

"I don't *believe* it," replied Houghton, "but I do think it is highly possible that such a culture did exist ... and that somehow their civilization came to an end through some great disaster. Who knows? It might have been caused by a nuclear accident, it might have been the ice melting at the retreat of an ice age raising the levels of the oceans.... Who can tell? But there is evidence, as I've discussed, that points to the existence of people who knew how to map the coasts of the world accurately thousands of years ago."

"Wow, wouldn't it be something if we could like trace them?" interjected Hanson. "Maybe we could find out how to avoid a similar disaster ... maybe they were, well, just anything ... like in touch with nature much more close than we are. It freaks me out!"

"Yes, it is intriguing, isn't it?" murmured Houghton. "What do you think, Bill?"

"Sounds a bit like *Alice in Wonderland* to me. I'll believe it when I see positive proof."

"Same old Bill," observed Houghton.

"I suppose there could be something in it, Mike," retorted Conan, "but we get so much ... escapism, I mean in books and films, nowadays. Look at all the fanciful gubbins that's hurled at the public these days, flying saucers and space wars, and all that damned claptrap about the Bermuda Triangle and paranoia-peddling piffle about man-eating sharks. Look, I've just spent four years having this bullshit hurled about around me, Mike. There's big money in it—at least if the people who churn it out are to be believed—who knows? Who can believe anything they say? All I know is that I'm fed up to the gills with sensationalism." Conan almost tripped over a mooring line on the edge of the dock. Houghton, although half-blind, sensed him stagger and quickly grabbed his elbow.

"It's as if they need a substitution for the God they no longer believe in," Conan continued, as he recovered his balance. "It's as if they have to have little green men with superior intelligence out there who are going to come down among them and save them from themselves ..."

Houghton rejoined, "Or as if, in order to escape from the pointlessness of their daily life, the alienation, they feel that they must be fed horror. One more pain to dull the existing agony . . . frustration, I suppose."

"I think they take it because they dig it. They like it," suggested Hanson. "Johnny Do-right is a funny guy . . . freaky, at least out on the Coast."

"From what I saw in my time ashore," Conan observed, "it's because they're so out of touch with nature and the natural world—how many people do you see, for example, in New York, ever looking up at the sky at night?"

"Or even in the day, I guess," agreed the American.

Conan said, "Many of them have been so dulled by all the barrage of crap flung at them day and night . . . then to insulate themselves they get wrapped up in themselves." They were above the vessels now. "Oh—what the hell—g'night, Jack!" Conan helped Houghton over the rail and placed himself below him, so he could be guided down in the dark.

"Yeah, see you guys at the reception tomorrow," came back the stentorian voice of the young American as he disappeared into the shadows in the direction of his own craft.

"You take the pit, Mike, I'll sleep up on deck." Conan unlocked the hatch door. "Pass me up a blanket, will you. There's a spare one under the berth."

"Young Hanson's a bit of a character, eh, Mike?" Conan commented with a grin. "Enthusiastic, I'd say."

"Can't imagine sailing with him," rejoined Houghton gruffly. "I'd need bally earplugs!"

"He'd be handy in a fog on a lee shore," joked Conan.

"Or in an argument with one of those dratted Turkish customs officers," said Houghton, chuckling. "It's true what someone said, you know, Bill, about American conversation as opposed to English . . . British." Houghton remembered Conan's Scottish origins.

"What's that?"

"Well, that our conversation is like a tennis match . . . you know . . . I biff and you boff, and it goes back and forth. But these Americans— their conversations are like . . . cycle races, with each one puffing and pedalling and forging ahead on his own bike regardless of anyone else."

"Some of them are quite good at argument," Conan said finally.

"Sleep well, Bill," called Houghton, later, as he laid himself down on the one berth, but Conan was already fast asleep under the dimmed stars.

Chapter 6

THE FOOD AND DRINKS for the race reception were paid for by the *London Globe.* The function was hosted by the Portuguese navy, who donated the use of the Maritime Museum reception hall and the services of the Naval detachments that guarded the museum, a group of personable young men, many of whom spoke English and French.

Before the "flower revolution" of 1974, such functions usually took place in the Yacht Club, but a worker's committee had taken over the operation of the club in 1975, as part of the worker's participation program. This had all been well meant, very idealistic, and finely intended. Initially the program had swung ahead in wild enthusiasm. The former bar steward had taken over the general management and one of the carpenters had been voted into the position of yard manager. The former management had been retired into limbo with a pittance of a pension.

By the end of 1976 it was obvious, at least to mariners, that the new order was not as ideal as it had sounded in the budding of the flower revolution. The former bar steward was drinking himself to death and the carpenter had taken into his employ, or been coerced into taking, half the lay-abouts of the Lisbon waterfront. The club, consequently, had fallen into a steady decline. The former steward had been packed off to an institution by the end of 1977 and the former carpenter had become a figurehead, whose only obvious function was to attend the weekly payment of vastly inflated wages to a vastly inflated staff, most of whom hardly ever appeared at the club except on paydays. Thenceforward, until the general election of 1979 when a conservative government was returned, the deterioration of the club houses and grounds had been accepted by all concerned as one of a growing number of irritating but seemingly, for the time being, inevitable facts of life.

In the spring of 1980 the worker's committee had been dissolved, and now, a year later, the club members and former staff were once more in charge. The first thing they, in their turn, had done when they took over, was discharge a good sixty percent of the "committee," generally retaining those who had worked at the club before the revolution, and who were known not to have been too "revolutionary," which in Portugal meant "wanting something without any effort." The club was still in a state of flux, as Conan put it "with everything like a midshipman's locker—all on top and nothing handy." The only things that still operated efficiently were the half-dozen showers, although the hot water boiler had been out of action for years. It was to these not-too-clean cubicles that Conan and Houghton repaired in the late afternoon on Wednesday, after a long day of checking, checking, checking everything on board *Josephine* that had not been checked the day before.

They arrived at the museum courtyard—it was only a five-minute walk from the boat—at dusk. The museum is right next to the Monastery of San Jerónimos, which was now floodlit a warm golden color. The carvings and statues and gargoyles of the monastery facade stood out in bold relief. Thousands of stone saints, the Virgin and the Lord, all floodlight bathed in golden beams, blessed the procession of very expensive cars which rolled up to the museum—Mercedes-Benzes, Cadillacs, and Rolls-Royces mainly, but with a few Ferraris and Alfa Romeos among them—to bring in them the more nonconformist members of the Lisbon *haute monde*.

Houghton was in his navy blue blazer and slacks, which he had carefully brushed down before stepping ashore. Conan was still in his customary light brown corduroys, but, as a concession to the social occasion, he had put on a clean light blue shirt and the Southern Counties Ocean Cruising Club tie. The tie was worn and shiny. The last time he had donned it had been in Falmouth for the party before the start of the 1976 transatlantic race. Ruth has insisted that he take it along. It was the only thing he had rescued from *Hobson's Choice*. He'd been wearing it as a belt.

They skirted around a large group of newly arrived guests, all laughing and greeting each other—the men in black tie and loud, the women in long ball gowns and sedate—and entered the museum main entrance. In the foyer they were received—challenged—by three husky Portuguese seamen. Houghton was busy explaining who they were when an English voice cut through the hubbub.

"Mike! Mike Houghton, good to see you again!" Conan saw a medium height fat man with long sideburns, a red face, and a loud tie grasp Houghton's hand. As he did so the fat man beamed at Conan. "Ah-ha," he exclaimed. "This must be . . . Phil . . . Will . . . Conan?"

"Bill," said Conan.

"Yes, of course," said the fat man. They shook hands cursorily.

Houghton intervened. "Bill Conan, this is Jeremy Findlay of the *Globe.*" He turned to Findlay. "You must be here to cover the start?"

Conan reflected to himself how Houghton was a great one for stating the obvious when he was bored. Houghton had told him how he dreaded these occasions. "It's like playing someone else's record collection for the umpteenth time."

"Everything on top line, old chap?" Findlay addressed Houghton.

"All ready for the off."

Findlay turned to Conan. "All the rum stowed away in the bilge, nice and safe, eh . . . got to look after the bubbly, eh, Conan?"

Conan distrusted journalists. He'd had too many run-ins with them, found too many of their accounts distorted, sometimes hurtfully. Some of the press had blamed, by innuendo, the *Hobson's Choice* episode on drink. He took an immediate dislike to Findlay. "I wrapped all the bottles up in old copies of the *Globe,*" he retorted.

Findlay glanced at him from under lowered brows. His smile stiffened. "Good idea," he said in a low voice. The fat man turned again to Houghton. "Find your way in, Mike. I'm waiting for the Polish chap. . . ."

They were accosted inside the glass doors by a young, very good-looking Portuguese naval cadet, who swept his eyes over Conan's glowering face and corduroys, then at Houghton's nautical blazer and distinguished mien. In excellent English he addressed Houghton in a high, piping voice. "Good evening, sir. May I see your entrance cards, please?"

Houghton handed the cadet their invitations and, his curiosity—and perhaps libido, thought Conan—aroused, leaned forward so as to see more clearly, through his dark glasses, who was behind the voice.

"Ah, Mister Conan," said the cadet, grasping Houghton by the elbow, "come this was please. The captains are all over 'ere, to meet the gentlemen an' the ladies."

Houghton started to say "But I'm not ..." as the youth insistently tugged him into the crowd.

Conan, grinning to himself, gently pushed Houghton's other elbow, as the club race-coordinator, now silent, lent himself to the jape. Conan watched as the cadet showed Houghton where to stand, at the end of a line of six men and one woman. Only Hanson, the young American, looked puzzled as he stared at Houghton in Conan's place.

Next to Hanson stood a young woman. Conan knew that she must be Mary Chatterton, the New Zealander. Over the heads of others he studied her for a moment as she smiled and shook hands with the passing line of Portuguese men and women. She was sturdy. She had chestnut hair, worn short, and was dressed for the occasion in a black dress. Conan stared at her. He was amazed that Mary Chatterton looked so ordinary. In sailing circles she was renowned, but if anyone saw her in a supermarket, or coming out of church, they would scarcely look at her twice. She could be someone's secretary, or shop assistant, or a teacher. No one who did not know of her record would ever dream that she was the first woman ever to sail nonstop alone from Fiji to England, nor that to do it she had survived two capsizes off the Horn. Now Hanson had seen Conan, over the heads of the crowd. The tall American grinned hugely. Conan, his eyes twinkling, raised an eyebrow at Hanson, then stepped back again against the wall. He watched as Houghton, who now had the young naval cadet in close, evidently amusing conversation, completely ignored the crowd. He looked at the other contenders.

A heavyset man with a black beard and the Royal Naval Sailing Association tie must be Joe Morgan. He'd met him before, of course, but it had been ten years before, and Morgan did not have a beard then. The slight man next to Morgan, with the startling eyes that stared as if he were mad, must be John Tyler. He was paler than the others. It was said that Tyler, who was something of a legend among "yachties," never, if he could avoid it, emerged from his cabin in the daytime. Even in harbor he did all his chores and took all his long hikes ashore, in the dead of night. Some people called him Batman, but always well away from Tyler's hearing. He was reputed to have a filthy temper.

Between Tyler and the woman stood a tall, bronzed man in his midthirties, Conan guessed. This, he told himself, must be Paddy Hunt, the Australian. He was one of the dark horses in the field of runners. Conan sized him up from his appearance as an affable, efficient, and when the chips were down, ruthless outbacker. One look at that face, with its aggressive hawk nose and chin like a bulldozer, and any man in the room would think twice before smiling at Mary Chatterton a second too long, if what Hanson had said—that Hunt and Mary had taken a shine to each other—was true.

On the other side of the woman stood the tallest man in the group. He was gesticulating violently as he conversed with a Portuguese naval officer and a beautiful woman. The tall yachtsman was good-looking, with short blond hair and blue eyes. Deep weather lines were etched on his face, so it was difficult to tell his age. As he spoke his mouth exploded into pouts, like a goldfish. Must be the Frenchman, Duplessis, thought Conan. Must be. No Briton could be that immaculately dressed while living on board a boat. Conan bet himself that Duplessis was a superlative cook.

Next to the Frenchman was another, shorter man with hair so blond that he seemed at first sight to be an albino. He was medium height, and Conan noticed that when he was not greeting people, he had that glum lost look peculiar to Scandinavians. When he was spoken to, his face lit up—almost broke up—into a wide smile punctuated by looks of deep gloom. Must be the Swede, Sven Larsen, thought Conan, a right child of the northern winter, that one, odds on he listens to Sibelius all night. He studied Larsen for a few more seconds. He noted the heavy shoulders of the Swede, and the way he moved them. Larsen would be a good lad in a tight situation.

Even as his eyes moved back to Houghton and the cadet, both of them now in an even closer huddle, like old friends, Conan heard the voice of Findlay. In a second the fat journalist, with a little red-haired man in his mid-thirties in tow, was alongside him, his face even redder. Findlay was perspiring heavily, his face even redder.

"Bill Conan," the fat man said, keeping his voice low. "What the devil . . . ? What are you doing here? You're supposed to be with all the others." Hurriedly he introduced Conan to Petr Bartusok, the Polish entrant, then, startled, Findlay stared over at the greeting line. He saw Houghton with his hand on the cadet's shoulder. "Good God!" Findlay shouted, then, recovering himself, said to Conan who was grinning at the obviously half-drunk Pole, "Come along, let's get this lot sorted out. . . ."

The fat journalist, with the two black sheep in front of him, herded them through the crowd and into line. As they squeezed and excused their way the Pole turned to Conan and winked at him, screwed up his lips, then grinned widely. With one stubby, scarred, and nicotine-discolored finger he prodded Conan in the chest.

"You Conan?"

"Yes."

"English," said the little man.

"Scottish, Scotland."

"Me Pete . . . Polish. Tomorrow"—he put one hand in front of him and made an undulating movement with it as he pushed forward— "zoom, zoom in der sea, yes?" The Pole walked unsteadily.

Conan laughed out loud. "Yes!" he said, and slapped the Pole on the shoulders.

Conan reached Houghton and tapped his arm. "Your friend Findlay's here. Come to take charge of you. Reckons you're in the wrong place."

Houghton turned, startled for a moment. Then he smiled. "Oh, really?" He leaned closer to see Findlay. The journalist waited, holding the red-haired Pole steady and upright. All around them an elegant gathering of beautiful people—many Portuguese *are* beautiful—jostled and introduced each other.

"I say, Findlay, old man," Houghton whispered hoarsely. "Shocking thing, got the tummy trouble. Look, be a good chappie, will you, and look after Conan for me? Manuel here . . ." he gently reached up and held the poker-faced cadet's shoulder with one hand, "Manuel is going to show me where there's a chemist's shop. . . ."

"Of course, Mike," wheezed Findlay.

"See you later—er, Bill,—I—er—Manuel has invited me to his family's place. . . . He says it's not far . . ." Houghton stammered, and before the astonished Conan could reply he was gone, gently guiding the young cadet by the elbow ahead of him.

Findlay looked at Conan. The journalist pursed his lips and raised his eyebrows in an unspoken question.

Conan thought of Houghton taking off like that. He said to himself *chacun à son gout,* and braced himself to shake hands and smile at and speak to most of the two hundred men and women in the hall.

The red-haired Pole by Conan's side weaved and laughed uproariously. He addressed everyone in his own language as he shook hands with the men, and bent low to kiss the women's hands as they greeted him. He left the men half-suspicious, half-envious, and the women, old and young, highly charmed and amused, even though no one had understood a word he said.

When the reception lineup was finally over Conan breathed a sigh of relief. He was basically a shy man. Meeting, however cursorily, two-hundred-odd strangers was, to him, a wearisome matter. It was not that he didn't like being among people. If he was left alone, to pick his own company, he sometimes enjoyed himself. Often, alone in a crowd, he was content merely to stand back and observe others. His own company he rarely found onerous. He had, over the years, learned how to recognize the onset of his own moods and how to guide and control his own direction away from or closer into them. Most of all, though, he felt happiest when he was with Ruth, even when they disagreed, even when they were both silent—perhaps even more, then.

As the crowd dispersed and sat at long tables in the middle of the great hall, and as the race entrants moved to a table just below the one reserved for notables and speakers, the little Pole again waved his hand palm downward at Conan. "Tomorrow—zoom zoom," he said.

Despite Findlay's shepherding them into seats apart, Conan managed to resist the journalist's ministrations and stick to the Pole's side. On the other side of him, at the skippers' table, he found Hanson, who stared around the crowded room for a moment, then turned to Conan.

"Hi, Bill. . . . What's with Mike? He ain't around?"

"He's got a touch of tummy trouble. . . . He decided to take off."

"Wow, this is something, huh?"

"Quite a spread. How's things going with *Sundance Kid*?"

"A-okay, all systems go! This—wow—these turkeys must be loaded," said Hanson. He glanced around the room. "An' some of these chicks— hey, Pete!" Hanson leaned over behind Conan and slapped the Pole on the shoulder. "Some foxy ladies!"

"Whatyousay?" The Pole, his eyes half-closed, focused them on Hanson.

The young American lifted his head, puckered his lips, and blew soft, hardly noticeable quiet kisses in the direction of the seated guests in the hall. The Pole smiled, hesitantly at first, then his face broke almost in half. His eyes opened wide. He leered at both Hanson and Conan. He moved both of his blunt-fingered, wire-scarred hands a foot apart, downward in front of him, and with them carved in the smoke-filled air the lines of an imaginary voluptuous female.

"Tomorrow—zoom zoom," he hiccupped. "You?"

Both Conan and Hanson nodded, laughing.

"You on der sea, yes? Come back Lisbon, yes?"

"Right on, man!" shouted Hanson.

The Pole prodded his own chest and hiccupped again. "Me . . . stop Tahiti . . ." He waved his hands downward again in the international code signal for unrealizable dreams. "Me . . . no more bloody Poland . . . me . . . bloody Tahiti!"

Conan burst out with a loud laugh. Hanson hit the table with one hand as big as a shovel. "Right on, right on, Pete!" he yelled.

The other skippers looked their way, half-smiling, wondering what the joke was among the obvious stag party at Conan's end.

As the first speaker rose on the head table to make noises suitable to the occasion, Hanson murmured to Conan, "Ya see, I told ya, Bill, Pete's a straight shooter. Man, that cat's a speed ball!" Hanson's voice rose. Everyone at the table stared at him. The Swiss—or was it Andorran?—naval attaché's voice droned in halting Portuguese. Hanson fell silent and Peter the Pole, leaning on Conan's shoulder, his elbows on the table in front of him, slept quietly all through the speeches, until it was time to eat.

Houghton was back on board *Josephine* at the crack of dawn. By six-thirty he had cooked a breakfast of fresh food which he had picked up at the Cais de Sodre market. He had made the taxi, which had been ordered by Manuel the previous night from their hotel, stop and wait for him a good fifteen minutes while he peered at and picked and chose and haggled for the best goodies he could find for Conan's breakfast and for the first day's meals at sea today and tomorrow.

"Morning, Bill. How was it last night?" were Houghton's first words as Conan awoke and smelled sizzling bacon and coffee. Conan sat on the edge of the berth. He had guessed that Houghton would not be back until morning.

"Not bad. Food could have been hotter and the speeches a bit shorter. The wine was excellent and the bar was fairly lively after dinner. I was with Jack Hanson and Peter the Pole. Pete's quite a card. You missed a bit of fun." Conan consciously played his part. "How's the tummy this morning, Mike?"

"Oh, much better, but I think I'll delay flying back. . . . Manuel's family has invited me to stay on for a few days . . ." Houghton handed Conan a cup of coffee. "Watch it, it's hot."

"Mmm, thanks. . . . Well, that'll be nice, Mike."

"Yes, it means I don't have to rush back right after the actual start of the race at noon."

At nine o'clock, Conan, as was his usual custom before sailing on a long voyage, walked ashore alone to commune with himself and the land and the things of the land.

He avoided the waterfront park. The memories of Ruth being there with him were too recent and raw. Instead he walked along the riverfront, toward the great granite monument to Prince Henry the Navigator, which thrusts out over the Tagus like a ship's figurehead. With his back to the river, he sat on the bottom steps of the monument. He gazed quietly at the trees and the bushes in the park, at the grass, the lampposts, the green bench seats, the mosaic paving of the paths, and the low brick walls. He gazed at all the little things that the people of the land take so much for granted—the wide highway, Avenida Brasilia, a steady procession of a score of different kinds of cars, blue, green, gray, brown, black, white. He stared at the trucks as they passed, and the busses, little green local busses and long, black-windowed busses, dreams of steel and chromium, which brought tourists from other lands—France, Germany, Italy, Denmark—to see the wonders of Belém. He watched the busses as they stopped outside the Monastery of Jerónimos and disgorged their passengers in front of the great silent porticos. He looked long at the beauty of the buildings beyond the park, the monastery and, next to it, newly constructed, but not clashing with the ancient beauty of Jerónimo, the Maritime Museum. His gaze went on up the hill beyond Belém, and one by one picked out all the villas, the mansions, and the tenement buildings and cottages of the poorer folk. As he gazed a jet plane, a huge transatlantic commuter, flew over and headed for the ocean in the west.

Conan reflected on all the artifacts that man makes and builds, all the seeds of dreams that have burst into ideas, into life, and that have been nursed and cosseted and developed and perfected and treasured, and that have made life for man a little more interesting, each one in its own way, a mite more of comfort, of hope, each one the symbol of a dream, the manifestation of someone's genius, each one a little step forward in the long, awful, bittersweet struggle from the cave to the stars.

Conan turned and stared at the huge monument. He walked around to see the heroic figure of Prince Henry pointing a huge finger away to the south and the dream of a world opened to knowledge and law and the idea of justice. His eye went back to the line of giant granite followers—courtiers, knights, priests, nobles, and peasants—who humbly trailed up the incline behind Henry.

Conan studied one particular figure. It was of a priest holding in front of him a cross. Conan was not a religious man in a formal way. His early memories, of his stern Calvinistic father and later the enforced hours of standing, aching, cold and puzzled, in the drafty chapel at the orphanage, had turned Conan away from chapels and churches and all that went with them. He knew, he was sure that there was some design—and therefore some intelligence—behind the cosmic scheme of things, the wonderful clockwork of the heavens. He knew these things beyond doubt. That it was man's fate to work and dream and strive toward the knowing of the unknowable was an integral part of Conan's faith—if faith it was.

Conan envied the old-time people as they were portrayed on the monument. They, with their unquestioning belief in the Holy Trinity, with their comfort of being able to seek aid and succor from a thousand saints and the Virgin Mary. They, the answers to whose problems and questionings, mental, moral, and spiritual, were so firmly settled on the bedrock of blind obedience to religion—how much easier it must have been for them to thrust into the unknown. Surely not as adventurous though, as is the quest of modern man, Conan asked himself, the search for what the carved saints of old times perhaps represented, the search for the Truth, for the Be-all and End-all, for the end of Doubt?

Conan turned to return to the yacht basin. In the morning sunshine he saw a running figure, long and lanky in the distant park. He recognized Hanson just as the young American turned and, without altering his steady pace, waved a hand at him. He waved back at Hanson without smiling. No point in it at this distance. He turned back to the statue and murmured aloud—there was nobody near—to the granite, blank-eyed figures, "Well, that's it, cheerio, chaps." He turned and made his way back to *Josephine*, which waited for him, sails all bent on the booms, mooring lines singled up, and seeming, to Conan's eye, to be crouched like a greyhound ready to spring from the trap. He returned the waves of the other entrants as he passed them.

At the race start there were boats and banners, balloons and bugles, bellows and bandying, a farewell drink, and a last minute cheer as the yachts motored out of the basin. Houghton gazed silently as *Josephine* slid through the harbor mouth. Then he walked away to watch the official start.

By one P.M. all nine of the entrant yachts were gathered on the line running due south from the Torre de Belém, a watchtower built during the days of Portuguese maritime glory in the sixteenth century.

They were not strictly drawn up in line as racehorses are; rather they gathered more or less near to the line. In a race lasting up to a year it did not matter if one boat was a quarter of a mile ahead of the others.

Most of the boats had their mainsails hoisted and hauled in close. They slowly tacked this way and that against a gentle westerly breeze. Two of them—the Polish *Blytskwtska* and the French *Etoile du Sud*—had their number one jibs, their biggest jibs, also hoisted, but with the sheets let fly so that the headsails fluttered in the breeze like the farewell waves of scarves and kerchiefs.

Conan, still in his corduroys but shoeless, hoisted *Josephine*'s number one jib as he waited for the starting gun to be fired from the base of the ancient tower. As he swigged the halyard to make it dead taut he glanced at the tower. Two men were bent over the starting cannon. It was almost time. He ran back to the cockpit, grabbed the jib sheet, heaved it in on the winch, and *Josephine* started to move forward, hauling as she did so into the wind. *Josephine* veered slightly. Then, in a beautiful movement which seemed like a sigh of relief at being free at last, she heeled over and bent her cheek in her first of millions of coming curtseys of obeisance to the gods of the wind and the sea.

At the very moment when Conan, gazing intently at the shore, found that he was on the starting line, the cannon boomed. A great cheer rose from the straggle of observers and well-wishers lined up on the waterfront. Conan, slightly ahead of all the other boats except the Polish yawl, which had wandered over the line three minutes before the official start, steered *Josephine* south, more off the wind, and eased her sheets. She darted like a hummingbird chasing a butterfly, crossed the bows of *Ocean Viking, Ocean Pacer, Southern Star,* and *Sir John Falstaff,* a hundred yards or more ahead of them, and was soon clear of the fleet, heading west-southwest, driving for the southern bank of the Tagus River, alone except for Mary Chatterton who did the same, two hundred yards upstream from the bigger craft.

Conan felt the tiller shiver under his hand as he veered *Josephine* even more off the wind. *Josephine* heeled over more and picked up speed. He leaned over the weather gunwale—the high side—and saw the red bottom paint exposed almost to the keel, as a great clatter of falling plates and parcels rose from the galley. He grinned to himself and almost cheered. Everything else except the sensation of sailing a fine responsive vessel was forgotten for the time being as *Josephine* laid to and started to smash her way to the freedom of the seas, to join her soul to the aching vastness.

By late afternoon Conan and *Josephine* were well clear of the rest of the fleet, all by now no more than dots scattered over the northern horizon. Cape Espichel was now twenty miles away on the port quarter and Cape Saint Vincent low and mysterious far away on the port beam. Conan reckoned his departure and entered it in the logbook. *Josephine,* as if she sensed she was casting off the land's trammels, charged ahead southwest.

On a broad reach across the fresh northwesterly breeze, *Josephine* bounded like a startled stag from one green sea to the next. With each bound she left the trillion-veined complexity which is the landsmen's world a little further astern, until at last, by nightfall, it was gone. *Josephine* was now alone, her hull caressed by the ocean waters. She leapt to the music of the night wind in her shrouds, her sails at times enchanted by the silver fingers of the filling moon which reached for her between the black flying clouds. Her whole being now was drawn forward into the night. Only occasionally did her rhythm break—when she gently slid sideways off a sea. It was as if the boat knew that Conan, even yet still in his corduroys, was thinking of Ruth and jealously was trying to nudge him from his regret, to comfort him as they sailed on under the dark clouds and the moon, together.

Part 2: Passage

"... one might conclude that the language of the dolphins is composed of two thousand 'words.' It is said that Racine wrote his tragedies with a smaller vocabulary. In any event the active vocabulary of the dolphin would be somewhat greater than that of many humans."

JACQUES YVES COUSTEAU
and PHILLIPE DIOLE,
Dolphins (Doubleday)

"... these Cetacea with huge brains are more intelligent than any man or woman."

JOHN C. LILLY, M.D.,
*Communication between
Man and Dolphin* (Crown)

Chapter 7

KWEELA'S VISION-MEMORY turned to Aka and to that day, so similar to this one, two years before.

Aka had courted her with great skill. She had known that he was following her for more than an hour. He had swum and gamboled and dived fifty yards behind her. It was part of the dolphin rites; he had signalled her—nine hundred clicks a minute as she counted—then he had sent her holograms, so that she, in her mind, could see what he was watching. It was, of course, *herself.* For more than an hour, with Aka patiently trailing her, she had taken delight at first in flapping her flippers, all the while watching herself through Aka's holographic three-dimensional images as they were received inside her own mind. Then, without sending any holograms back to Aka, she had doubled up as she dived, and she had gyrated as she rose to the surface, and had fallen on her back from her leaps above the surface. All the while she had watched herself, through Aka's holograms in her own mind, and had been delighted with her own grace and power and beauty, and pleased that Aka was seeing her thus. She had not once looked back at him. She had not needed to, because she had known that Aka was receiving her acoustic pleasure waves which, despite her attempts to douse them, had been escaping from her to the broadly tuned acoustic receivers of all the other dolphins within five miles of her. All the world loves a lover.

They had played thus until Aka, in a steadily rising crescendo of urgent acoustic and sonar signals, which became stronger and stronger as he focused on her, had suddenly darted to her and intertwined his flippers with hers. He had held himself pressed against her as they swam, slower now. All the other calfless females of her school, keeping up their speed of ten knots, had pulled away from them. As Aka's tail had oscillated more and more slowly, so Kweela's, too, had slowed down, until she and Aka, locked together flipper to flipper, tail to tail, had been almost stopped. Out of breath then, Aka had ascended to the sea surface, drawing Kweela with him. They had risen through the water, blue, then emerald green, until they were resting with their blowholes above the surface of the sea. Aka had taken a deep gulp, then he had blown a playful spout of water—about ten gallons—into the air, so that it had fallen down on her, and she had rolled over and over a dozen times, daring him to let go of her.

When he had first come close to her, the great scar on Aka's head had alarmed Kweela, but as he gently led her below the surface again, still with his flippers entwined in hers, she had felt better about it. She even had the temerity to "ask" him about the scar. This she had done by placing her lower jaw against his and making noises that to a human would sound like the opening of a creaky door. "Why are you different?" She knew that abnormally born babies were abandoned by their mothers. Members of the tribe who erred from the tribal laws—for example, any who attacked another dolphin for whatever reason—were exiled from the tribe, in effect a sentence of death; a dolphin cannot live alone in the sea. Exiles were known to trail their former school for days, miles astern of them, not daring to come near them, and to gradually pine away and die of hunger. Hunger for food; a lone, exiled dolphin will not eat. Hunger, too, for friendship and affection; without them, what good was food?

Still clinging to her, as they rose again to the air, Aka had told her of how he, only three migrations old at the time—twenty years before—had strayed among the boats, great monsters that carried on their backs Man, and that dragged long, cruel nets made of wire cable astern of them. Aka, on his low frequency sonar, terrified, had suddenly "seen" one of the boats ahead of him. He had dodged, swimming fast this way and that, frightened, and sent garbled holograms of what caused his fright back to the tribe. Several males, including old Oba-of-the-legends, his mentor, had tried to come to his assistance, but the noise of the boats and the wicked look of what they dragged had kept the rescuers well back, far beyond eyesight, but within range of their long distance sonar signals, by which they could anxiously "watch" his every move.

The boat had changed course and the net had wrapped itself around Aka in a wide arc. He, scared into a wild panic, had hurled himself at the net as he would at a threatening shark. He had been trapped in the metal wires which, as the boat moved ahead, sawed into his head so that his blood blinded his eyesight and his signals to the waiting males made no more sense except of fear and pain. Slowly the net had dragged him, deep in the water, unable to breathe. Then, drowning, almost at the end of his air, he had found the mad strength to twist and drag his head, somehow, backward out of the trap. He had been almost unconscious by then, but instinctively his body had sought the surface. There, in blind panic, with blood streaming out of the wound, he had gulped air as deeply as he could. The blood had cleared momentarily. He had seen the boat, terrifyingly close. It had a tail, Aka had assured her, which brutally smashed around and around and there was a roaring noise, and Man—several of them had been riding on the boat, shouting and pointing at him.

All this Aka's eye had taken in during a matter, in human terms, of two and a half seconds. Instinctively and desperately Aka had thrown himself right over onto his back and, upside down, had pushed himself down under the surface, down, down, obliquely away from the boat and the net, down into the dark gloom, deeper and faster than he had ever been before, until his lungs screamed for air. At last he had risen up, up through the blackness and the purple and the blue and the green, and surfaced a mile and more away from the flailing horror that had almost killed him. Another gulp, two gulps of air, and he had turned toward the now fading sonar signals of the tribe, which had abandoned him for lost. Speeding just below the surface, in bursts of twenty knots, he had caught up with them, still sick with fright. He had approached his mother, but she was feeding a new calf and had ignored him. He had appealed to other females, but they, because of his scrambled, panicky signals, had avoided him. Then old Oba had sent him a signal to stop. It had been so strong that the urgency of it subdued all Aka's fears of Man and he had slowed down until he was almost dead in the water. Oba had appeared—the biggest dolphin in the tribe, twelve and a half feet long, thirty years old. Oba had swum straight at him, at an angle from one side, and had butted Aka, firmly but gently, in his sick-churning stomach. He had spewed out all the fish he had eaten that day. Oba had pushed him ahead, toward the small group of the oldest, most authoritative males in the tribe, who swam ahead of the rest and a little to one side.

Except when he had been mating, Aka had stayed with the Wise Ones ever since. He had learned from them all the hazards and dangers of a dolphin's existence and of all the joys and beauties of their legends. From the Wise Ones, Aka had absorbed into his memory all the dolphin history, from the hazy dawning of their time, twenty million years before, when the dolphins still had four limbs like Man and when they still sorrowed and grieved over things that were external to them, just as, said the Wise Ones, Man still did. Things that the dolphins had left behind them on the land, so that they could be free.

Kweela's memory turned again to her mating with Aka. On the surface once more, after thirty slow rises and dives, Aka then had placed his head on Kweela's body, just behind her head, where a human would say her neck was. Breathing slowly, they had swum thus together sedately on the surface. Then Aka had wrapped one of his flippers right around her body and made love-signals—a riot of pleading groans—through his lower jaw. The tympanic sensation on her neck had been more than pleasant to Kweela, and she, in her turn, had wrapped her flipper around Aka as far as she could. Aka, suddenly, had leaned his head away from her neck and nipped her snout, but gently. She, becoming excited, had dived, dragging him, passive, with her. A hundred feet down she had turned and bent her body right over him and nipped his free flipper, not as gently as he had nipped her, but that was only natural. He had strengthened his grip on her and dragged her again to the surface of the sea and the air. There they had floated side by side, almost stopped in the water, for fifteen minutes, while Aka slapped her with his flipper all over her body, while she rolled over and over for him and he whistled and cried to the sky and to her.

The mating itself had been very quick and much less tender than the courtship. Aka had abruptly torn himself away from her and had swum for about fifty yards. Then he had turned and rushed at full speed at her, as if he were about to ram her head on. At the very last moment of his charge, when he was but a hairsbreadth away from her, he had turned at right angles to his line of charge, so that he skidded to a halt alongside her. His body and hers, both covered in gray, satinlike, highly sensitive flesh, had rubbed and pounded together vigorously and violently. Aka's penis, which was flat and triangular, and ordinarily stowed in a sheath in his belly, had been willed to emerge and become erect by Aka during his rush. In a moment, during the rubbing, he had entered her. He stayed so for only fifteen seconds, his pelvis moving rhythmically. At the moment of climax, which she had known because for a rare time in her life her four signal-receiving systems went blank in her ecstasy, Aka had slid under her and with his head and chest almost at right angles to her, dangled down into the ocean deeps. He had wrapped the hind part of his body and his tail right over her in a gesture of utter loving. Then he had left her to find another female. It was the dolphins' way.

Now the mother-group with their calves, as if on command, all rose to the surface again. Her calf, Om, still stuck by Kweela's side, exactly six inches away from her. She remembered his birth and how her friend Sheena had stayed with her, away from all the tribe. Om had already been one third her size—two and a half feet long—at the moment he was born. The umbilical cord had broken itself as Om, tail first, had come away from her and Kweela had violently twisted her whole body. Sheena had been close by, below her, looking up, in case the cord needed to be bitten. As soon as Om was out of her he had started to sink; there was no air in his lungs. Sheena had caught the sinking calf on her snout and gently nudged him toward Kweela. Then they both, together, had swiftly lifted the baby to the surface. Sheena, well-practiced after six calves of her own, had butted Om's belly to make him start to breathe as Kweela anxiously looked on, with her snout close to Om's. Om had gasped in air, his blowhole had closed, it had opened again, and Kweela, delighted with joy and affection for Om, had taken him, balanced on her flipper, for his first dive. He had been never far from her ever since that day eighteen months before. It was long ago, in the shallow inlet between the lonely rocks atop the undersea mountain far away to the south.

Like all her kind, Kweela was a devoted mother. She watched Om night and day, above water and below. The memory of his birth was always with her. For all the joy, it had been painful. Om had been born one third of her own weight, fully formed. Only hours after his birth she'd had to defend him against a prowling gray shark until Aka and three other males had raced to the scene and butted the shark again and again, at full speed, all four of them, and left the predator limp and dead on the bed of the inlet, to be eaten by the crabs.

Kweela had fed Om with her own milk every fifteen minutes for a year and a half. After nine months he had started to feed himself between suckling at her. Now he was hunting and eating all his own fish, but he was still suckling occasionally. In another four months he should be completely weaned, and she would be ready to conceive her next calf when they returned north again next year.

For the first few weeks after his birth Om had remained permanently pressed to his mother's body, feeding from her, ingesting her rich milk at frequent intervals, as soon as there had been any room in his stomach.

Om, from a few hours after his birth, had been sexually aroused by his closeness to his mother's body. By the end of the third month he had aroused her, in her turn, so much that she finally laid over on her side and encouraged him to copulate with her. But it was merely a mother-son relationship. Om would not be mature enough to give her a calf until he would be seven years old. It was a simple matter of passing on to Om his first lesson in sexuality. It was the dolphin's way.

Now, again the mother-school glided up to the surface, all as one. Again the leaps and bounds, the rolls and somersaults, the clicks and squeals as the sun colored the falling spray. Again they all dived and slid down into the dark green depths together. The school of mothers and their calves again flattened out their dive and, tails beating in unison, swam even faster now in the direction from whence came a steady pulse of sonar signals commanding, guiding them. "Here . . . here . . . here is food. Here is where we will eat. Here . . . come here!"

As if on a radio-direction guide beam, all the different schools of dolphins, the mothers, the young female calves, the young males, the mature males, the odd males who did not mate with females but preferred to stay in each other's company, the older females, too old now to bear calves, the full-grown males in pairs and threes out on the fringes of the tribe who scouted for herring and pilchard, all of them changed their courses and headed in the direction of the command signal. It was so strong, so authoritative, so firm, that every one of the 142 dolphins covering an area of almost a hundred square miles knew immediately it was the call of Aka, and every one of them turned immediately to obey the call.

As she raced along, rising to the surface to gulp air and diving every five minutes, Kweela turned frequently to send a short-range sonar search beam into Om. He still occasionally suffered from wind. When she beamed him she could "see" in her mind a perfect three-dimensional image of Om's insides. By regulating the beam with shorter or longer waves, infinitesimally fine adjustments, she could "look" at different depth-layers inside Om's body. She could "see" her calf's skeleton, with its long, pointed skull, its short neck, and the deep ribs. She could see Om's brain, now fully grown to 1,700 grams (250 grams bigger than a human's).

She noted the short-distance "sonar" brushes in Om's beak—a mass of fine nerves under the granite-hard external shell. Om used these when he was homing in on fish close by.

Kweela could "see" the long-distance sonar "echo-location" chamber on the front of Om's head, a great bulge just behind and above his beak. It was filled with a waxy substance. Suspended in the wax was a network of tissues by means of which Om controlled the incidence of his sonar-wave receptions.

As Om squeaked and squealed his complaints to her, Kweela saw a string of bubbles rising from his blowhole and streaming out behind him. It was from the blowhole that Om "talked," controlling his acoustic signals by means of the massive sphincter muscle inside. Between dolphins further away, but not so far as to need holograms, "words" were whistled in a range that varied from a groan to pitches so high that even a dog would not receive them.

To a human ear, the sounds from other dolphins around Kweela as she swam on with Om by her side, merely the ones within her range of hearing, would be a cacophony of noise ranging from that made by a forest of falling redwood trees to the row that emanates from a pork-butcher's slaughterhouse. Yet Kweela was able to sort out all these sounds and retain only those that concerned her or the mother-group. The sum of an adult dolphin's communications system is approximately that of a human station equipped with two sonar sets—one long range and one short range—two radio broadcasting and receiving systems, a loud hailer, a television receiver and transmitter, and a very high capacity computer memory and retrieval bank.

Kweela could inspect Om's two flipper bones, still somewhat resembling a human arm and hand bones, and the long spine which ran seven feet all the way down to his tail, almost to the edge of the split between his horizontal flukes. She could "see" his conical teeth, all 130 of them now, which Om used to hold the fish he caught, and his powerful jaw, with which he could crush his catch into a cylindrical shape, so that it would slide easily over his larynx and into his esophagus. She could follow his alimentary tract all the way through Om. And all this she could do in what humans would call the "twinkling of an eye." Om was not yet old enough to signal to her much that made sense, but he could, and very often did, signal pain, distress, or discomfort. She beamed his stomach again as the mother-school dived. She "saw" a bubble of air in his upper stomach. She turned her snout toward the calf and butted him gently. Om burped. She "saw" the bubble move up into his throat. She butted him again and the air, now in tiny bubbles, emerged from Om's snout and streamed out behind him. Speeding along very close to the sea surface, so they could breathe about every half minute, Kweela and Om caught up with the mother-school and ploughed along, with clear ocean water streaming off their backs, in the direction of Aka's signals. As they did so, they passed the faint gliding shadows of the tribal shoal herders, males in their prime, sent out by Aka to drive the moving underwater clouds of herring and pilchard into the area where the tribe was even now gathering, circling impatiently on the surface of the moving waters, slowly in the shadows of the gently drifting clouds overhead and swiftly in the sudden patches of sunlight.

Soon Kweela's mother-group had joined the waiting herd as it circled round and round Aka and his three companions, the Wise Ones. Round and round they went, keeping their blowholes just above the surface of the water, waiting for the sixty shoal herders to chase fish in their thousands toward them from whatever direction. All seventy-nine waiting dolphins, in eight cohesive schools, the mothers and calves, and their male guards, the youngsters, the odd males, the old males, the old females, each school keeping time with the others, circled round and round only a hundred yards from Aka, who himself, beaming his powerful sonar transmitter-receiver as he did so, circled his three "henchmen." They, stock still and dead in the water, faced in different directions, weaving their heads from side to side so as to cover 120 degrees each of the "horizon" with their sonar.

Suddenly, as the tribe steadily swam on, Aka stopped. He waited. The flowing tribal ring slowed. Heads turned toward Aka. Then, after a great leap eighteen feet into the air, Aka smashed down into the water and, tail flailing the surface, flung his five hundred pounds toward the north. He sped through the now stopped circular procession of bottlenoses. In a second his three companions were on his track, close behind him, soon reaching Aka's speed of thirty knots. As Aka and his three companions cleared the circle, the others, all still in their separate groups, raced after them. It was only a minute before they were above a five-mile-long, two-hundred-yards-wide shoal of pilchard. Sounding with their short-range sonar beams as they went, the dolphins were down among the fish, darting and snapping and crushing as they flashed into the depths; then up again, back through the exploding shoal, catching and biting, swallowing as they surfaced. Quick gulps of air into their blowholes and down they went again, as the pilchard shoal scattered in panic in every direction, with dolphins at their tails.

By the time Aka's command had gathered the tribe in again, the sun was well down. As it sank below the ocean edge the satiated dolphins gamboled and dived and played with their young. The older ones swam in graceful arched curves up and down and, turning their bodies this way and that, rode on the tops of wind-driven waves, while the nonmating males frisked with their favorite companions and nipped at each other's snouts in fond friendship. Then it was time to sleep and the tribe split up into little groups of a dozen dolphins to doze through the night. Each group was guarded by two adults who watched it carefully lest one of their number should not wake in time to breathe every few minutes, and so, airless, sink and drown. The dolphins dozed, all but the guards, facing toward Aka.

The sun had disappeared. The moon, almost full, was high in the black sky between the scudding clouds when Aka's alarm signal alerted the night guards. Moving as one, the guards threw themselves bodily at the groups of dozers and woke them. In a few seconds everyone was still. The whole tribe waited. Aka beamed again, toward the polestar. Every adult dolphin received his hologram. It was vague at first, but as it defined itself it was clear to all, one after the other, that what they were "seeing" in their minds was a boat. One of the Wise Ones broke into Aka's signal. "Noise?" he asked. They all studied the boat. It was not as big as the ones that dragged the death-dealing nets, nor the ones that chased the whale. It made little noise, only the sound of its body pushing through the water. No more noise than their friends the killer whales. On its back it had . . . fins? Wings? . . . Sails! *Sails!*

Aka told them, "One of the quiet ones. I have seen its like before. It may be dangerous—it is Man's."

"Distance?" an odd dolphin asked, and was immediately chided by one of the Wise Ones. Such questions were out of place at a time like this.

All signals dissolved. There was a blank. Aka beamed the boat again. "Not sure . . . wait."

They waited, not moving, resting, still, on the surface of the black twinkling sea under the moon, like a hundred-odd floating corpses. They waited five . . . ten . . . fifteen seconds, then Aka signalled them, "Close, very close, but wait!" They waited, all except for their leader, with their beams, acoustic and sonar, blank, all facing in the same direction, which Aka signalled to them.

Then they heard it; with their fur-covered ears, incredibly sensitive to direction, they heard it. A steady rhythmical sloshing noise and the thin jingle of something moving. They all, as they picked up the sound, stared in its direction; Aka slowly changed his angle to the guide stars above. There was a nervous agitation at the northern quarter of the ring of dolphins. One of the young calves was the first to visually see the boat. He jumped in fright toward his mother. She quietly, gently butted him into calmness. The rest of the tribe, one after the other, sighted with their eyes the cause of the noises. It was a boat swimming on the surface, past them, heading south. A hundred and forty-three tails slowly changed direction as the thing passed them a mile away. Two hundred and eighty-six eyes, old and young, followed the phantom shape silently, fearfully alarmed, for four or five minutes.

On a sudden Aka jumped. He hurled himself up and backward. The splash splurged thirty feet. His signal smashed into the minds of every dolphin in the tribe. *"The boat has changed course! It is heading for us!"* Within a second the whole tribe had flung itself sideways and back and downward into the dark depths of the sea and was, blindly at first, racing away from the menace of Man. It was half an hour before they stayed on the surface of the heaving waters long enough for Aka to be sure that the boat had changed course once more and was heading south again. The tribe waited, floating on the surface of the black waters under the moon, until Aka ordained that they might doze again, under the watch of the wary night guards and a million stars gleaming in the black velvet sky.

Chapter 8

CONAN HAD NOT CHANGED out of his corduroys and into his canvas sailing pants, cotton shirt, and wool jersey until an hour before sundown. Then he had quickly decided to don his windbreaker, too. *Josephine* was going well west-southwest. He had not more than roughly plotted his course and position. Time enough for that in the morning, he told himself. He cleared up the mess of fallen food in the galley, made the last-minute stowages, and sent the first radio signal to Lisbon—"all well, fifty miles west-southwest." Then he settled back to enjoy the sail. At seven he heated up the stew, which Houghton had made for him that morning, and found it tasty. At eight o'clock, an hour after sunset, he decided to check the automatic steering gear. It was a good idea to exercise in the moonlight. Besides, he loved night sailing.

Up on deck, in the cockpit, Conan found the steering-gear trip line and pulled it. The wind vane, released from its bondage to the gears, the helm, and the rudder, swung free with a low clinking clatter. Conan, exhilarated, gripped the wheel as moonlight broke through a gap in the clouds. With a fifteen-knot breeze this would be a good night-sail. As he took over steering, *Josephine,* momentarily out of true control until Conan could "feel" the helm, fell off the wind and changed direction for a matter of seconds. As soon as she did so it seemed to Conan that the whole dark night horizon ahead of him exploded in a blanket of white spray. There was suddenly a moving curtain of white water right across the curve of the ocean ahead of *Josephine.*

Instinctively, violently, Conan spun the wheel to steer away from the eruption. As he brought the boat onto the wind he heaved the jib sheet, strained at the winch handle with one hand, grasped the wheel to hold it steady with the other, and all the while he stared, gazed, until his eyes ached with strain, to leeward, to where the night horizon had seemed to disintegrate before him. His first startled thought was that it was an uncharted reef—but he had immediately dismissed that assumption from his mind. That was impossible, here in the Atlantic Ocean fifty miles off the Portuguese coast. Anyway, he told himself, there were no coral reefs this far north. For a moment he wondered if what he had witnessed had been the result of an underwater volcano, but then he realized that was highly unlikely, for there had been no tremendous upheaval of a swell. As *Josephine,* close-hauled now, clawed to the west, away from the phenomenon, whatever it was, Conan muttered to himself aloud, "Must have been a couple of whales skylarking. . . ." He considered making a note of the event in the ship's log, but decided against it, or to do it in the morning, after he had thought about it some more. He was wary. He knew only too well that there were many strange visual effects at sea on moonlit nights.

Conan eased *Josephine*'s jib sheet and mainsheet and, peering into the dim red light of the compass, steered southwest. A few seconds later, when his eyes had again become accustomed to the night, he found a low star approximately in the southwest, laid the luff of the jib against it, and settled down to enjoy his first night's sail alone with a vessel and the wind, the sea, the moon, the stars, for longer than he cared to remember. By midnight the loom of a million and more Lisbon city lights was now merely a faint pewter-colored glow, dulling steadily, over the northeast horizon, astern. The wind was rising as *Josephine,* her skirts lifted, trooped on to the southwest. Conan decided to leave the number one jib hoisted for as long as possible. He was crossing the main shipping lane from Gibraltar and Capetown to northern Europe. The sooner he was over it the better. There was no sense in courting danger. He would press on. Now he was sighting ships heading south and north at more frequent intervals. Sometimes he saw only the white masthead lights, and the red or green navigation lights of cargo steamers or tankers. Again, he saw three brightly lit passenger ships, faster than the freighters and looking like moving towns as they sped for the sunny Mediterranean or the Canary Islands from the still-chilly climes of Britain and northern Europe.

As he stared at one liner Conan envisaged the people on board. He conjured up visions of excited honeymoon couples, retired post office owners and stationers, a couple of football-pool winners, and perhaps a crusty old dowager and a gouty retired major-general who had sat in their deck chairs side by side all the way across the lively, gray Bay of Biscay, and sipped their gin and bitters, and fumed and fulminated about the shocking mores of the younger people.

Conan grinned to himself, casting his glance now and then at the dull-red glowing compass and then at a star ahead. When the liner was hull-down over the horizon he gazed around, searching for any sign of the other race yachts. There was none. At ten o'clock he thought he had seen a single bright light, which might have been a competitor's bright masthead light (they would all display them while they were crossing the shipping lanes), but it had been only a suspicion, perhaps a trick of vision. Now there was nothing but the topmost lights of the liner, low on his starboard bow, as she steamed southeast for Gibraltar.

Conan was glad he had not drunk too much the previous night at the race reception. He felt a pang of pity for Peter the Pole, who, he thought, must be suffering. Conan's stomach invariably revolted on the first few hours at sea, if he had been drinking any amount previously. But perhaps, he asked himself, the Pole had a cast-iron stomach? If his insides were as hard and tough as his exterior appeared to be, thought Conan, Peter would be all right—he was right now probably snorting his head off below, even despite the dangers of collision in the shipping lane. He looked the type who would get away with it, too, he concluded.

An hour later Conan decided it was getting a mite chilly. He held on to the wheel with one hand and with the other searched for the steering gear trip-lock line. He found it draped over the counter. He pulled one bight of the line and heard the steering gear lock in. It would hold, approximately, the course he had set. He let go of the wheel. The boat steered herself, but slowly veered and yawed a few degrees either side of the course.

Conan peered into the night around the unseeable horizon again. Particularly he stared astern and on each quarter. Only novices, with car-driving habits, pay more attention ahead than astern in a sail craft at night. There was nothing—only the driven seas, steepening now little by little, and the black gleams of the moving ocean waters between the shadows of the scudding clouds all driving to the southeast, at an angle across *Josephine*'s scending bows. Satisfied that all was well, he stepped into the companionway and went below. He switched on the night-light over the navigation table. The cabin was bathed in a low, warm red glow, soothing to his senses, like the firelight gleams in a darkened room. He imagined how Shaughnessy or Tristan would have described it—"like a bloody opium-den on a fairground switchback." Conan grinned to himself as he glanced around the cabin. In the dull-red glow, with *Josephine* heeled over ten degrees more or less to port and plunging up and down, fore and aft, it looked and felt, he thought, like any landsman's idea of a waiting room in purgatory. Conan rummaged around in his duffel bag and pulled out a woollen bobble cap which looked black but was light blue. He donned it, staggering all the while to hold his balance. It was still too early for Conan to have found his sea legs, for the balance tubes in his ears to coordinate with the rest of his body and signal instantly to him where and what "vertical" was. It would take forty-eight hours, if the past voyages were anything to go by, for him to be able, at all times, instinctively, to maintain his body perpendicular to the earth's center, regardless of what angle the boat might be at. In the meanwhile it was a matter of conscious effort, short, awkward staggers; holding on to any convenient fixture; patience and perseverance.

Conan clambered up two of the companionway steps. He stuck his head up above the hatch and gazed around into the night again. You couldn't be too careful in a shipping lane this busy. He found all was well. He stepped down again into the cabin and decided it would be a good time to practice lighting the stove in the night-light. It was a kerosene stove, which meant that the burner had to be heated up with alcohol, so that the kerosene, as it flowed down to the burner, would vaporize and ignite. He had lit the stove in the harbor, when it was steady, and earlier that evening, when it had been swinging slightly on its gimbals. Now the stove was swinging, more or less still horizontal, while the rest of *Josephine*'s little world was heeled over. Conan found the matches all right, stowed in their watertight box above the berth forward of the galley. Shaughnessy had taken in five hundred boxes of matches, there were thirty thousand matches on board. Very important, matches and canopeners—there were four of those on board, too, he remembered.

Finding the alcohol container, a cylindrical brass can with a long, thin spout, something like a miniature watering can but without the sprinkler nose, was a bit more difficult. At first Conan couldn't recall where it was stowed. Eventually, after five minutes muttering and patient probing around the galley he compromised and grabbed a flashlight from the navigation shelf. The flashlight body was yellow rubber, waterproof, and it would float if it was dropped overboard, but if its short lanyard was wrapped around his wrist there was slight chance of that.

Soon Conan had found the alcohol—he knew there were three spare containers anyway—and had the stove burning under the kettle. He had five hundred gallons of water in four separate tanks and ten jerry cans on board, he remembered. He must try to keep down to a gallon a day. He would do this by using seawater for most of his cooking, and for washing himself. He would merely rub himself over with a fresh-water-damp cloth after his "bath." There was not much dirt at sea, anyway, so it would be only once a week. He decided it would be Mondays to mark the new week. On Sundays he would, weather permitting, make himself an extra specially good meal and drink some of the three-dozen bottles of Bual wine which Shaughnessy had stowed in the bilge, all in square plastic bottles. He reckoned wryly there were four days to go for a "wash" and three for a drink. He looked around at the cabin, which, now that his eyes had become accustomed to the night-light, he could see much better. He decided not to compare his home in *Josephine* with those he had known before in other boats. He tried to dismiss from his mind the remembrance of the dear old *April Love,* the first boat he had ever owned alone. She had been sixty-five years old when he bought her—or rather the wreck of her. Mahogany on oak, she was, built like a London pub, and by the time he had finished pouring skill and love into her, *April Love* had been the coziest boat on the British south coast. All white painted below, with brass lamps and fittings, and a little wood stove with a ceramic tile surround, and a "charlie-noble"—a stove pipe—which he'd blackened with a vile paste every week . . . now, *April Love* again surrendered him for the time being to *Josephine.*

One thing about her, *Josey,* as he now called his new home, did not pretend to be anything else than what she was—a sailing machine, fitted now for maximum speed and efficiency and for minimum comfort. Her American designers had at first, he knew, included in her many refinements, some of those life-easing gadgets of which many, most Americans are so fond, and which most of the time at sea do nothing but clutter the vessel up with useless decoration. There had been a refrigerator—unnecessary now that there were freeze-dried foods and treated milks and cheeses which would last good for months. There had originally been teak cladding over the ship's side down below to hide the rough-looking fibers of the GRP hull and to make her look inside like a wooden boat. There had even been fixtures made for a television set. All these had been ripped out of the boat when the club had taken her over. Conan reflected that Shaughnessy had probably had an enthusiastic hand in that operation. He imagined the little Irishman gleefully tearing away the varnished cladding. "Now yer man can see ye, me foine beau-

ty—now he can git at ye if a whale or any other monstrous crature of
the broiny deep stoves a bloody hole in yer foine integrity!" Shaughnessy loved to blarney his boats, Conan recalled with a grin.

At the foot of the companionway was the galley, where the burner
now cast a flickering yellow reflection around the blood-red cabin, and
on the other side was the chart table. Above the table, which extended
right back to the ship's side, was a narrow shelf for pencils, dividers, and
such, and above that were the lockers, crammed with books: nautical al-
manacs, star tables, *Sailing Directions for the World*, Admiralty Pilots—the
eastern North Atlantic, the west coast of Africa, the east coast of South
America, the western South Atlantic, the southern Indian Ocean—the
line of dark blue books, with their golden titles, told the tale of the far
spaces that lay ahead of *Josephine*, the long, long trail of blue and gold,
down through the trades to the smoking graybeards of the unforgiving
Southern Ocean.

Above the navigation library, under the side decks, all the way along
the starboard side of the cabin, there were wide, shallow, wooden cupboards full of charts, the maps of the sea, 128 of them. Some of them
were blank ocean charts with little on them except lines of latitude and
longitude and a few figures where, God knows how many years before,
someone had heroically made soundings. Most of the charts would never
be used. They were the ones that showed the ports and coasts where ref-
uge might need to be sought . . . the Canary Islands, ports in Morocco,
ports in the Windward Islands, Recife, Ascension Island . . . Rio . . .
Capetown . . .

Running down the starboard side, below the chart cupboards, was the
starboard berth. This had been crammed with food-stocks: heavy canned
food below, inside the stowages, and lighter stores, such as cereals and
dried potatoes, lashed down on top. As much as possible, Shaughnessy's
wife, when she had helped him store the food on board, had arranged
it all so that one day's food supply at a time could be easily got at. Each
day the supply would be taken from alternating sides of the ship, so as
to keep the weight equally distributed.

Down the center of the cabin, on top of the floorboards, yet more food
boxes, each with several days' supply of food in them, were stowed,
three abreast and three deep. This severely restricted movement in the
cabin, as it brought Conan's headroom, when he was stooped on top of
the boxes, down to just under three feet. An easier way to get through
the cabin, from the galley to the forepeak, was to climb onto the port
berth, the one used for sleeping, and walk along that. There was almost
four feet of headroom there.

The port berth had been left clear for sleeping. It had been provided with a leeboard on its inboard side, which could be bolted upright when the ship was heeled to starboard, and so prevent Conan from crashing out of his bearth whenever the ship lurched.

Forward of the cabin, the door to the forepeak had been replaced with a strengthened aluminum door. This was so that in case of heavy damage to the bow the forepeak could be sealed off. Hopefully this would keep the vessel afloat and enable her skipper to reach haven. The possibilities of collision with whales or heavy balks of timber were being taken more seriously now by the powers-that-be in ocean racing and cruising. Six clips closed the aluminum door. Just abaft the door there was a head—a lavatory—with a hand basin and even a shower outlet, in a small cubicle on the port side of the door. All the water connections to these had been blanked off—there were six rubber buckets, black, red, and yellow on board now. The head cubicle was used for storage of sailmaker's gear and inflammable ship's supplies—kerosene, ten gallons of it, alcohol, three gallons, paint—and a good supply of distilled water for the batteries.

Conan envisaged the inside of the forward cabin. The two berths had been removed and the space was mostly taken with sail bags, fat and lumpy, which were crammed into the cabin, one on top of the other. Forward of that was the forepeak, which contained two anchors—one heavy and one lighter—and their rope and chain. If all went well, neither anchor would be used until the return to Lisbon . . . nine? . . . ten? . . . eleven? . . . months hence.

Conan made cocoa in his tin pint mug, remembering to only half-fill it, and slowly and carefully made his way topsides again. He stared around the horizon. The wind was yet rising and hauling around more to the north. The steering-gear wind vane had followed the wind round and set *Josephine* on a more westerly course. Conan was tempted to change back to his original course right away, but then he remembered . . . no rush. A few miles to the west wouldn't hurt. He'd still be in the Portugal current, which was carrying *Josephine* south at a knot and a half, anyway, even if he sailed due west for the rest of the night. He decided to finish his cocoa and then adjust the course. "All in good time," he said to himself aloud, as he sat down on the low lee side of the cockpit. He was immediately aware that he had spoken clearly to himself aloud for the first time this trip . . . or was it? He grinned slightly. By this time next week, he knew, he'd be talking to himself often, and in a month's time he would be doing it much of the time. It didn't worry him.

Some people, he thought, if they knew he talked to himself, might think he was a bit crazy. Conan knew differently. That doctor—Conan tried to remember his name—what was it? Conan wracked his brain, sifting through a million trillion bits of information. Suddenly the name came to him—Lilly, that was it. He was British. He'd done a study on single-handed sailors, a psychological study, to see just how nutty they really were. Lilly had come to the simple conclusion, Conan recalled, that ocean solo sailors must be sane because a mentally disturbed person by definition cannot cross an ocean alone. True, there had been some crazies who'd had more than their share of luck, but a loony—anyone who was not completely sane—would be highly likely to make serious errors of judgment and of navigation, and in heavy weather he would be more than likely to break down completely. Conan knew, from hard experience, that the amount of physical and mental stress that he had endured when the ocean really had let loose was almost enough at times to tempt him to drop down on his knees and scream, weep and plead and beg to God—and the devil if need be—for cessation and safety, for just one infinitesimally tiny moiety of comfort, just one more, before he was beaten, a bloody, raving pulp, into the black void of an unknown death. That he had not done this, that he had resisted the temptation to do it, even when hope was but one last ragged thread stretched to break-ing limit, was his badge of sanity. Conan, after a pitch-poling hell of brute violence in the ocean, had viewed askance the landsmen's plaints of woe. To him a broken-down air conditioner or ten-cent increase in the price of gasoline soon found their proper place in his scheme of priorities.

Conan gazed astern again, quickly scanning the whole sweep of the horizon, which was now invisible under the herding clouds. He finished his cocoa and spoke to himself, again aloud. "So why the hell am I doing it?" The empty mug, which he had placed on the seat, beside him, clat-tered into the cockpit well as *Josephine* suddenly lurched to starboard. Conan ignored it. He was not a fussy, tidy man, except where it mattered.

There's the money, he told himself. That would come in handy. It would give him time to write a book without having to worry about deadlines. A really deep one. He could get onto the track of Conrad, ex-cept he would write for a generation that was forgetting how to read. It would have to be—he searched for a word—sculpted for the TV-watching crowd. The money mattered, said the Scotsman in Conan. But then he knew that even if he didn't win, he still wouldn't want to be anywhere else than where he was at that blessed moment . . . apart from being away from Ruth. That was his only regret, so far. As for the writing and New York, it was good to be away from it all, the crowding, the juggling for money and position and power. Out here, whatever the drawbacks, there was none of that. There was, as far as the sea was concerned, only two positions, only two levels—afloat and under—and the sea didn't give a damn which level he was on. As for money at sea, he knew that when the going got rough, say in the Southern Ocean, with fifty-foot seas and the wind blowing a storm ten days out of ten, it wouldn't matter if *Josephine*'s keel had been cast out of twenty-four-carat gold and her winches were made of solid platinum, and if he owned all the oil fields of Texas—it simply would make not one whit of difference to the gray hurtling waters and the wind of the roaring forties, because they just didn't care a—a—*monkey's tit.* The lower-deck phrase came through, despite his momentary search for another one.

He peered around the horizon again. To the west the clouds were thick, black, and menacing. He remembered a phrase his father had once used. "As black as John Knox's breeks." He watched them for a minute and saw not one silver moon-sliver on the ocean below the clouds. He glanced at his Omega watch. Two-thirty. It would soon be false dawn, three hours to go, he told himself. The mainsail was straining, the noise of its fluttering leach—its trailing edge—was like a faraway machine gun. The big jib was pulling like a brewer's dray horse, full-bellied and heavy with wind. *Josephine* flung herself from one sea to the next, each fling now a full-bodied rugby tackle on the shoulders of the driving seas. With each crash, spray drove in tiny sparklets over the bow, the shining droplets in their thousands reflecting the red and green of the navigation light glares.

Conan determined to leave the number one jib aloft all night, this side of a roaring gale, until he had logged another twenty miles—and if all was well, he decided, he would drive her even in a gale. If the low pressure was approaching too fast, he would change to the smaller number two jib at daybreak. He would be clear of the shipping lanes by then, he reckoned, and there would be much more light to see his way around the pounding, heaving foredeck.

He settled himself down again, drawing the collar of the windbreaker up around his neck and ears. A spray dodger was fitted above *Josephine*'s companionway, a hood, which could unfold up and aft on an aluminum frame, which could protect him from the cold night wind and odd dollops of seawater that now and again slapped against the leeside and, like errant precocious children, urgently sought for his attention before they fell back into their parents' arms. But Conan left the dodger down. He wanted to observe as closely as he could, this first night out, how *Josephine*—all of her—her sails, her rigging, and her hull, behaved in a rising sea and wind. There were clear plastic windows in the canvas of the dodger, but they would still be obscured by the spray and the salt that would be driven onto them.

Conan thought it was again time to delve into himself, to find his motivations. His own self-significance in the world had little place in them. He'd tried to figure that out long ago. It might have had a lot to do with him making his first voyages—he was much more romantic then—but now, he concluded, it didn't matter all that much. He knew he was important to Ruth, that mattered a great deal. He was of interest to a few publishers and, he supposed, to his agent and some of his readers, but he didn't imagine they would go into paroxysms of grief if he failed to return. More likely the publishers would have a field day publicizing his nonreturn and issuing another edition of his books. Conan, with a wry laugh to himself at his own cynicism, wished them luck.

Conan asked himself about fame. His mouth tightened as he stared ahead from under the drawn-down bobble cap. He frowned. He even shrugged his shoulders slightly. He came to the conclusion that he would much rather make something worthwhile to leave behind him— a book, a record, a legend—than make nothing of use to anyone and be famed. He saw again in his mind's eye the vacant faces of some of the "celebrities" he had sometimes forced himself to watch on the TV talk shows. Loud, arrogant, and semi-literate men whose only claim to fame had been the ability—the brutality—to batter another man senseless or to kick a piece of leather over the ground for immense sums of money, or to wiggle their hips over a dance floor to moronic noise, and graceless women (and men of a sort, too), of startling cosmetics whose only assets, evidently, had been a glib tongue, cynicism, a seemingly insatiable sexual capacity, and a collective lack of probity. There were those, too, who were intelligent enough, evidently, to know better, yet who practically fell over themselves to kowtow to the false idol of opportunism and join in a continuous barrage of falsehoods and fancies, which twisted history to serve the ends of mammon. Conan shook his head in the dark. No, he told himself, if being famous meant being mixed up with some of that crowd, then the sooner he got to the Philippine hills or again back to sea, the better.

Curiosity he discounted, too. Conan supposed there was always something new on every voyage. He would be surprised if this one didn't turn up a few curiosities. If it didn't, that fact in itself would be curious, he concluded.

The need for independence was a different matter. That's what he needed the prize money for in the first place. But to be able to earn it while retaining his independence, the control over his own destiny, that was important. There were far too many people leaning on other people nowadays, he told himself. That he would never do—he would literally rather starve. Conan's Scottish Calvinism, even after decades of semisubmersion, rose to the surface like the sword of Excalibur. He heard his father's voice again roaring, "You, you and yourself alone, are solely responsible for yourself, let nothing come between you, laddie, and your Creator!" Conan frowned. The old man had been dead a month later, killed by a falling ship's side plate in the Glasgow yard where he had labored as a riveter.

Conan did not consider that, like Peter the Pole, he was escaping from a society he could not agree with, or that did not agree with him. He himself could fit in anywhere, and was old enough now to be able to make allowances for what he saw as others' failings, and to hope they did the same for him. Besides, anyone who imagined that going to sea in a small boat on a long voyage was an escape was either a fool or simply did not know any better. Physically, life ashore was much easier. So many things are done for the landsman that, most of the time, he does not even think about, much less appreciate. Here, he was his own grocer, water supplier, cook, doctor, dentist, policeman, engineer, navigator—here he was king, president, and prime minister of his own little state, all rolled into one. Here the buck not only stopped—it started too.

Adventure, Conan told himself, was definitely in it. The sense of the limitless spaces ahead of him, the outwitting of all the mighty forces ranged against *Josephine,* the out-guiling of storms and calms and currents and even the passage of time itself, the careful rolling of the dice each time the odds were raised against him; all these spiced his sense of adventure. Without that sense, Conan knew in his heart, life cannot be lived to its fullest. Adventure should have been his middle name.

Conan remembered an account he had read once, of a weekend motorboat sailor on the south coast of England, a bank manager. Back in 1940 the man had answered the call for volunteers to go with their boats to the Dunkirk beaches to bring back the defeated troops of the Allied armies. When the bank manager turned up again for work after the evacuation was over, he positively glowed and claimed that it had been the finest weekend he'd ever spent in his life. He had come back from Dunkirk with his boat riddled with shot. That sums up the effects of adventure very well, Conan reckoned. Of course the psychiatrist's couch crowd would make noises about masochism and all kinds of nonsense, and they would never admit that a damned good struggle, with a good dose of fear thrown in, was sometimes the best medicine ever concocted for man or beast.

Next Conan considered competitiveness. Although it existed in him—he'd love to beat the Englishmen if it was only for Scotland's sake, but he suspected that he might feel regret if the woman or the young American lost. He knew that the prize for him would mean that he would probably be settled for life, but he did not thirst at the brim of the great silver winner's cup which had been so prominently displayed at the race reception last night. He had only taken part in three races, the disastrous transatlantic one among them. By nature he was not competitive with other humans. Perhaps, he told himself, it was because most of his competitive spirit over the past two and a half decades had been pitted so much against the forces of nature. Time, the sea, and the weather were his real competitors, even now. He knew, deep down, after he had considered it for a while, that if any of the others were in distress and he could reach them, he would go to their assistance, even if it meant abandoning the race. He was a dyed-in-the-wool cruising man, he concluded, and to try to assist anyone in distress at sea is the first tenet of a true cruising man's faith.

Competition, Conan felt in his bones, was one of the stumbling blocks of shoreside existence. There was too much trying to outdo, to vie with, to beat others, and not enough trying to relate with each other. To Conan, the contention that competition with others brings out the best was only a half truth, because often, except in the case of a biological choice of mating partners, perhaps, a person's best is not always the best for others—sometimes not even for himself. True, at sea, in a solo race, it was somewhat different. Here he was isolated from the competition, so he could not actually harm them. But if he let ruthless ambition turn his head he could surely allow the sea to harm him, through his own foolhardiness or downright blind stupidity. The thought came to him that the reasons that other species—especially the sea creatures—survive was that they did not compete, except for mates, with each other within the species, but that in all other circumstances they related to and assisted fellow creatures of the same species. He would try to run the race as fast as he could—that was as far as Conan's competitiveness went.

The thought of the months of solitude ahead was not onerous to Conan. He was quite happy in his own company. It would have been nirvana, he considered, to have Ruth along, but he knew that could not be, and so he accepted his solitude. He recalled that he had sailed with many other people, probably over a thousand of them, in one vessel or another over the years. Some, if they turned up now, he would greet with open arms, others he would jump over the side to avoid. Conan could be an introvert or extrovert, depending on his mood or the circumstances, but he had a need which perhaps only true sailors, writers, and monks know, for inner reflection and contemplation. He knew that these can only be achieved in isolation. He knew that when sailing alone his perceptions were vastly heightened, and that the absence of other people brought his experiences to him much less diluted, more vivid, more sharply defined, and better remembered. For these reasons, the company of others he was willing to sacrifice.

Conan knew that his lack of fear of solitude was a curiosity to some of the landsmen he had met. Indeed, in some it even aroused a certain hostility, a resentment, a suspicion that because he did not succumb to society's incessant clamor to deny his own personality, to submerge it in society and "cooperation" (yet essentially "uncooperation"), there might be something wrong with him. He was certain that in his solitude he had always been able to perceive much more clearly the richness and meaning of what is in the world and all around it, and in his silent contemplations he had grown in mental, moral, and spiritual stature. Besides, he considered a fear of being alone to be nothing less than a symptom of childish self-pity, and to Conan self-pity was the deadliest sin of all, the root-base of most of the twentieth century's problems.

To Conan, there was simply no sense in feeling sorry for himself, merely because some Viennese cocaine-addict had said he ought to, and so he didn't, ever. He generally considered that he existed for solutions, not for problems. Conan was usually fairly sure of himself, and now that he was alone at sea, he knew he was sure of himself and that he, and he alone, was in charge of his destiny. Many people never—not even for five minutes of their lives—know the joy of that, he reflected.

With a shiver, Conan looked over to starboard, to the southeast. There was a purplish tinge in the blackness of the sky, low down, just above the clouds which piled onto the horizon. Dawn was hauling itself west against the spin of the world.

Conan watched the purple patch in the east, a mere suspicion of a smudge, for a minute, and thought of the last motivation. The most mysterious one of all. The one that always defied expression. It was as if the sea beckoned him to her, as if the sea knew that part of him belonged to her, as if the sea called him, and he, tasting her in his own sweat, knowing the salt of her in his own blood, was unable to deny her call. It was almost as if his body—not he but his body—remembered a time when humanity belonged to the sea, and as if the sea, like a mother whom he had abandoned, was drawing him to her, with open arms, strong and undeniable. He gave up trying to resolve what he felt about the sea. He didn't love it; respect would be more the word.

Conan shivered again. The false dawn now was slashed across the eastern sky. As if she had a bit in her mouth, *Josephine* plunged on ... on ... on. There was a thick taste in his mouth. He picked up the empty, fallen mug from the cockpit well, hooked his safety-harness lifeline clip to a heavy ringbolt, and leaned over the port side. He scooped a mug full of water out of the sea, put the mug to his lips, and drank a mouthful of the ocean. He swirled the water round and round in his mouth, tasting the flat bitterness, then spat it out again into the sea. He emptied the cup. "Cheers," he said aloud.

He made ready, holding on tightly as the boat's bow and stern rose and fell, to change the jib. He glanced at the log: 122 miles sailed over the water. At this rate, he told himself, *Josephine* would make between 150 and 180 miles a day in fair conditions. He did a quick mental calculation. At this speed he would be back in Lisbon in 195 to 250 days. He made up his mind, again, to drive her hard.

"So that's it," he spoke aloud as he clambered down to drag the number two jib out of its stowage. "The prizes: money, independence, adventure, and solitude." He had worked out his motives. "Four reasons—four for the gospel makers ..." he sang to himself.

It was typical of Conan not to have calculated his reasons for joining the race, consciously, before putting out to sea. With him the "who, what, when, and how" always came before the "why."

He smiled to himself as he thought about it. Finally, as he hauled himself forward to the foredeck with the sail he said aloud, "Well, Houghton did say it was a pierhead jump, after all!"

All of a sudden he saw the other sailboat, a tiny white blob in the pale dawn, low down, in the west. The first rays of sunlight on its sails contrasted them starkly with the chimney-black clouds beyond, over the rim of the world. He stared at it for a moment intently.

"*Josey*, lass, we've got ourselves some company," he said aloud, but quietly.

He gazed at the tiny faraway apparition again, as he balanced on the foredeck. Then it was gone under a cloud and, with sea spume driving onto his legs over the bow, he set about, slowly, methodically, and very carefully, changing the headsail.

Chapter 9

AKA'S TRIBE MOVED STEADILY SOUTHEAST. Sometimes, when the fishing was good, they stayed in one area for hours at a time. The fish shoals on which they were feeding were moving also south, and they moved with the fish. All the time the current, running south and east, steadily carried them with it, at least when the dolphins were near the surface.

Off Cape Saint Vincent, one of their favorite hunting areas, Aka's scouts found a great shoal of bonito, and for five hours in the morning sunlight and down in the dark green depths, the whole tribe—all eight schools—carried havoc with them into the fleeing fish and gorged themselves. All the rest of that day and all the following night they had followed the coastline over the edge of the continental shelf at a steady pace of ten knots. They had been only too well aware of the many fishing boats in the area to send out shoal scouts, so by the time Aka leapt up eighteen feet and recognized Cape Trafalgar forty miles away they were hungry again, and the calves were becoming more and more insistent and peevish with their patient mothers.

All day they had been accompanied by a school of tuna, which swam in line with the dolphins, directly below them. This habit was not unusual. Among tuna fishing boats it often leads to many dolphins being caught in the nets and drowning. The dolphin does not eat tuna, and tuna has a poor sense of direction, so trusts the dolphin to guide him. The tuna did not realize that Aka's tribe were following the coast to hunt. It was not until the tribe approached shallow water, then headed out again, that the tuna finally left them, shortly to be caught, all of them, in the long nylon nets of the Spanish fishing boats slowly trawling around and around out in the Straits.

A careful, long-range sonar sweep by Aka of the sea around them turned up the presence of two fishing craft and two killer whales, fifteen miles off, to the southeast of the cape. Aka ordered four male scouts off in that direction to form a line—a sonar chain—between the tribe and the boats. He guessed that the whales themselves were, by the frenzied tracks of their image-blips on his sonar receiver, probably too busily preoccupied with a hunt of their own to bother to compete with them in their attack.

Apart from some men, the killer whale is the most maligned creature of the sea. The killer whale is not a greedy glutton like the shark, who if he has the chance will kill and eat almost anything that swims. The only sharks who are not craven cowards are the great whites, the blackguard tigers of the Southern Ocean. Their bloodthirsty ferocity leaves the killer whales looking like grazing sheep.

As the guard-scouts fanned out to take up their warning positions, Aka and the three Wise Ones turned their attention to the area north of them, back along the shallows by the shore, northeast of Cape Trafalgar. Slowly all four of them swam ahead of the shoal herders and the remaining scouts, who were themselves a mile ahead of the main body of the tribe. After half an hour of slow, steady approach, in complete acoustic silence, Aka's sonar caught the shadows of three immense shoals. They were, he knew, in water generally too shallow for fishing boats to operate. Aka stopped dead on the surface and scanned the shoals again and again as they moved very slowly southeast, only a hundred yards or so from the low coastline. He "ordered" the shoal herders to move out fast, parallel to the coast, until they were on a line a mile and more either side of the fish shoals, and then to turn in at full speed and place themselves between the fish and the shore. Then, as the rest of the tribe moved in on them, they were to drive the shoals out toward the attacking dolphins. It was a classical dolphin strategy.

The shoal herders, eight of the fastest males, turned, flashes of gray and silver, and sped off to obey Aka's command. Four raced off to the southeast, swimming on the surface most of the time, all in line together, until they were almost level with the center dolphin of the flank guard. Four others sped off to the north, until they were four miles away on Aka's flank. There, both schools waited until Aka gave the "close-in" signal. Then, like hunting dogs let from the slips, they were off toward the shore, each team racing in line ahead, keeping perfect time with each other, keeping exactly the same closing distance from the shore by means of the up-current leader's acoustic signals to the down-current team's leader. As Aka followed both schools with his long-range sonar, he "saw" that they were synchronizing their approach to the shore, so that both jaws of the trap would close behind the fish shoals at precisely the same moment.

In fifteen minutes the two schools had reached the shallows by the shore at two points six miles apart. All the while the main body of the tribe had spread out in a long crescent-shaped line, with Aka at the center. This line gradually closed in on the shoals of fish, its two "horns" moving steadily to the points where the flanking shoal herders had reached the shallows.

Suddenly, there was a flurry of commotion among one of the shoals of fish, a darting this way and that. Aka knew that the fish had sensed the presence of the herders between them and the shore. With a tremendous mental blast on his acoustic transmitter he gave the signal to attack.

The herders threw themselves into the fish shoals, not bothering to kill yet, only intent on spreading alarm and confusion. The three shoals, as if all the fish in them were controlled by one nerve, turned seaward and scooted away—straight toward the new rapidly closing-in crescent of hungry dolphins. The dolphins, each pinging away at the highest frequency on his or her sonar range, homed in on the thickest groups of the now scattering shoals of—for Aka knew now—garfish, young barracuda, and pilchard. Even before the terrified fish had seen the long line of gray shadows rushing toward them, the dolphins had switched to their short-range sonar. This had locked on to every darting move that most of the millions of fish could make, and within seconds the dolphins were among them, from ahead, from the sides, from the rear, and from above and below. The shoals, after thirty seconds, were widely scattered and reduced by roughly eighty percent of their former number. The last remaining stragglers from the shoals blindly groped their way in the dark gloom far below, out to seaward. These, the now returned guard dolphins located with their sonar and made short work of, while the rest of Aka's tribe, grouped together on the surface, waited for them to eat their fill.

As the sun lowered itself in the western sky, the tribe again sent out guard-scouts all around them to seaward to range a long arc up to five miles offshore, while the rest of the adults and calves frisked and gamboled and leapt over the tiny wavelets of the calm sea all around Aka and the three other Wise Ones. Aka's companions moved slowly with him on the surface, round and round in a wide circle. They "discussed" with each other their legends of this part of the ocean. When they raised their heads above the surface they could see the far-off Atlas mountains to the south, a hazy khaki in the afternoon sunlight. They knew that immediately to the north of the range of high mountains was the strait that led into the land-surrounded sea. That was where the Sea Kings of Atlantis in ancient times had gone when the waters had overcome their home long, long ago.

Aka recited to them how the great carved ships, with their purple sails, had traded with this part of the world long, long before the cataclysm. They had loaded the ships, the dolphins remembered, with great bales and balks of shining wood, brown and black; and ingots of metal, gold, and silver. The dolphins knew, too, that just as their own relatives in widely flung oceans were different, so was Man. The crews of the ships had been of many races—Atlantis had sent ships to all the oceans and gathered people from all over the world. This the dolphins knew; the ancient Sea Kings had worshipped them and communed with them. The dolphins of the tribe had gone out with the purple-sailed ships and kept company with the Sea Kings as friends and helpers for voyages that had lasted for many years in some instances. "The ships," said one of the Wise Ones, "took dolphins with them to send shoreward when they reached unknown lands, to search for fish and shallows and reefs, to bring back reports of the best places for the ships to anchor, and to scout for pirates and wild savages."

"After the rising of the waters, when the very last three ships left the now almost disappeared Atlantis," said another of Aka's companions, "the whole tribe accompanied them this far, to the mouth of the strait— which then was much narrower, so long ago was it—and here they parted company with much sorrow on both sides, and the Sea Kings sailed on into the landlocked sea to the place where their predecessors had founded the temple in honor of the dolphins—Eh-ee. From then on, although the dolphins came here every year after parting with the Sea Kings, they had seen no sign of them for many thousands of years. Eventually, a few ships similar to those of the Sea Kings, but much cruder and slower, and with dirty-white sails, had passed them close to the shore."

"One of them," interjected Aka, "had a golden animal skin nailed to its mast, according to what Oba told me when I was young. Oba said that those men were the descendents of the Sea Kings, and the ancestors of Man who now rode the fishing boats and the great noisy steamers."

All at once the outlying sonar guards sent in alarm signals on a broad band, at low frequency, so that the calves, too, would receive them. The fishing boats were heading their way, but not fast.

Aka ordered the tribe into convoy again, all the different schools to take their places and the scouts to range ahead. Then he and the three Wise Ones, a hundred yards ahead of the main body, started to swim southwest, swiftly, while the outlying sonar guard withdrew to a position two miles astern of the tribe, where it could maintain watch as a rear guard. They headed out, then, for the open sea and spent the rest of the day and most of the night wending their way between fishing nets and waiting, stopped still and wary, while great freighters and passenger ships, all brightly lit charged noisily across their track, ahead and astern of them, temporarily blinding their sonar and acoustic "sight."

It was early morning before they could at last doze in reasonable safety, among the current-ripped rocks below the great cliffs of Cape Spartel. There, while the remainder of the tribe dozed, the guard dolphins kept watch against deadly moray eels as well as numerous gray sharks who hovered, cowardly as usual, off the sea-beaten boulders of the very northwesternmost tip of the shoulder of Africa.

For the next eight days Aka directed his now wide-flung tribe south over the shallow, sandy-bottomed waters off the coast of Morocco. The tribe members were more free ranging now. The waters were clearer than they had been further north. There were few dangers—even the sharks were so well fed and passive that the tribe ignored them, letting them pass peacefully through the dolphins' own ranks.

The fishing was excellent, mainly pilchard and mullet, and each day when the dolphins sighted shoals by the shore, they practiced the crescent attack, and they all ate their fill.

Now and then some of the adult dolphins, whose ears can pick up 150,000 hertz, perceived even the noise of flying fish leaping miles away. Off they went in fast pursuit, sometimes reaching a speed of thirty knots, across the track of the flying fish, catching them in midair, swallowing them whole.

At other times, for sport, when they sighted fishermen working from the beach on the desert shore, Aka sent the shoal herders out to gather in a swarm of fish—mullet as a rule—and all the dolphins took enthusiastic part in driving the fish into the waiting nets. Then they watched, as the fishermen, before they dragged their nets in, dropped to their knees on the sand and bowed their heads down to the ground, over and over, again and again, to the dolphins, who by this time were themselves gorged with freshly swallowed mullet and were merely eyeing the black fishermen out of curiosity. This game was a tradition within Aka's tribe and had been carried on for thousands of years.

Sometimes a fishing boat was sighted, and then the whole tribe formed up and moved off at speed, with guards before and after, out into the ocean. When the menace had passed, the tribe moved in again to the shore and the profuse food in the waters along it.

There were many fishing boats off the Moroccan coast. Aka's tribe were very careful to keep well out of their way. They had learned to scatter now if a fishing boat headed for them, in case the men thought there was a school of tuna below them. Often a boat came charging over in their direction when they were in tribal formation, but as soon as they scattered and showed the men they were doing so by leaping and flailing the water, the fishing boat would change course and leave them alone. That this maneuver was successful they had learned over two decades at much expense in dolphins' lives.

After four days of fish-swallowing orgies, playful gambols, games with the men on the shore, and comparatively safe dozing at night, Aka, after a brief consultation with the three other Wise Ones, decided that it was time for the tribe to head west to the Island of the Whistling Men. "This was the place," said Aka, "where according to the old dolphin legends, the Sea Kings of Atlantis taught the islanders to talk to us by whistling sounds very similar to some of those we use among ourselves."

It was the law of Aka's tribe that each year before they set out on the last, long trek through the ocean back to their home in the south, they should visit the island that men call Gomera, which, with its sister island Hierro, is the most oceanward of the Canaries.

For the dolphins, swimming at about ten knots, it was a two-day passage from the coast of Africa to Gomera. They kept their usual formation, the scouts ranging far out on each side and the schools formed up behind Aka and the three Wise Ones.

Now, when Aka leapt above the sea surface to get his bearings of the sun in the day, or the moon and the guide stars at night, there were far fewer clouds in the sky, and those that did pass were young and light and fluffy and flew overhead fast before the northeast trade wind. The wind itself, new-sprung from the great Sahara Desert, still carried with it minute grains of sand, which gradually fell out of the wind and settled on the moving faces of the blue, white-topped seas.

For the dolphins there was plenty of sport with flying fish here, on the first day out from the coast. By now even some of the calves and their mothers were joining in, chasing the tiny, elusive creatures as they scooted swiftly from the crest of the sea, skimmed lightly over a dozen other seas, only barely touching them with their bellies, all gleaming silver in the sunshine or the moonlight, and then, twisting to one side in lovely curves, landed again, either into the sea or into the beak of a grinning dolphin. Then the dolphin leaped, twisted right around so he could in a flash inspect the whole of the area around him, and threw himself, swift as a rifle bullet, straight into the flight path of yet another flying fish. Sometimes, in wonderful horizontal lunges of twenty feet or so, the dolphin caught the flying fish while he himself was still in mid-flight. It was a game that would make the average water-polo match look like a funeral gathering.

An hour after sunset the tribe formed itself up in schools for dozing. Aka was in no hurry, and he knew that all the dolphins had tired themselves with the day's swimming and sport. No one was hungry. He decided to let the tribe doze until sunrise and the faithful night guards relieved each other frequently, so that all could rest well.

Just as the false dawn broke the eastern sky into a purplish orange haze, Aka was awakened by the steadily increasing sonar bounce of something moving down on the dozing tribe from the north. He alerted the night guards. They all turned in the direction that Aka was facing. The guards, too, beamed in on the intruder. Aka gave them the order to wake the whole tribe. Soon all the dolphins were awake, swimming slowly around Aka. Now the first rays of the sun were slicing the sky to the east. Aka turned and started to move westward. The scouts shot out to their stations and the rest of the dolphins fell in behind Aka and his three companions. The signal from the intruder was increasing rapidly. Aka found, with his furry ears, the azimuth of the signal source. Then he leaped into the sky to compute in an instant the visual situation. Even as he did so the rays of the sun, now merely peeping over the horizon, caught the white sails and blue hull of a boat. . . . Then Aka, suddenly, as his mind ingested the signals from the boat, realized that it was the same one that had so alarmed them ten nights ago. He signalled to the scout in the north to move in closer to the boat and observe it.

Ten minutes later, as Aka and all his followers hovered still, waiting, the acoustic signal came back from the scout. "No Man, no net."

All the while the scout sent back a hologram, which, fuzzily at first, gave Aka a complete, three-dimensional picture of the boat. It was longer than a killer shark, but not as long as an adult rorqual, and its body was blue. It had two big fins, both white, and the fluke on its vertical tail faced the wind. There was no sign of Man on the boat's back. It seemed to be guiding itself.

Now the scout was much closer. At first he sent back acoustic signals of trepidation, but then, as the boat passed much closer to him without turning to attack, they became more confident. Bravely, the scout swam in toward the stern of the boat, deep in the water. He looked up and sent to Aka the hologram of the bottom fluke of the boat's tail, which moved gently. The scout swam rapidly under the boat and surfaced ahead of it, momentarily, just long enough to breathe. He dived again and rose beneath the boat's bow. Immediately, as the boat's bow-wave pushed him along through the water without any effort on his part, he sent back acoustic pleasure signals. "Good. Likes to play."

There was a relaxation of tension in the sonar and acoustic waves all around Aka. One or two dolphins were already moving toward the boat—seconds later they were followed by a few more of the males and a couple of females, Sheena among them. As the first school started toward the boat the others all followed them, slowly at first, then rapidly. Soon the boat was surrounded on all sides except the stern by over one hundred dolphins, all ploughing their undulating way through the sea on the same course as the boat, and slowly, shyly, moving in closer to her.

Aka, too, moved in closer to the boat. Swimming alongside her, about twenty yards away, he leaned his head to one side and studied her with his right eye. In three seconds he had taken everything in from the gently rising bow, right up the luff on the jib, the masthead with its chrome-plated light, the mainsail, the backstays, the steering gear, and the full length of the blue hull. The shapes of all were stored away in his memory.

Aka watched as two males, more daring than the rest, moved in under the boat's bows and actually rubbed them with their bellies, squealing, and let the bow-wave throw them forward, rolling themselves over as they did so. Aka watched as the two males did it again and again, and as other males and Sheena joined them, so that soon there were eight or nine dolphins on either side of the boat's plunging forefoot. Suddenly one of the males, carried away with the exuberance of the games, sped away from the blue hull, about fifty yards off. Quickly he turned, and as if he were going to mate with the boat, dashed toward her at full speed. An inch from the hull the male turned at right angles and then with the full length of his three-hundred-pound body, pounded away at the hull. Almost immediately, he fell back, squeaking and squealing for all he was worth, into the merrymaking of eighteen fully grown dolphins, transported with joy and delight, rolling in the bow-wave.

At this moment Aka dived to inspect the boat from under her stern.

Kweela had rushed over with the second wave of dolphins. Om was at her side, still complaining of wind. She had been too preoccupied watching the boat and the fun around the bow-wave to turn and inspect him. Right now she was looking at the underwater fluke of the boat's tail, which waggled in the sea in a fascinating way.

Om nipped Kweela's beak. She paid no attention but remained staring at the boat's fluke as she swam on. Om nipped her hard beak again. Still she paid no attention. Then Om, piqued by her lack of attention, dropped back alongside Kweela and angrily bit the tender skin of her body, just ahead of her tail. Kweela involuntarily lurched with the pain. As Om swam up abreast of her again she lifted a flipper and walloped him just in front of his dorsal fin. Then, turning on her side to do so, she grabbed her seven-foot-long son with both her flippers and, holding him in a viselike grip, took a deep breath and turned over on her back. With her immense strength Kweela lifted all 170 pounds of Om while swimming upside down, and held him clear out of the water, up in the air. This was punishment for Om, who, like every other young dolphin, was frightened of being out of the water, and hated it. Kweela swam thus, weaving her head from side to side slowly so that she could breathe through her blowhole, for five minutes, while Om screamed all the time, in fright at first, then in apology.

Kweela let go of Om and righted herself—and found that she was staring directly at a Man, only a few feet away from her on the boat.

Kweela was still so angry with Om that at first she hardly noticed the Man. Then Om nudged her and squealed again in complaint. She turned to him and "saw" yet another wind bubble in his stomach. She gently butted him. The bubble rose and streamed out of his mouth. Then she turned again and looked at the Man. He was staring at Om. Startled now, she gave an alarm, but the pleasure signals, squeals and squeaks and billions of clicks, coming from all around her were far too strong. The only reaction was a slight moving out of the dolphins who had swum close to the boat's belly. Still the Man did not move. Then Kweela knew all was well because Aka was swimming ahead of her, studying the Man, while the Man turned his head this way and that as if in astonishment. Aka would know if there was danger.

Aka gazed intently, curiously, at the Man. He thought at first that the Man was almost the same color as himself, but then he realized, when he focused his eye closely on the Man's head, that it was covered with hair. The Man had his mouth set widely and his teeth were showing. The Man was obviously watching little Om, who was, he knew, swimming behind him, beside his mother. Aka lowered the frequency of his holographic signal system wondering if Om were still in pain, trying to tune in to Om's baby talk . . . and accidentally tripped over low, blurry signal waves coming from the Man. The Man was actually sending out some kind of a love-signal! It was about the frequency and modulation of a baby calf's signal of affection for a fellow calf! Aka "tuned" down again. No doubt about it. This seemed to be a good Man. . . . Perhaps he was the descendent of the Sea Kings of Atlantis, who so long ago had worshipped the dolphins? Aka decided he would discuss it later with the three Wise Ones.

In the still increasing welter of excitement and joy coming from the dolphins riding forward with the now boiling bow-wave, Aka accepted the Man and the boat, and himself joined in the fun, until he tired of it. Then, having received from the scouts signals of three fish sightings, all the dolphins raced off to join their patiently searching comrades, leaving the Man and the boat to plough and plunge along peacefully in the morning sunshine, alone again, while they themselves headed for the Island of the Whistling Men.

Chapter 10

CONAN UNHANKED THE NUMBER ONE JIB from the forestay and dumped it on the plunging foredeck. Then he dragged it aft and laid it out on the lee side-deck, ready for bagging later. He glanced now and then in the direction of the sail he had seen, but there were rain patches in the west, obscuring the horizon. Now that only the mainsail was pushing *Josephine*, the wind-steering gear was making a heavy job of keeping the boat on course and she veered widely to port and starboard, with the bow rearing and plunging the while.

After his first night out at sea in months, and awake all night at that, Conan was feeling . . . it was not tiredness, more a numbness, as if his body were wrapped in some kind of soft shell, but he forced his mind to remain fully alert. He decided to slow down and consider what he was doing more carefully. There was no sense in him rushing things, even with the wind now at twenty-five knots and the seas rising fast. He sat on the side of the coach roof to bag the number one jib while he thought out the situation. He pulled his bobble cap down low over his ears and securely buttoned up his windbreaker around his chin.

A running sail change is not an easy thing to achieve at the best of times. It means keeping the vessel on course, with the wind full on the sails, while the jib sheet is eased off. Then, with the strain still on the sail hanks, the halyard is cast off and the fluttering, whipping sail has to be dragged down the forestay. But Conan somehow, swearing, managed it alright with the jib. He had clipped his harness through and around a foredeck cleat and set to, but it had been heavy, difficult, and very uncomfortable, leaning out over the bow pulpit, with the wind tearing and plucking at him.

Conan decided that in the future, in a wind this strong, he would stop the boat—heave to—when he changed sails. As he stuffed the last of the big jib in the bag he decided to heave to even now, so he could get the number two jib up taut on the forestay wire. He reflected that he was not as nimble, nor as strong, as he had been—he would do it the old man's way. It was safer and easier, too.

He staggered his way aft with the bag, dumped it down the companionway, and clambered into the cockpit. He seized the steering gear triplock line and hauled it; the wind vane apparatus clattered out of gear. He took the wheel and spun it. Then he secured the wheel lock and the helm held to windward. As *Josephine*'s mainsail shoved her nose round into the wind the mainsheet eased off. Conan grabbed it and closehauled the mainsail. Now the vessel was almost stopped in the water and rode with her bows to the wind and sea. As Conan returned to the foredeck and hoisted the number two jib, *Josephine*'s bow passed through the blind eye of the wind. The high mainsail fluttered and flapped like a great white butterfly's wing; the blocks shook and clattered. The wind caught the port side of the mainsail, and she heeled over slightly, started to move forward, then sailed herself back very slowly through the wind.

In a few minutes, working more easily now, Conan had the smaller jib halyard well swigged up hard against its sheave in the masthead. He then eased off the main halyard a few inches, and as *Josephine* passed through the wind again, he inserted the reefing handle into its gear and rolled the foot of the violently flapping mainsail boom until the sail was three feet shorter than before.

Then he stowed the reefing handle carefully in its rack and went aft again, hauled in the jib sheet, and eased off the main. He put the boat back on course, south-southwest. Next he locked in the wind-vane steering gear, with its rudder straight on the course and its wind vane pointing into the eye of the wind.

Conan stood for a moment, checking the compass against the course, made sure that all was well, and he clambered down below. He stowed the sail bag in the forward cabin, lit the burner on the stove, put the kettle on, and, still puffing, made some tea.

As the kettle boiled, he thought for a moment about last night's strange occurrence, when the sea had seemed to brew up. He decided to ignore the matter. He told himself it had probably been either whales or a hallucination. He'd had hallucinations before at sea, he remembered, only not this early in a voyage—not the first night out. The very few he'd experienced had all been after several weeks at sea on his own. He had never told anyone about them—not even Ruth—but he understood that it was by no means uncommon for solo sailors to see and experience things that simply could not have been there, or happened. Dr. Lilly had written that it was nothing to worry about—and he'd proved it by conducting experiments where, in simulated conditions ashore similar to a small craft at sea, he had made people hallucinate after only a few hours.

It was still difficult for Conan to accept one of his recurring "daydreams" at sea as *déjà vu*, though. These were the visions he had thought he had seen, while at sea, fully awake, of steamers. Every time he had "seen" the ships . . . later, sometimes several hours later, sometimes days later, that particular ship which he had previously "seen" steamed into view. It had only happened after he had been at sea for many days alone. He had never mentioned it to anyone else, but he had met that strange Welshman—what's his name? Griffith Evans, that was it, in New York. Griffith had spoken frankly to him about seeing things that were not there, and that appeared later, and he did not seem to mind if people might consider him a little crazy. Typical Welshman, Conan thought.

For no particular reason, except perhaps that Griffith loved the poet, he recalled a line from Kipling, which Griffith had quoted that day:

> . . . 'e's all 'ot sand an' ginger.
> An' probably shammin' when 'e's dead . . .

Conan could not recall the rest of it, but he wryly thought it would make a great epitaph for the Welshman. The scruffiest, most unlikely romantic, the most perceptive, the most self-effacing "living legend" he had ever met, and he'd met Griffith years before, all over the world, in some *very* unlikely places. He'd once, years ago, helped him to "rescue" a beautiful power boat, a seventy-footer that the Algerian government had seized from her French owner. They'd actually snaffled the boat out from under the Algerian guards' noses, he recalled with a grin. A rum one, a real laddie, that one, thought Conan, as he poured the hot water in the china teapot, one of a dozen that Shaughnessy—a typical Irishman—had stowed on board.

Conan was pleased with the amount of milk Shaughnessy had ordered. He had concluded lately that the times he had hallucinated at sea had always been when there was no milk left on board. He hadn't thought about that angle until Griffith had casually mentioned it that afternoon in the Lion's Head pub on Sheridan Square.

Conan, with his mug of tea in hand, clambered back up to the cockpit. A shower had passed quickly overhead and had washed much of the night's salt and sea dew off *Josephine*'s topsides. His throat and his nostrils, salt-stiffened, welcomed the tang and the steamy aroma of the tea. As he sipped the hot brew, Conan gazed over to the west, but still saw no sign of the sailboat. He concluded that whoever it was, he or she— and he suspected it had been *Flagrante Delicto* with Mary Chatterton at her helm—was now heading further out into the Atlantic, further away from any possible encounter with ships in the steamer track.

The seas around him had now worked up into swiftly moving humps of white-topped green water. Conan looked up at the sky. The clouds which earlier had been a black mass in the west had broken up into light gray streamers scudding high overhead. Conan recited to himself the old seaman's rhyme:

> Mare's nests and lamb's tails—
> Make tall ships haul down their sails.

Josephine plunged on from one green sea to the next. Conan decided that he would not need to swill the decks down. There would be seas enough washed on board in the next few hours. For a moment he watched the length of the boat as she rose and plunged, scudded and wallowed, and as the bow bit into the seas and was, in turn, pickled and rinsed with industrious regularity. His eye ran over the rigging wires, now as drum-tight as violin strings, and over the sails, full pregnant with the half-gale. He felt happier now, with himself, with the ship, and with the watery world around him. For a few moments, with his body pressed against the wheel column, Conan held the steaming tea mug in both hands, like a priest offering a chalice at mass. He sniffed deeply now of the pungent salt air, always strongest at dawn; he sniffed at other odors—so well remembered, so loved—of saturated canvas and cordage. But the fragrance of the tea was the sweetest of all and he held it up, under his nose, while he inspected the compass, now askew in its gimbals. His eyes rose again and swept over the ocean, toward the new dawn. The air was so fresh and the blue glow on the horizon so clear and delicate that it was as though creation had happened only moments before. The sun that had been a small, glowing coal had grown and was now circling the slate-colored sea in a ring of silver light. The black horizon clouds in the east had turned to gray and, even as he watched, were breaking up, turning white and starting across the sky.

Conan turned, crouching, and slid down the hatch, content that his first full day at sea was well underway.

Down below he made his breakfast, while he waited to radio to Lisbon at seven o'clock for relay on to Lloyd's of London. He decided to request that Lloyd's inform Ruth, in New York, of his progress every three days. When he had suggested this to her, she had protested to him about the cost, but he would do it anyway. That way, he thought, he might feel a little less alone.

Like many single handers when at sea, Conan usually slept—half-slept is a better expression for the sailor's doze—during the day. He dozed, in three sessions, one from dawn until six, one in the forenoon, from about eight to eleven, and one after taking the important sights at noon, until late in the afternoon. He had several reasons for preferring to stay awake at night and to sleep during the daytime. During the time that the vessel was ploughing through shipping lanes, Conan was awake during the dangerous hours of darkness. Most ships keep a good lookout, but in some the automatic pilot is in charge and the bridge watch are half-asleep, or reading, or playing rummy. Some huge tankers simply cannot change course in less than half an hour. Conan knew that for any small-craft man who is alone to sleep at night while there is any chance of one of those blindly charging leviathans being around is ultimate foolishness.

He reflected also that another good reason for sleeping during the day in the tropics is that the nights are cooler, down below especially, and less sweat is expended in working effort, so less fresh water is consumed to replace it. The night, especially in the tropics, is much kinder to the eyes. A few days of the sun's hot glare reflecting from the ocean seas can half blind a man and roast him with ultraviolet rays, causing all kinds of problems if he has any sensitivities.

Back in Lisbon, Conan and Houghton had briefly discussed the best course for *Josephine.* Houghton was too experienced himself to have laid down any hard and fast rules about it. "The essence," he had said, "is to get around the Cape of Good Hope as soon as possible, before the southern deep winter really sets in around the end of June. East of the cape you'll have the hard winter winds and seas, of course, but it will be a clear run all the way east, south of Australia and New Zealand to the Horn, and you should get there around mid-southern summer, about December, and have a fair rounding of Cape Stiff, then a good run up the Atlantic and so back to Lisbon around March or April . . . even February if your luck holds out. . . ."

Conan, as he remembered the offhand way in which Houghton had mentioned the prospect of him battering his way around the Cape of Good Hope and riding a wild bronco for six or seven months before the everlasting gray, charging, relentless, angry-crested sea mountains of the Southern Ocean, laughed quietly to himself. He listened to the shipping forecast from Niton, in Britain, on the shortwave receiver. The low pressure system to the south was not very deep. It would dissipate by evening and the weather would ease off again to the usual fifteen or twenty knot wind, from northeast to north.

Conan hauled himself up and across the cabin to the chart table. The small-scale chart for the eastern North Atlantic Ocean lay before him. He had, before sailing, drawn a line that curved south from Lisbon in the direction of Tenerife. If he stayed on that line or east of it, the Portugal current would give him an extra two knots—forty-eight nautical miles a day—and he would pick up the northeast trade winds sooner than if he headed out into the ocean further west. Then, with Tenerife past, he would steer, still close to south, on a beam reach across the northeast trade, until he joined the North Equatorial Current somewhere off the Cape Verde Islands. This current would carry *Josephine* west in its drift, so he would then have to change to a close reach and try to hold to the line that ran from the Cape Verde Islands to St. Paul's Rocks. There would be a few hundred miles of doldrums—the Horse Latitudes—to work his way over, around the equator, until he encountered the southeast trade wind, which would enable him to drive down as far south as Rio on another broad reach. From the latitude of Rio both the wind and the current would push and carry *Josephine*, with various degrees of liveliness, eastward again across the South Atlantic and so around the Cape of Good Hope. Conan frowned slightly as he remembered the old Portuguese name for it—the Cape of Storms.

That was his strategy, and the tactics would be a day-to-day, week-to-week, month-to-month, affair. He knew—he guessed—that some of the other participants would already have headed further out into the ocean to escape the shipping lanes and to avoid any possible problems that might crop up near or among the Canary Islands ("If you can see it, it's too near" is an ocean sailor's adage), but Conan knew the currents and winds around the islands as well as he knew the Solent and Long Island Sound. The extra mileage which the Portugal current would give him would, he concluded, be worth any extra risk he might incur steering straight for the Canaries. That night, when he was well clear of steamer traffic, he would change course to south-southwest-by-south. He made again for the ladder.

Conan took one more look around topsides, then, still fully dressed except for the windbreaker, he lay down on the port berth. He glanced around at the cabin, now much more shipshape, patted his bobble cap, thought of Ruth and the loft bed in the Manhattan apartment for a few minutes, then he went to sleep fully stretched out with head forward, his right arm pressed by the heel of the boat against the blanket he had folded against the ship's side.

Conan rarely dreamed ashore and never at sea. Out here his mind never completely shut itself down enough in deep sleep. It was always tuned to the boat, even on the first day's sleep. Images did reveal themselves to him, figures and numbers did occur to him, but they were never unreal, never fanciful, always they were related to the present reality. Things, ideas, *occurred* to him in his sleep.

For example, on this first full rest it occurred to him, while he was unconscious, that he must take his vitamin tablets, especially vitamin C, every day, and a touch of garlic with all his main meals to help his digestion and keep the scurvy away. Through his mind ran images of all the "fresh" food he had on board—potatoes, onions, carrots, apples, tomatoes, bananas—and he determined, still sleeping, to eat through them before the weather became too warm and he lost them. He had other foods that would not go off too quickly—nuts, cheese, rice, macaroni, soy beans, lentils, wheat germ, granola, margarine, eggs, dates, figs, raisins, apricots, prunes; and Shaughnessy had left a box of glass jars in which bean sprouts were growing even now ... and he would set out the trolling line that evening on. He might catch a nice fat dorado in these waters.

The food images faded then, as Conan slept, and their place was taken by *things*—boat's gear. Lines, spare sheets, wire cables, blocks, tackles, vang gear, preventers, pumps, buckets, bailers, sewing and sail repair kit—it fell open in Conan's "dream," out tumbled thread, twine, marlin, needles, fiddle, spike, palm, tape, patches, beeswax, sail slides, hanks, sail shackles, leather, cotton, all over the cockpit well. Then the electrical tape, copper wire, flashlight batteries, circuit tester, soldering iron, solder, radio spares—a whole compartment full of valves and transistors. Then the plumbing kit appeared—hoses to fit all through-hull fittings, hose clamps, spare parts for all pumps, siphon hose, gaskets, nipples, packing, grease, diaphragms, flap valves, and tapered wooden plugs ... now the items as they passed through his mind were no longer in kits, but higgledy-piggledy scattered all through the cabin—caulking cotton, bedding paste, seam compound, foam rubber, plywood sheets, common putty, cup grease, soft metal sheets, plastic steel, self-curing urethane putty, Fiberglas tape and resin, spare canvas, spare Dacron, epoxy adhesive, alternator, starting motor, fuel filters, solenoids, fuel pump, injector feed lines, gauges, spanners, starting handles, lube oil, spare stove burners, stove prickers, patches for the life raft, adhesive for the patches ... bits and pieces for the self-steering gear ... screwdrivers, pliers, wrenches, hammers, wood saws, hacksaw, blades, wire cutters, angel hair, bolt cutter, wrecking bar, hatchet, brace and bits, tin snips, chisels, files, plane, clamps, vise, crimping tool, monkey wrench, stillson, end wrenches, socket wrenches, chain wrench, water pipe connections ... Conan woke with a start. He looked around through half-closed eyes, then turned over and went to sleep again to see all the rest of the things on board, just as he had checked them over with Houghton during the previous three days, and as he dropped away into the sailor's twilight, he knew that outside the wind was dropping and the sea had stopped rising, and that it would soon be time to change the headsails again. He recalled the date ... Friday, April third ... *was it only the second day?*

Conan wrote the date on the top of the page of the logbook. *April twelfth.* Sunday. He looked forward to his special weekly meal that evening, and the wine. He now had the habit of writing out the log in the very early morning, after he had charged the batteries and before he turned in. Then he could start each day afresh at noon, which is the sailor's way. He made his entry.

"Wind northwest-by-north. 12 knots. Sea moderate. Passed through the channel between Gran Canaria and Tenerife during the night. Still heading more south than west, hoping for a wind shift to northeast in the next couple of days. Miles run since noon 11th April—108. Average speed during the night—6 knots. Total miles run to date—1,218. Made extra chafe guards for after lower shrouds and repaired frayed stitching on tack of No. 2 jib."

Conan frowned. He wasn't doing too well. The gale had helped *Josephine* along; the fine weather had held her back. For three days the previous week the wind had dropped to mild breezes and light airs. *Josephine* had wallowed, stopped dead for hours in between creeping along at three knots. But he was confident that he was doing as well, if not better, than the other boats in the race, all of whom, he now had learned from Lisbon, were much further out in the ocean. He had the current still giving him an extra mile or two an hour, south. Now that he was through the Canaries, the way ahead was wide open, except for the shipping lane outside the islands. Once across that he would have the whole central Atlantic Ocean before him open and free all the way to Brazil, except for the rocks of St. Paul ...

Bang-wallop! The whole forward end of *Josephine* lurched slightly and reverberated with shock. Conan, who had been bending his head pensively over the chart table, jerked his head back and sideways, grabbed the companionway ladder, and started up. But even as he climbed he knew that whatever had happend was not serious; the vessel was back in her regular rhythm again. His first thought was that the boat had collided with a tree trunk or a big balk of timber—or perhaps even glanced off a whale. These are infrequent, but regular occurrences near coasts or islands. Then, as Conan's head rose above the coach-roof level, and he unconsciously turned to look forward, the sight that met his eyes almost made him stagger with wonder.

All around the boat, as far as two hundred yards, in the gentle dawn-puce-colored seas, *Josephine*, as she plunged and danced, was surrounded by—at first he thought they might be porpoise . . . but one of the creatures close by raised its head . . . and the mischievous grin of a bottle-nosed dolphin, a great twelve-foot-long animal, blackish gray, with gleaming eyes right behind the hinge of its long, wide grin, corrected him.

Conan looked ahead. The sight of almost a score of dolphins playing in *Josephine*'s bow-wave delighted him so much that he stared at them as they, without making any movement of their bodies, flippers, or tails, passively let the wave carry them forward as they rolled over and over in a welter of spray and spume, then dived, swam aft, rose again, and headed for the bow-wave once more. Conan grinned. Involuntarily, a habit by now, his head lifted and he gazed at the sky. It was clear blackish blue, with not a cloud in sight. The sun was yet only an orange-purple haze tinged with gold over the pure curve of the eastern horizon. All around, the sea was now turning from puce to gray to blue, and on the starboard side of the ship the sunlight struck the light gray of the dolphins' backs and the opaque green sheen of the water which streamed off them as they humped and thrusted and lunged their way forward, all at the same speed as *Josephine*.

Conan balanced atiptoe on the ladder to watch the antics of the dolphins under the forefoot. They rolled and dived, twisted and turned, squiggled and squirmed and tried to nudge each other at the plunging bows. He laughed aloud. He turned around to watch the dolphins on the port side. As Conan watched them pitch and toss, pound and plough, hump and dive, he stiffened. At first he couldn't believe his eyes. One dolphin close by was swimming upside down; he could plainly see its whitish belly, and it was actually holding another, smaller dolphin up in the air with its flippers! He stared, astounded. This was a new trick.

He had seen thousands of sea creatures, but this act he'd never seen before. He wondered to himself, just as the lower dolphin rolled over and released the upper one, if the upper one, the smaller one, was perhaps ill, or wounded, or crippled in some way. He leaned further over the cockpit coaming to watch. Now the smaller dolphin was swimming all right along the surface, still next to the larger one. The larger one turned to the smaller one and clouted it with its head, quite hard it seemed to Conan. Then it dawned on him—this was a mother and calf, and he felt, for some strange reason, compassion for them both. Life for them seemed to be much more of a serious matter than it did for those clowns around the bow-wave. He felt a pang in his heart as he wished Ruth was with him. Conan supposed that the revellers were all males. There did not seem to be any calves among them. He looked around at the other flashing bodies on the port side, a good two dozen of them, he estimated, and he felt a real, deep fellowship with them all. He was moving with them.

Suddenly even as he thought of Ruth not being with him, he found himself *being inspected closely by a particular eye.*

It was the eye of an extra large dolphin which swam steadily, with powerful, slow thrusts of its body, ahead of the mother and calf. The big dolphin now and then raised its head and looked directly at him—it appeared to Conan straight into his eyes. Conan for a moment was astounded by the eye of the old dolphin, for by now he had decided that the big creature must be an old male. He noticed the livid scar of the old male, a white gash right across the top of its head. He gazed at the eye. The eye gazed at him. It was not like the humble eye of a dog, nor like the rather stupid eye of a monkey, nor the arrogant eye of a cat. This eye had an extraordinary look of . . . *intelligence.* Wisdom seemed to shine through the eye from the inner depths of the gray skull behind it. There was recognition in the eye, a lighting up, as if it belonged to a person who had suddenly met an old long-lost friend. It was a friendly eye, with a world of good humor in it, and Conan thought it looked at him as if the mind behind it was wondering when he was going to jump in the sea and join them. It was—Conan searched for a word—a *benign* eye.

The eye had behind it not only intelligence and wisdom, but also, it seemed to Conan, as the eye gazed at him, *experience.* Glinting among the sparkles coming from the eye, there were certain signs: gleams, sometimes mere hints, sometimes penetrating beams of intellect, curiosity, wit, shrewdness, acumen, and sagacity. Whatever it was that he could see in that eye, Conan knew that he was being surveyed, sized up, weighted, reckoned, examined, and judged; every expression that he displayed and every move that he made, and he somehow was certain that *Josephine*, too, from her stemhead to her steering gear, was not being merely observed—scrutinized—but also being *recorded*. It occurred to Conan that he had noticed the same gaze in the eyes of some of his writer acquaintances at times. It was a look of objective interest, of wondering what was going to happen next, and yet of all the time having calculated full well what the next act, the next word, was likely to be. It was a look that knew of the humor in tragedy and the tragedy in humor, and yet in it there were the signals of faith, hope, and . . . was it love, charity, or compassion? Conan did not know, but it was very like the gleam he had also seen in some older sailors' eyes. *Understanding*.

After a good three minutes' mutual staring with the old dolphin, Conan carefully and slowly moved aft. He grabbed the wheel. The eye tracked his every move. The old dolphin even dropped back a few feet so he could observe Conan better. Conan lifted one arm and held it over his head. The eye followed it, then came back to Conan's eyes with, it seemed to Conan, a twinkle of amusement. Conan, with his eyes fixed on the big, old dolphin, slowly made his way forward, holding on to the coach roof as he went. Steadily, the old dolphin kept up with him, his eye closely watching Conan's hands and legs sometimes, but always returning its gaze to his eyes. Conan reached the bow. He placed his hands on the forestay turnbuckle and pretended to fiddle about with it, all the while watching the old dolphin. The eye focused on every move he made, even when Conan tired of watching the acrobatic antics of the animals under the bow and turned to look at the dawn.

For long moments he watched the miracle of the sun's earliest rays touching, with golden fingers, the twelve-thousand-foot-high peak of Tenerife, more than one hundred miles away over to the northwest. In the northeast he saw, faint and glowing in the early light, the long, low black silhouette of Lanzarote, and, on his leeward side, closer to the west than Tenerife, but still far away, the startling emerald green of Hierro, a tiny, long jewel rising up to a peak from the blue ocean depths. It looked like a lost child to Conan, lonely, as if it would have been cozier if it had been closer to the great volcano of Tenerife, and could, perhaps, have held its hand once in a while. Then, with the dolphins still playing around the boat, and that eye still inspecting his every move, Conan checked the course and went below to make breakfast and to sleep.

When he returned topsides to take the noon sight, the dolphins were gone. The blue sea under the hot sun was empty, except for the skittering flashes of occasional flying fish. Now, to Conan, it was not nearly as friendly.

Chapter 11

AKA DID NOT HURRY on the way to the Island of the Whistling Men.
The fish that the dolphins sighted, bonito and mullet mainly, were scattered in small, widely spread shoals or they were swimming alone.
When they left the company of the sailing boat, Aka ordered his tribe
into open formation. The advance scouts raced away until they were
about eight miles ahead of Aka, just within range of his acoustic signals,
then the main body dropped back until the eight schools were strung
out four miles apart, one behind the other. The lead school, the dozen
odd males, were five miles behind Aka. Behind the last school the rear
guard of four adult dolphins kept a distance of six miles from the main
group. Consequently, for most of the day Aka's control signals, relayed
from one school to the next, and the search signals sent to him, extended
over an area seventy miles in length, twenty-four miles wide, and six
miles deep.

Only when they "sighted" fish with their long-distance echo location
did a dolphin break formation; but not before passing a signal to Aka.
Then, when permission to chase was received, the dolphin banked away
from his cohorts and, bringing his tail into top gear with a great thrust
down and up, off he went at full speed. Sometimes they chased barracuda—great eighty pound to a hundred pound fish, up to seven feet
long—for miles. On these chases hunter and prey reached speeds of up

to thirty knots, both the dolphin and the barracuda, until the fish flagged. Then the chaser was on the fish's tail and with a mighty snap of his conical toothed jaws, the dolphin bit clean through a foot and a half of fish-flesh and bone and the chase was over. The dolphin then, all in a flash, used his ears to find the azimuth, his brain to calculate the present position of his school (they would have moved up to six or seven miles by now), and his acoustic signal receiver to reckon his position relative to Aka. All this not merely on one horizontal plane, but also taking into account his depth in the water. To a human observer, it would appear that the dolphin quickly turned after his meal, moved his, head up and down and sideways, and raced off, as straight as a cleaver-cut, back to his school, wherever it was now within the forward moving tribe.

When the sun was high overhead, Aka signalled playtime to the main body, which until now had been as orderly and soberly disciplined as a regiment of foot guards. Within seconds of the signal the wilder spirits were off, racing this way and that, thrusting for the surface and up in the air, speeding pell-mell at other schools and only at the last split second turning aside or leaping to avoid crashing head on into them. After a minute the whole tribe, except the wary scouts, were at it. Some of the older adults even dived right down to the black waters of the two-mile-deep sea bottom and brought up squid. Others scooted away at high speed, chasing the odd flying fish—forbidden game while the tribe was in formation.

As, one by one and school by school, the dolphin tired, they took up again their convoy positions, still in open order, until the moment that the sun was at an angle of forty-five degrees to Aka's meridian. Then he commanded them all into closed ranks. It was legend-telling time.

In a matter of minutes, all the main body closed up, one school close to the next, all grouped around Aka and the three Wise Ones. The advance guard kept their positions six miles ahead and the rear guard trailed two miles astern. Now the area that Aka could survey through relays was a mere sixteen miles long and twelve miles wide, but the depth-sounders of the whole tribe still swept down to the ocean floor two miles and more below them.

Kweela, in her accustomed place at the rear left side of the mother-group, with Om at her side, now quiet and content, saw Aka's hologram. The story was told every time the tribe passed through these waters on its way to the Island of the Whistling Men. She herself was beginning to remember much of the tale, but as the pictures formed in her mind there were still episodes where she could not quite recall what was to come next. Now, swimming in tight formation at five knots, keeping precise time with the group, rising for air every five minutes, her sonars, her long-distance sounder, her acoustic signal apparatus, her short-distance acoustic sounder-receiver, and her azimuth finder all tuned in on their different wavelengths, and all the time "talking" comfort and encouragement to her son, Kweela settled herself to watch Aka's hologram, clear pictures in her mind.

"In the days of Aye-ee, our ancestor, the most renowned dolphin leader of old," signalled Aka, "eighteen of the Atlantean ships, all with purple sails and golden dolphins on their bows, sailed on the annual voyage to the land-surrounded sea. It was a voyage that took many weeks, so all care was taken by the Atlantean Sea Kings in their preparations.

"Atlantis was high, with green shores surrounded by the ocean. The heights above the golden roofs of the white palaces and villas of the city were, first, farmlands, all brown and yellow, then further up pastures green, then woodlands and black-gray rock, and finally, at the very top, two bright sparkling white pinnacles which glowed silver in the dawn, and salmon pink, even red, in the evening twilights of long, long ago.

"The nursing ground of the dolphins was a holy place, a deep fjord in the side of a mountain. The Atlanteans had built a long deep wall out into the sea to almost close the fjord; and they guarded the entrance with a strong net to keep the marauding sharks at bay. Every month, at full moon, the good men and women came to the nursing ground. Oo-ee-ah and the other high priests then conversed with Aye-ee, the leader of the dolphins, and the Wise Ones. The following days after the full moon, the dolphins chased fish" (Kweela "saw" millions of fish in vast shoals) "into the Atlantean's great harbor. When the harbor was full the dolphins kept guard outside the entrance until the men closed it with another vast, fine net. The fish were trapped and were scooped up, a thick, squiggling mass, by the Atlanteans, who laid the fish out on the long sandy beaches to dry and turn brown in the sun.

"When the eighteen ships sailed on the voyage to the great inland sea the dolphins had accompanied them, as usual, to act in their traditional roles of weather forecasters, pilots, fishermen, and scouts to watch for the bloodthirsty pirates who infested the strait into the inland sea.

"The voyage of the eighteen purple-sailed ships lasted three months, for they visited many lands on the shores of the ocean. The ships parted with the dolphins at the strait with a promise made between Oo-ee-ah, the king of Atlantis, and Aye-ee, the dolphin leader, that they would meet again in three months for the voyage back to Atlantis.

"The waiting dolphins mated, fished, played, and slept around the shores of the strait for three moons, and then, on one joyful morning, they sighted purple sails with the Atlantean insignia—the circle around the cross, gleaming silver—driving back out through the strait. Puzzled, the dolphins saw that there were only three Atlantean ships returning. Oo-ee-ah explained that all the rest of the ships and their crews were remaining in their new home, another island at the far end of the inland sea, where the ocean dolphins were forbidden to go.

"The voyage home from the strait to Atlantis went well for the first few days. Aye-ee's tribe brought the brightly dressed crews of the three ships food galore—mullet, dorado, bonito, and shrimp. On the first day south from the strait one of the dolphin calves fell sick. It was taken on board Oo-ee-ah's ship and in two days nursed back to health and then handed back to its mother while the ships' musicians played their musical instruments and the crew made obeisance to the golden dolphin on the ship's bow, and hung garlands of sea flowers around it.

"Seven days south of the strait a great storm arose. The three Atlantean ships opened their sail slats more and more, but try as they might to keep company with each other, and try as the dolphins might to guide each to the others, the ships were scattered. Mighty winds and seas drove Oo-ee-ah's ship onto the sea-pounded rocks of one of the islands of the fierce war-canoe savages. In despair Aye-ee and his dolphins watched as the ship hurled against the rocks. Time and again the dolphins rode on the piling seas, trying to reach Oo-ee-ah and his crew to rescue them. Time and again the undertow hurled them back among the wild waters. So it went all that night. Aye-ee decided that the only way Oo-ee-ah and the Atlanteans could be rescued was from the shore. Aye-ee looked up and saw a line of naked brown men, all shorter than the Atlanteans, all with wildly unkempt hair and stringy beards, all waiting with spears and knives in hand to kill any Atlanteans who managed to get ashore, for the savages, the Atlanteans said, ate their own kind.

"Seeing the situation, Aye-ee ordered his dolphins—all three hundred and eighty of them" (*dolphins were many more in those days than they are now*, signalled Aka) "—Aye-ee ordered them all to signal the savages to help Oo-ee-ah and his crew. Aye-ee knew that men could only hear the lowest-frequency whistles of the dolphin acoustic range in air, and so they had all leaped from the rough seas and whistled their lowest notes for many minutes, until Aye-ee saw one of the savages pointing in their direction. The dolphins then approached the perilous shore as close as they could, all whistling plaintively. Then, as they leaped, the dolphins saw the savages drop on their knees one by one, and bend their hairy heads to the ground in their direction and then in the direction of the wreck. Still the dolphins leaped, until some of the savages ran away along the cliff, to return shortly carrying crude lines and ropes. They hurled a line, a thin one at first, tied to a stone, at the wreck. Oo-ee-ah's men caught it and pulled down toward them a thick rope which they tied on the mast. Then, as Aye-ee's dolphins all looked on, leaping for joy, the Atlantean crewmen and women, one by one, climbed the rope to the cliff top and were received with open arms and shouts of praise and welcome from the chief of the savages, most of whom bowed low before the new arrivals and shielded their eyes from their sight.

"Oo-ee-ah and his Atlanteans were taken to the savages' village, on the shores of a wide, shallow bay on the calm south side of the island. Aye-ee had followed them, first sending a few of his fastest males to find the other ships and to inform them that Oo-ee-ah was safe, and to guide the ships to the island.

"As soon as they reached the islanders' village Oo-ee-ah and all his men came down to the shore to thank the dolphins, with loud whistles and hymns of praise and gratitude, while the islanders, awed, looked on.

"During the time that he and his men waited for the other two Atlantean ships to sail to the island, Oo-ee-ah, in friendship and gratitude, taught the islanders the parts of the dolphin language that he himself knew, those parts that are within the very restricted human range of sending and receiving. Aye-ee's dolphins then amused themselves by conversing, in childish terms, with the brighter islanders, including their chief, who ordered a dolphin god to be carved from wood and set up on the beach.

"Some days later the two other ships of the fleet arrived within a few hours of each other at the island. Their sails were now patched in places, and their hulls had been badly battered, but all the crewmen were safe and the ships were still fit for the further weeks of homeward voyage to the south. The following day Oo-ee-ah sent for the finest vestments in the fleet, and the musicians with all their instruments, and all the crews in their most colorful raiments to come ashore.

"There, on the beach, before the astonished and delighted islanders, the Atlanteans and over a thousand leaping dolphins in the bay made music and prayers and consecrated the wooden dolphin. Then Oo-ee-ah made the dolphin-promise, speaking first, then whistling loud and slow so that the chiefs of all the erstwhile savages and all the dolphin Wise Ones could hear him plainly, and understand him clearly.

"Oo-ee-ah stood on a rock by the sea, all the humans gathered around him, with his arms stretched out toward the huge tribe of surfaced dolphins. 'Each year,' he signalled, 'on the third quarter of the April moon, the dolphins will visit this island and they will drive so many fish into this bay that people will think that they can walk on them. This promise we make, Aye-ee,' he pointed at the dolphin leader, close to his rock, 'and I, for you,' he waved his hand over the islanders, 'and for your children, and for their children, for all time to come, as long as there are men on the land and dolphins in the sea, as a sign that men and dolphins shall always love each other.'

"Aye-ee, in the dolphin sign of agreement, thrust almost all of his body out of the water, up and around in a grand twisting movement, and signalled to all the vast dolphin tribe, 'So it shall be forever, as Oo-ee-ah, the king of Atlantis, has promised, so the dolphins promise!'

"The next day, after a night of feasting and rejoicing, and after the exchange of many gifts with the islanders, Oo-ee-ah's two ships, with their escort of a thousand dolphins, sailed again for the Atlantis in the south. When they reached the ocean area of calm seas and little wind, the three ships, with their battered sails, found they could make little headway. Long lines from each ship were passed around the strongest dolphins, thirty to a ship, and Aye-ee's adults towed the ships through the doldrums. They all reached Atlantis safe and sound, after a passage from the Island of the Whistling Men, in just five weeks, and on their arrival there was much rejoicing among the Sea Kings and their families."

It was late in the afternoon when Aka's scouts reached the southern shore of the Island of the Whistling Men. By the time the main body of the tribe had joined them by the rocks under the high cliff, the last golden red rays of the sun were striking the undersides of cottony clouds over the western edge of the ocean.

Aka ordained that the tribe should rest, in preparation for the next day's hard activity. So they dozed in their schools, and the night guards circled round and round, until they were relieved by others.

Before the dawn's first lightening of the sky, Aka sent thirty-eight of the fastest dolphins out as shoal herders. As they slowly followed, the rest of the dolphins took up positions widely apart, on two lines, six miles either side of the track that the shoal herders had taken. The sun was well underway on his daily passage across the sky by the time the shoals of pilchard and mullet were herded into the lane between the two lines of "fence" dolphins.

As the great mass of several shoals crammed into the lane, actually darkening the sea from the surface to the rocky bottom, the "fence" dolphins turned inshore, like prisoner escorts, and guided the unthinking fish toward the wide entrance of the harbor which had been built above the sunken bay. Soon all the fish, a great swarm almost three miles long and three miles wide and half a mile deep, were gathered outside the harbor, which itself was a mile higher than the bay where the dolphin-promise had been made long, long ago.

Aka—for it was his right as leader—leaped. Time and again he sprang into the air, waiting for the Man-signals. As he leaped and dived he saw small figures running along the wall toward the houses in the village. After a while people, men, women, and children, hurried out along the wall, where they crowded at the very end. Then Aka, with his acoustic receiving frequency turned down almost as low as he could manage, heard the whistles of the Man-signals. It was a series of sounds that was older than the history that Man knew. It came from the lips of a dozen men and women, all over middle age, while the younger ones stood by them, listening carefully, learning the sounds so they would know them well later in life.

"Welcome, holy ones of the sea," said the Man-signals. "Welcome to the island upon which Oo-ee-ah and Aye-ee bestowed their promise of beneficence. We have kept our promise never to harm the dolphins!"

Aka heard the greeting a dozen times. Of a sudden he gulped air into his blowhole, dived down fifty feet into the sea, turned toward the harbor entrance, levelled out, and thrust himself into the highest leap he could manage. He broke the surface in front of the waiting crowd on the wall, only a few feet away from them, and thrust with all his might up ... up ... up forty feet into the blue sky, so high that his eyes were level with those of the delighted people. Then he whistled to them. *"The dolphins, too, have kept their promise never to harm Man!"*

Aka fell backward into the sea with a mighty splash of rainbow-colored spray. As he fell he heard the people cheer. Then he gave the signal, a piercing, very high frequency command, 150,000 cycles a second, for ten seconds.

All the dolphins of his tribe, all acting as shoal herders now, all moving as one, sped at the almost solid mass of fish. They threw their whole bodies at them, they lashed their tails at those escaping, and brought them back into the silver-gleaming mass. Slowly at first, like a running brook, then like a rushing stream, then like a roaring cataract, the fish liquidly spilled through the narrow entrance into the harbor, millions and millions of them, until the harbor was choked in every part of it, from the oil-streaked surface to the rusty-iron-strewn bottom, from the harbor entrance to the feces-spewing outlets of the innermost open sewer drains. The dolphins pushed and shoved, lashed and nudged, flippered and tail-lashed the mass of silver fish until there was no room for more in the harbor. Even so the dolphins kept up their pressure on the edges of the slippery heap of shining panic, until at the harbor entrance the fish started piling up one layer on top of another, until the topmost were a foot above sea level!

The dolphins held the mountain of fish jammed into the harbor for the whole of the time of the rising tide—four and a half hours. Only when the combined weight of a billion fish and the water of the outgoing tide oozed out on them with overwhelming weight, like a landslide, did they relent from the pushing, herding, heaving, shoving, butting; and, surrounded by clouds of fish blindly escaping the huge trap in nerve-deadened daze, swim calmly away at Aka's order, their promise to the Whistling Men fulfilled.

The diesel ferry boat was crowded with tourists of twenty nationalities.

"It's a pity we couldn't have flown here, Elmer." Mrs. Gurber complained. "You know how ridin' in boats upsets my stomach so." She was about sixty-five and thin as a marlin spike. She wore a flowered dress and a wide-brimmed hat, so as to keep the hot sun from the air-conditioned sallow pallor of her deeply lined face.

"No airfield on Gomera," Elmer informed his wife for the fifteenth time that day. He was white haired and chubby, with a well-fed, red face. He wore a soft sailing hat perched on top of his head. When he removed it, to wipe the sweat from his brow, a classical crew cut went, as inevitably as dawn and day follow night, with his loud Hawaiian shirt, his dark tartan knee-length shorts, his white socks, and his running shoes.

Their ferry was now fast returning past the southeast point of the island, on the two-hour trip back to Tenerife. As yet the sea had been smooth, ever since they had left the tiny port. Mrs. Gruber glanced at the tiny watch on her thin wrist. As she raised her hand the scrawny fingers closed, so that it reminded a passing Spanish crewman of a dead hen's claw.

"We're almost two and half hours late," she said petulantly.

Elmer removed his cigar from his mouth. His lips grinned. His eyes frowned. "It's not surprising is it, honey," he said, "with the harbor jammed stiff with all those li'l fishes?"

"They should have arranged the ceremony so it started earlier. Then the boat could have left on time," she declared.

"Gee whillikins! Wasn't that something . . . huh?" Elmer observed.

"I didn't appreciate the smell all that much," she replied.

"But all them fish . . . hot diggety!" he exclaimed. "There musta been a thousand tons o' fish in that li'l old harbor!"

"I still think they should keep us tourists in mind—"

"The guide—what was his name, Manolo?" asked Elmer.

"Some such name. He was a deal too flighty with the other girls if you ask me," Mrs. Gruber observed, brushing Elmer's shirt collar.

"Well, Manolo told me that it happens every year . . . every gosh-darned year, honey. The porpoise just turn up and drive those li'l old sardines right on into the harbor . . . and the folks back there, why, they just scoop 'em on out with buckets an' such." Elmer replaced his cigar and drew a puff. Then he said, "Say, wouldn't it be somethin' to have a kinda floatin' bulldozer an' grab crane out there? Gee whillikins, they could load every fishin' boat in Europe all at one time, an' freeze the fish an' take 'em to all those starvin' people. . . . You remember, Tangier, last year?"

"Elmer, don't mention that place to me. You know how I feel about it. All those filthy beggars, panhandlers . . . and pleading children . . ."

"Okay, honey, but those fish sure were a sight. It all happened so fast! One minute the main street was sorta quiet, only us tourists about—"

"You mean that loud Mrs. Streicher and that flibberti-gibbet daughter of hers—"

"—and all of a sudden these kids come runnin' up the street an' all the folks leave what they're doin' an' run down to the waterfront, the village priest an' the cops among 'em, an' before you can say Jack Robinson there's the porpoise leapin' an' the gold-darned harbor just as full o' fish as can be—"

"And smell, too." said Mrs. Gruber.

"Well, everyone forgot about Christopher Columbus's li'l ol' house, and headed right on down there and photographed the fish an' the porpoise like crazy."

"Did you get any slides of the Columbus house, Elmer?"

Elmer clenched one fist and hit his knee with it. "Oh, gosh-darn it, honey, no . . . I completely forgot about it . . . but I got fifteen rolls o' shots o' the porpoise to show the folks back home. . . . We can give a slide-show party."

"Don't invite Mrs. Streicher. I swear she's the loudest woman in the state of Kansas!"

"Of course not, honey."

"Nor her daughter. She got pictures of Columbus's house."

"Nn-nn." Elmer shook his head. The ferry gave the first of fifty thousand slight pitches yet to come on the smooth passage back to Tenerife.

"Oh, oh." Mrs. Gruber stood up groggily. She staggered and grabbed Elmer's shoulder. "We're facing the other way. Now where's the bathroom?"

But she had to find her own way, muttering to herself. Elmer was too engrossed in watching the splashes of a hundred and more leaping "porpoises" as they broke the calm sea surface, now . . . and now . . . and again . . . and again . . . and again . . . and there . . . and there . . . and over there . . . and again. . . . In silence, now that Mrs. Gruber had left him, Elmer, as if transfixed, watched the shooting fountains of silver spray and the leaping, twisting bodies as they grew smaller and smaller, until they finally disappeared in the direction of the fast-running sun away in the west.

Long, long after the ferry boat had rounded the headland and turned north, all the while Mrs. Gruber was in the "bathroom," almost until they entered the little port in Tenerife, Elmer stared over the same spot on the ship's side rail at the far distance, with a dreamy frown on his face, as if he were trying to remember something he had forgotten long ago . . .

"Elmer, don't forget to tell the hotel about that noise from the bathroom."

Elmer turned to her, smiling. "Okay, honey," he said quietly. He took her arm and led her gently to join the groups of peeling British noses, Swedish shoulders, and German elbows clustered early around the gangway rail so as to be first ashore, to see and film the most.

Chapter 12

CONAN SHOT HIS AFTERNOON SIGHT OF THE SUN as it eased itself steadily down, still high in its arc, across the sky to the northwest of *Josephine*. To do it he wedged himself, sitting down firmly on the bouncing, rearing, starboard side of the coach roof. All the time he carefully shielded the sight glass and mirrors of the sextant from any spits of spray flying aft across from the port bow or the starboard side.

Below, at full volume, Chopin's First Piano Concerto (in E minor, Opus II) played from the tape deck to the sway and dance of *Josephine*. She soared and descended, as if she were keeping time to the music. The offshore wind from Morocco was a steady blow, keeping the sails bellied and pressing. The blue seas, as they piled on before the wind in their numberless ranks, caught up with *Josephine*'s stern and fitted themselves, as if guided by some celestial pins-in-mouth tailor, two at a time, along her now greenish waterline; and always as the forward sea ran ahead of her from her bow, another sea was sliding in under her stern. *Josephine* leaned over, as if she were straining away from the desert shore far away in the east. Her sails were on a broad reach, with everything on her side—the rigging wires, the sheets, the spreaders, the halyards—taut as a bandsman's drumskin. She scooted and slithered, plunged and ploughed, slid and slammed onward and onward making her southing. This was sailing!

As Conan took a quick check of his stopwatch, which he held in the palm of one hand, its lanyard safely around his wrist, he grinned to himself. He looked away from the sea's sun-glare for a moment, then with his right eye closed he quickly raised the sextant eyepiece to his left eye, gently waved the sextant about a little to catch the sun in the mirror, adjusted the arc with the hand that held the watch, and, after he had rocked the sun's image on the horizon for a second or two, his thumb clicked down the watch stop-lever. Conan then opened both eyes and looked at the sextant arc. He mentally noted the reading. He took two more shots of the sun to check that the first one was not wild, and, still shielding the sextant from the spray, slid aft, swung himself over the bucking coach roof, jumped down into the cockpit well, and slithered down the ladder.

The first thing Conan did down below was turn to the chart table, grab a stumpy pencil, and make a note of the sextant and stopwatch readings. Then he stowed the instruments away in their teak boxes, which were screwed to the chart-table partition, and turned to make himself some tea.

While the kettle boiled, he worked out the sight and marked a line-of-position on the ocean chart spread out before him. This, with the morning line-of-position, and the noon latitude, and the log reading of distance run, enabled him to plot his assumed position within a mile or so of actuality. As his range of vision around the boat to the horizon was about four miles from on deck, a slight error of a mile or so was acceptable out here in the open ocean. When he neared the land, or any ocean hazards such as St. Paul's Rocks, for example, it would be a different matter. Then Conan would take several sights and note the readings carefully before he was satisfied with their accuracy.

Having marked off the line-of-position on the chart, a minute line on the almost blank chart sheet of stiff paper, he reached for the logbook and entered the date and his position.

"April 13th, 1981, 1,620 hrs. 24.50N–17W. Wind NE 5. Sea confused."

He reached for the small scale chart which showed the whole bulge of the Atlantic coast of northwest Africa, and on it marked, with a tiny dot, his assumed position. Then he took the dividers and measured off the distance from the shore. *Josephine* was about 115 miles northwest of Villa Cisneros, in what used to be Spanish Morocco. Now was the time to change course and head out into the ocean west-southwest. Conan decided it could wait until he had finished his tea and biscuits. He brewed the tea and settled down to perform a British rite which was, he reflected, sanctified by time, custom, and wanderings, from the shot-holed, blood-soaked ramparts of Cawnpore to the freezing polar steppes at the top and bottom of the darling world. He grinned as he broached another can of Peek Frean's fine assorted and dumped half a dozen biscuits on the berth. As he sat down on the one available seat—the berth—he rubbed his hands together in pleasurable anticipation. "That's the ticket, Bill, my lad," he said aloud. "Everything stops for tea!" Then, leaning over to where he had set the teapot, on one of the now diminishing midship's food boxes, he poured himself tea just as carefully as he would have done on the terrace of the Southern Counties Ocean Cruising Club back in Sandleston, and enjoyed it more, he was fairly sure, than he would have on that (to him) rather stuffy esplanade.

The next morning was much the same as all the mornings that followed for the next week. Conan had changed the steering gear attitude to the new course and braced the twin headsails out on opposite sides of the double headstay, with the aluminum light-weather running poles, "wing and wing" as the sailors say. The northeast trade wind now blew over *Josephine*'s starboard quarter. So fine on the quarter, it almost blew directly over her stern. This made heavier work for the steering gear, as the seas running under her stern made the vessel yaw heavily from side to side, but after a few hours of trial and error during the first evening on the new course, Conan had balanced the rig so that yawing was minimized.

The following morning, just after dawn, the northeast trade stirred himself from his night's doze and sent in the seas. *Josephine* threw up her bow to the first of them, as with thrusting urgency the wind streamed into her winged sails. They filled as smooth and full as a puppy's belly. *Josephine* laid her cheeks down to the ocean waters and started to smash her eager way to the comparative openness of the deep ocean. She lunged over traceries of spume, dived, swung in the trade-wind chop, rolled her winged-out sails over vast, shadowless space, all the while tense with movement, sedate and restrained, dancing rather than speeding, and left it all up to Conan to calculate the results. At noon he reckoned he was two and a half degrees—150 miles—farther west than the previous noon of the greenwich zero meridian, which is named after such an unlikely, dull place on the banks of the river Thames.

In the late afternoon Conan sadly sighted some tiny land birds driven out by the wind, fighting to stay aloft, but flagging, dropping downward—and when they went down they never ascended again. One of them made a gallant try for *Josephine*'s bow. Eventually, after a half-hour struggle with the wind, it fell, exhausted, only ten yards ahead of Conan, who, holding on for dear life to the plunging bow pulpit, tied to a ringbolt with his safety harness, had tried to save the bird. Try as he might, he had been unable to reach far enough with the boathook to save the fluffy brown-feathered tiny heart and pluck it from its watery grave.

For seven days and nights Conan touched none of the boat's sailing gear nor once did he take the wheel.

With the exception of a few huge tankers ploughing their way north and south, the second and third day out Conan saw nothing except the sea and the life near and on and above the surface of the sea. The few birds he had seen when he changed course diminished in number, until by the fourth day there were none at all. Conan was alone with the boat and the sea, a few squadrons of flying fish, especially in the high-sun hours, a few leaping mammals—dolphins, porpoise, killer whales, and on one occasion, a giant blue whale. Once a small school of small squid came flying on board *Josephine* from aft. They shot past Conan's head and struck the sails and rigging wires with such violence that some of their heads and tentacles were knocked off. For the rest the only other life he saw were the squirming dorados which, almost every morning, he dragged in on his trolling line and cut up bloodily on the transom.

Dawns and sunsets, out in tropical waters are God's own delight, but familiarity breeds casualness. By the end of the first week on the ocean run Conan was scarcely noticing the celestial displays. He thought about this and decided it was a pity. If these sights only occurred once every ten years people would pay thousands merely to come and look at them. He made up his mind to stay on deck every morning to watch the dawn. Each dawn he marvelled, silently, as the velvet black of night, still star-laden overhead, trembled on the eastern horizon through veils of paling purples, hues of gray from puce to slate and then through all the shades of azure, delicate rose, and flashing gold to the imperious blaze of His Majesty the sun, risen again from his litter over the shining silver curved edge of the eastern sea.

"And sunsets . . . ah, the sunsets," he said to himself every time the fast-dropping monarch of the tropics lowered himself in the early evening over the western horizon and shot shafts of scarlet and red across the length and breadth of the sky, and transformed the great rounded, scudding trade-wind clouds into gaudy, flaunting petitioners awaiting word of their fate in the anteroom of their black-robed nemesis, inevitable night. Each evening, as soon as the fiery sun had stowed away his spears of blazing light, the western sky changed to peach, then orange, and finally glowing scarlet. At the same time the sky in the east changed from duck-egg blue, to purple, and finally to indigo velvet, and the change of color crept right across the sky, as if it were synchronized by a celestial choreographer to the dying rhythm of the sun's fading.

When the night was bedded into the sky, Conan looked down at the sea, at the brilliant phosphorescent displays in the blackness of the moving waters. Sometimes a marine creature—what it could be he had no inkling—left a streak of sparkling galaxies behind it, and when one of them stopped the water all around became phosphorescent. On several occasions each night the ocean just below the surface was a vast multitude of phosphorescent head-lit highways, ten to fifteen feet long, for as far as Conan's eyes could see across the faces of the heaving swells. In calmer spells, it was sometimes as if the whole ocean was an undulating black field bearing clouds of snowdrops, on others as if all the galaxies in the heavens had fallen into Earth's waters.

Then, coal black sea after shining sea towered up on all sides, and a gleaming myriad of tropical stars drew a faint reflection from plankton in the water. Then the world, the universe, was to Conan simple—*stars in the darkness.* He lived, and that he felt with an alert intensity. He was sure then that life had been full for men before the technical age also— in fact fuller and richer in many ways than the life of most modern men. As he gazed in wonder about him out into the night, time and evolution ceased to exist for him: all that was real and truly mattered were exactly the same tonight as they had always been and would always be. On these nights Conan was consumed by the absolute common measure of all of the history of the firmament—an endless, unbroken darkness under crowded, swarming stars.

It was no wonder, then, on one holy night after a throbbing sunset, as the boat veered and yawed her way west, her sails reflecting the silver sheen of the moon and the sea, Conan, suddenly overwhelmed with the heart-wrenching beauty of it all, cried into the star-scattered sky, "And God *did* say 'let there be light!' "

Each night, after the evening performance of sun, sky, planets, stars, and the moon, the trade wind, as if in anticlimax to the magic show, weakened like an exhausted giant and breathed over *Josephine* more softly. Each night Conan listened to Bach or Debussy or Brahms as their notes rose and joined the sighing night breeze in the shrouds and echoed on the ghostly pale sails under a million trillion bright stars and stately planets coursing overhead in all their black-velveted magnificence. He sometimes felt as if his heart would burst asunder under the staggering yet welcome weight of the wealth of the nights.

Each dawn, with the rising of the sun, the wind always seemed to heave a sigh of relief that he could commence heavy work again. Soon after sunrise he was at it again, breathing powerfully, like a road laborer wielding a shovel, once more piling and throwing the seas ahead of him, and *Josephine* with them, as he ranted and roared, huffed and puffed . . . puffed, like a celestial shirt-sleeved trade unionist, in cosmic concern at the world's turning against him. Conan stayed awake long enough each morning to feel the full force of the wind's efforts, then satisfied that the sails would deal with the day, he went below to think of Ruth, and to sleep again the doze of a sea rover.

On the early morning of the twenty-first of April, eight days after Conan had changed course and headed out into the high ocean, the northeast trade wind roused himself in an unmannerly choler. In the east, low on the horizon, as the sun balefully glared up from behind them, torn, ragged black clouds told their tale of the raving hounds of hell to be shortly let loose upon his world. Conan tapped the glass below; low, low. Then, working as fast as he could on the plunging foredeck, he lowered the twin headsails and changed back to mainsail and number three jib. The mainsail he braced out to starboard, right out hard against the shrouds, so that the boom end, hovering way out over the blue running seas, was now and again submerged for seconds, and rose from the waves streaming with flying spray. The jib he winged out to port from the headstay, using one of the four long, strong, solid wooden running poles, which he locked into its gooseneck low down on the mainmast. He poled the jib out well forward, so that now both the sails made a line aslant the vessel's topsides, as if their course was slightly different to that of the hull.

By the time Conan had eaten breakfast, both wind and sea had worked up into what Mike Houghton would, with his typical understatement, have called "quite boisterous," which meant that it was as if every red-eyed, fire-tongued, iron-armed, bloody shackle-forger from the nethermost pits of the Inferno were all hammering *Josephine* at once. She yawed, she veered, she swung this way and that. Conan hung onto the wheel now, to steer her by hand, for against these chasing devils it was beyond reason to expect the steering vane, a device based on pure reasoning, to deal with forces that cared no more for reason than did a wild bull for a mouthful of buttercups.

By mid-forenoon the condition of the sea would have concerned Captain James Cook himself. An hour later, with Conan grimly heaving the wheel to keep *Josephine* from broaching, the wind at times was reaching states of maniacal fury and the seas were rapidly piling into jumbled heaps of frothing foam. Conan decided that he would have to trust the steering gear long enough to reef down sail again, or at least long enough to unship the running pole. Quickly, fumbling as spray driving over the stern blinded him momentarily, he locked in the gear and adjusted the vane to the wind direction as best he could. Then he clambered up forward, his safety harness clipped to the long running line which ran the whole length of the vessel, and made his way—was bodily pushed by the gale—forward. A second after he grabbed the coach-roof handrail, hand over hand on the plunging, rising side deck, *Josephine*, with a wild, agonized lurch, broached—turned sideways-on to the wind and sea.

The gale from astern momentarily shifted direction, for less than a few seconds, to the north. The mainsail caught the full blast and slewed her full around, spinning her like a compass needle on her own axis. As the boat now pointed south, so the treacherous wind veered right around to the southeast—again only for moments. The jib slid through the wind, with the gale now on its forward surface, backed. Then with a juddering crash of an explosion the running pole, almost six inches in diameter in its thickest part, cracked and shattered and the jib sail, free of the iron control of the pole, smacked across the foredeck. As the jib flew back, so its sheet line parted just below the tack, with another crack from the depths of doom, and let the jib fly free, stuttering like a machine gun, on the lee side of the boat.

During all the three seconds of time in which the foregoing events were taking place, the mainsail, braced forward to a cleat on the foredeck and aft by the mainsheet, cocked itself into the wind like a weather vane, and the reefed sail shook so violently that the whole boat shuddered even as she rolled drunkenly from side to side, with her port side high above the sea and her leeward side submerging and rising, streaming green, in the sea.

Conan's first thought was to unclutch the steering gear. It was useless, in fact downright dangerous, to expect a machine as finely constructed and efficient as it was under normal conditions to deal with anything as crazily illogical as a wind generated by a deep local tropical depression. It flashed through Conan's mind, as he struggled forward now on the crazily jerking side deck, that for him to expect the steering gear to react as quickly as a man to the moves of the vessel, to keep a sharp eye, like a man, on every sea as it rolled threateningly to the stern, to gauge, like a man, every rise and fall of the wind in such a sea as this, was a bit like an Inns-of-Court barrister sending his office boy to the Old Bailey to defend a multiple murderer.

Conan's next priority was to lower the jib before it frapped itself to a rag. It took all his strength and agility to bring the wildly shaking sail down onto the foredeck, and he was forced to stand on the writhing

thing as he unhanked it from the forestay. He dragged it aft to the companionway and ruthlessly stuffed it down the hatch higgledy-piggledy. He clambered over the cockeyed, spray-lashed topsides and eased the halyard of the shaking mainsail, slowly, a little at a time, and with difficulty, reefing it around the boom as he did so. Soon the mainsail was down to almost half its full area, and Conan released the preventer, grabbed the wheel, and heaved in the mainsheet to take up slack. *Josephine*, as her mainsail gathered the wind, heaved her bow, smashed down vengefully onto a running sea, as if to hit it back, and was underway again.

Conan, his shorts and cotton shirt stiff with salt, worked away at the wheel to keep her running before the charging seas. He was shaken, he was tired, the helm was hard labor, and down below the cabin was a shambles, but he felt elated. *Josephine* and he had come through their first real crisis together.

Conan made up his mind to hand—to lower—the main at dusk and hoist the number one storm jib, if the wind did not drop by then, but, if the gale strengthened he would, instead, hoist the spitfire jib. He glared back astern at the serried ranks upon ranks of angrily heaving seas and the racing black clouds charging at him from the northeast across an angry sky. Again he heaved the wheel as a maverick sea pushed *Josephine*'s stern over twenty degrees. As he labored, Conan looked over the deck and grinned to himself. "She's a good 'un," he grunted. *Josephine* yawed in reply and buried her lee deck, staggered, shuddered, and labored like a thing in agony, but the crushing blows, from astern she took on her sweetly rounded hull, where they lost their destructive force as they ran forward and so away from her bow.

But even as Conan settled down to a day's and possibly a night's hard work, he considered the wind. He knew that it was not the wind that was the enemy in these battles of will. The real enemy was the seething, leaping, and appalling humps of ocean coming at him from astern. All that waste of tumultuous power was the enemy, and it was always alert on the grab and on the pounce. He looked astern again. As far as his eyes—slitted against the wind—could see, menacing white demons surged with the seas, and flung up fingers and flashed their teeth. There was the threat of steel-eyed devils with grabbing claws and gleaming tusks, and drift slashed off sharp from the tops of the seas and flung flat with the scooped scud, and sheers and jerky scurries and stomach-lifting dives and sudden glides sideways and forward of the boat. But *Josephine* somehow seemed to find her way, guided by the hand of the savage in Conan. He looked up at the mainsail. As she lifted and descended in the heaving seas, there was a strain on the sail's shoulder, then a pause, then an urge, then a surge, then a seething of sea forward along her lee gunwale, with spray spitting . . . and Conan cursing as the boat lurched yet again and he struggled with the helm to keep the crazily swinging compass lubber line nailed to the course and chained to his will . . .

Conan was lucky that time; the gale was of short duration and by the very early hours of the next day, the twenty-second of April, it had almost blown itself out. *Josephine,* during the gale, sailed—was hurled—180 miles south-southwest. Conan, after a solid twenty hours on the wheel, was able to unreef the mainsail, hoist the number two jib, and clutch in the steering gear. Then, after making sure that all was well, he went below, clambered over the dumped jib still at the bottom of the ladder, heated up a can of beans, hungrily scoffed them, and sank wearily into his still wildly plunging berth. He slept for four hours, until it was time to work up the dead reckoning and to radio Dakar, which was now relaying his messages on to Lloyd's of London.

As the sea relented and the wind steadied, and as he spliced the broken jib sheet, after a good breakfast of porridge, ham, and eggs, Conan reflected on the hazards at sea for a single-hander. Collision did not worry him overmuch, for he mostly slept in the daytime. If, by any chance he was forced to sleep at night there was a very efficient strobe light on board, which could be slung from the backstays, and which could flash a strong beam for many miles, depending on the conditions of visibility, and which could be seen for 360 degrees around the whole horizon. Conan was not sure that the strobe was legal under the International Rules of the Road, but he knew that when Shaughnessy had stowed the strobe on board, the uppermost images in the Irishman's mind had not been of legal documents, but of a "bludy great monster of an oil tanker" bearing down on him at twenty-five knots on a dark, rainstormy night off the Cape of Good Hope. Conan was not at all sure that he would ever use the light, though. Its quick stabbing flashes might arouse the curiosity of some Levanter captain skippering a Liberian or Panamanian tramp, and he could do without eastern Mediterranean curiosity on a dark stormy night, especially if it was at the helm of twenty thousand tons of steel.

As for other collisions, such as with heavy flotsam or floating balks of timber, Conan was happy about the Simpson Gear on board. This is an umbrellalike gadget that can be thrust, closed, through a hole in the hull from inside the boat. Once through the hole the "umbrella" is opened, and the canvas of the "umbrella" is pressed by the weight of the sea against the ship's side, hopefully covering the hole long enough for a patch to be fixed over the hole from inside the boat.

Collision with whales was another matter. Conan was fatalistic about it, but he dreaded being anywhere near the creatures. He recalled to himself the time when in the Bay of Biscay off the coast of Spain he had found his twenty-five-foot sloop among a herd of finback whales, all more than three times bigger than the boat. They were feeding on plankton, heading straight for the boat. The sea had been still lively from a previous hard blow, but the wind had been light. Having no engine, there was nothing Conan could do, with a dozen whales charging in his direction, but try to sail across their course and take his chances with their flukes. He had rattled his boathook on the deck and yelled at the finbacks, but they came on at him, with their great mouths wide open, and he could plainly see their blowholes, which had looked wide enough for a man to crawl into. By the time the finbacks were within a few yards of the boat, Conan had merely stared at them, paralyzed with fear. Then, about fifty feet off, the whales had started to lash around with their tails, making the sea boil as they sank slowly. Conan had thought they were going to sound, and had felt relieved, but then they swam right under the boat and rose to the surface all around it, blowing for all they were worth and all heading in different directions, but very slowly. As Conan's boat jiggled along in the weak breeze, the whales had moved with her, rising, blowing, and sinking all around. This had gone on for fifteen minutes, with the whales boiling the sea, causing the boat to swing this way and that, completely out of Conan's control, as he stared, his heart thumping and scared out of his wits all the while. Then, one by one the whales had left the scene, except for one more stupid, more loyal than the rest. He stayed with the boat, directly under her keel, only inches below it, for another fifteen minutes, until he at last had decided to follow his huge companions and Conan had been able to wipe the perspiration from his visage on that cold February morning.

Even now Conan found himself shuddering as he recalled being almost completely hemmed in by those tremendous creatures, those tons upon tons of bone and muscle, with little headway on his boat and the water all around boiling and foaming, and the boat whirling so fast that the compass looked like it, too, was going crazy, and the creatures blowing their misty breaths right over him and the boat the whole while. . . . Conan comforted himself with the thought of the watertight door between the main and forward cabins. At least if he hit a whale head on and the bow was smashed, he stood a good chance of keeping *Josephine* afloat, and even of sailing her into some haven or other.

Two of the most common worries of sailors did not bother Conan at all. These were groundings and lee shores. On the route he was going there were no possibilities of grounding, and there would be no shores within hundreds of miles of *Josephine,* except when she rounded Good Hope and the Horn, and even then the coast would be over a hundred miles away if Conan had anything to do with the matter.

Rigging failures were a concern. But all the stays and shrouds on *Josephine* were doubled up, so the chances were that if one of the wires went its twin would hold until fair weather set in and Conan could effect a repair on the broken wire.

As for dismasting, which is always a possibility in any ocean voyage, Shaughnessy had worked out a very good jury rig which he had drawn up and written about in the logbook. It meant making a new mast out of the main boom. The heavy boom was to be erected by fitting one end of the boom into the mast step on deck and resting the other end in the erected boom crutch. Then a line was to go forward from the top of the boom to the bow and back to the sheet winch aft. Guys, to hold the rig steady while it was hauled up, were already cut and stowed on board. The genoa would serve as a jury mainsail.

Conan felt confident. There was plenty of food and water and a good medicine kit on board, all the boat's gear, except for the busted running pole (one of four), was sound, the boat had proved herself, and ahead of him now was the probability of good, fair weather all the way to the latitude of Rio de Janeiro. The only navigational concern he had was to steer clear of a hazard now a mere fourteen hundred miles to the south in the middle of the Atlantic, practically on the equator—St. Paul's Rocks.

Chapter 13

AKA'S TRIBE moved steadily south at an average rate of five knots after fulfilling their millennia-old promise of annual tribute at the Island of the Whistling Men, and having, afterward eaten their full of bonito and grouper, mullet, and pilchard.

Aka discussed the blue-hulled boat they had met and played around, and with the Wise Ones in agreement, came to the conclusion that the good man on board might indeed be a descendent of the ancient Sea Kings of Atlantis.

"For what other men," they asked each other, "would feel such compassion for the sufferings of young Om?"

Aka said, "Not fishing boat men, nor men we sometimes see on big oil tankers, nor on silent submarines when they surface, nor on rushing warships. Those men were, most of them, merely amused. This man was different, like some others we have seen sailing alone in tiny craft under sail. This man had true compassion, almost as if he were one of us. He emoted—he even thought something like a very young, very ignorant calf, but still he had compassion."

Even though the dolphins gorged themselves for three days around Gomera, there was no aggressiveness as they chased and darted for their food, nor was there greediness in their efforts to keep full their twenty-pound-capacity stomachs. They were matters of pure necessity of survival. The dolphin—in fact all of the scores of different subspecies of the Cetacea, including the dolphin's huge cousins, the whales—*cannot drink salt water.* Their kidneys, just like man's, cannot deal with salinity, so as the dolphin needs a steady supply of fresh water, he gets it from the fat he stores in his body. A blue whale can store six months' supply of fat; a bottle-nosed dolphin can store but six or seven days' food and fresh water.

Aka and the Wise Ones knew from lore and experience that their prospects of catching fish would diminish each day they moved south, until they reached the Cape Verde Islands, a journey for them of a week. Wisely, Aka would not let them hurry, lest they use up their supply of protein and fresh water too soon, and be too weak to tackle the fish shoals when the tribe arrived at the north side of the islands.

As the fish supply diminished, so the tribe fanned out more and more until by the fourth day they were in their widest formation, a "net" twenty dolphins wide and five deep, sweeping and searching the whole depth of the sea, from the blue waves, down through green opacity and cloudy purple, right down to the complete blackness of the sea bottom two miles and more below the surface. Thus the moving curtain of searchers could rummage with their sonar the whole depth of the sea in a band 12 miles long fore and aft, 2 miles deep, and 130 miles wide. Nothing in that area of search escaped them. Nothing that moved was not chased or rooted out of the rocks on the murky bottom, tasted—a quick incision of the conical teeth—to test for poison, and, if edible, eaten.

All the while, Aka or one of the three Wise Ones, in turn, in their role as navigator, would swim just below the surface, rising regularly to breathe and to scan the sea's surfaces. Down in the water, the navigator would swim with the edge of his tongue pushed out slightly between his teeth, with his lips slightly open. This was so that the taste buds all around the edge of the tongue could taste the seawater as a major aid to navigation.

The navigator, as he swam along, continually tasted the water flowing through the cracks between his lips, tasting for traces of the feces of other mammals and fish, or the infinitesimally faint effluvia of distant rivers—yet indiscernible to even the most advanced of human instruments. Or he might taste the pollutants dumped in the sea by man from ships or distant industrial cities. As he tasted, his brain accepted the information sent to it by his taste organs, computed comparisons to taste patterns stored long before in the same waters and in other areas of the ocean, and then, together with all the information received from his other navigational organs, such as his ears and his long-range sonar, produced a conclusion as to the geographic position of the tribe, which was seldom more than a mile in error.

In comparison, a human navigator at sea, in the same calm conditions, moving at the same speed out of sight of land and aided only by the *senses within himself,* would consider himself or herself fortunate if the assumed position were within ten miles of the actual whereabouts after only one day at sea. The expectation of accuracy could diminish by about fifteen miles each day, so that by the time the boat had been at sea for three days, moving around in different directions at speeds close to thirty knots, she would be extremely lucky if she was not completely lost.

As the tribe drew close to the northernmost of the Cape Verde Islands, they sighted more and more fishing boats. In their hungry eagerness to chase bonito and mullet, three of Aka's young males darted straight into long hempen nets. Only one of them was lucky enough to untangle himself, much as Aka had done many years before. The dolphins had watched as the other two struggled in the cruel nets for long minutes before they finally gave up twisting and flailing, until they at last quietly drowned, their last agonies multiplied a thousandfold by the dolphins inherent horror of drowning at sea. A drowning dolphin will rather throw himself on the beach than descend into the abyss of the sea.

The escaped dolphin, with streaks and trails of blood streaming from his head, his dorsal fin, and his tail, with one of his flukes almost torn away, came limping back to the tribe.

Aka signalled two of the males to escort the wounded dolphin to a position very close behind a mature adult. Then, as the front dolphin moved forward he caused, because of his exquisite streamlining, a swimming-pressure pattern so powerful that it drew the invalid behind through the water along with it as it moved forward. Thus the wounded dolphin was "towed" for several days, with different "tugs" relieving each other every few hours, until the invalid was recovered enough to manage again on his own, at least for short swims. He never did recover completely. The damage to his tail made it impossible for him to swim fast or to leap. For the rest of his life he would remain in the nursing grounds with the twenty other permanent invalids, all disabled by fishing nets. There he would never mate and so the survival capability of the tribe was maintained. Nature does not need a damaged fluke to influence, however minutely, a possible mutation, and this hard edict was "written" deep into the law of the dolphins.

While he was under the surface, Aka tasted the water continuously to follow the course—a direct line south-southwest, which headed straight for St. Paul's Rocks over two thousand miles away. At night, when he rose to the surface to breathe, his ears and eyes sensed the azimuths and altitudes of the guide stars—up to five of them at a time—all within a period of seconds, before he dived again to taste the waters. So Aka kept his tribe's line-of-march heading direct for the far-off nursing grounds. It was a straight and true line which even took into account the slightly distorted curvature of the earth. Even while some of the Cape Verde Islands intervened on the course between the dolphins and their destination, their line-of-march was directed always exactly, precisely, at the distant rocks in the middle of the ocean. When they were within a mile or so of an intervening island they swam around it, fishing as they went, and when they reached the southern side they all converged again to take up formation on their original rhumb-line just as surely as if they had been pulled back onto it by some great celestial dolphin flipper.

Aka's outriders picked up the echoes of all moving bodies in the sea, and these they relayed on to the leader. Each and every time, from the huge bulks of the seventy-foot-long sperm whales as they sounded down to the bottom like sinking ships, to the tiny pink sea horses as they rose and fell with their perfect little horses' heads upright, stiff and proud over their swelling terra-cotta chests, the image of each and every living organism on the surface, in the sea, and on the bottom, as they came within range of the dolphins' sonar beams, was passed on back to Aka and the three Wise Ones.

Among the Cape Verde Islands the tribe encountered other dolphins. Most of them were of other breeds. As Aka's tribe passed them there would be some saluting—swift rises and leaps and dashes toward and away from the strangers by some of the friskier of Aka's mature adults; but when they met schools of other bottle-noses, then it was a watery circus, a rowdy, roaring riot of movement.

All hell—heaven to the dolphins—broke loose very soon after the scouts picked up the echoes of other tribes of bottle-noses. As they ranged around, up to six miles away from Aka, the scouts' heads changed attitude continually, and they sent their three-degree-wide long-range sonar beam in all directions—all around, up, and down. Suddenly one of the dolphin scouts, two thousand feet down in the green opaque silent-to-humans-only never-never depth which suspends between sea surface and sea bottom, almost stopped dead in his tracks. Swiftly he moved his head from side to side, in ever diminishing arcs, until it was merely trembling horizontally, as if he were vehemently denying an accusation. Then he flayed the blackness all around him and shot forward, toward the far-off shadowy blips he had "seen" eight miles away. As he went he twisted and flung himself backward time after time, toward Aka, swiftly sending his excitement and joy along his long-distance, high-frequency acoustic beam. "Olo's tribe—old friends!" His frenzied anticipation emanated all around him through his low-frequency, short-distance sonar and acoustic emanations to every dolphin within two miles of him. Instantly, the receiving dolphins knew that brother bottle-noses were in the area. Instantly, they knew where the new school was, at what depth, in what azimuth direction, at what angle, at what speed it was travelling, and in which direction; and instantly they flung themselves in the same direction as the scout and passed on in turn their "whoops" of excitement. Within seconds of the first scout's detection of the strange bottle-noses, every one of Aka's tribe of 141 dolphins was rushing at full speed to meet and greet the strangers.

As the 93 bottle-noses of Olo's tribe detected the images of dozens of blurry shadows all converging on them, they in their turn hesitated and digested, mulled over and reacted to the movements of the images, all in the fiber breadth of a splinter of a split second, and rushed themselves toward the oncomers at their fastest velocity.

Now the combined speed of the two fleets of dolphins, as they aimed for the already computed and transmitted target area where they would meet on the surface, was 63.5 knots—almost 75 miles an hour.

The distance between the forward scouts of the two tribes rapidly closed, now only a mile . . . a half mile . . . a hundred yards . . . then they all, in both teams, changed their angle of direction slightly upward and sped for the same half-mile-diameter plot of water and air on the surface of the calm blue sea.

Within fifty yards of the target area the forward scouts of both tribes hurtled upward at a steeper angle, all with their short-distance sonar at full strength, and at exactly the same time they fractured the surface of the sea in a tremendous welter of spray spume and falling water.

Within ten seconds 234 gray-white gleaming bodies from one hundred to three hundred pounds in weight, were leaping, hurling, twisting, falling above the surface. Below the surface of the sea, they rushed among each other pell-mell at full speed, missing each others' great bulks and delicate skin-coverings by millimeters, spinning, turning, gliding up, sideways, down, and upside down from the opalescent transparency near the surface to the opaque smoky emerald below, an almost solid column of silver-gray muscle and movement, whirling, darting, dancing, whizzing at high speed, shooting up again, and again, leaps of joy and curiosity, stranger inspecting hurtling, gliding, sliding, glistening stranger, all rising, falling, lashing, flashing in the twinkles of 468 eyes; brother, sister, sister, brother, brother . . . brother . . . sister . . . sister . . . old . . . young . . . old . . . old . . . young . . . young . . . all together, all apart, leaping, hurtling, twisting, twirling; tails swinging, swirling; flippers flapping, flying, falling; eyes blinking, batting; beaks opening, grinning, closing, spitting; blowholes blowing, water spouting up . . . out . . . sideways . . . away, the sea all among them, around them boiling; the waters below bubbling, swirling, up above—above—misty rainbows falling—an effervescent ebullience of excitement, jumping jabbers, hurtling harmony, darting dashes; a million explosions of exhilarated exuberance until, exhausted for the moment, both tribes, on a signal from their leaders, after an hour of seeming utter confusion, finally separated one from the other in a matter of seconds, and parted.

And all the while this extraordinary high-speed circus performance was going on, Aka and Olo and the Wise Ones of both tribes reported on everything they had observed during the past year, since they had last met in this area. Aka and his companions described their long trek up through the West Indies and across the Gulf Stream and so down the Portugal current. Olo recounted how his tribe had journeyed from their nursing grounds around the islands of Fernando de Noronha, in the Atlantic off the northeast bulge of Brazil, down the east coast of South America, east across the southern Atlantic Ocean, past high, lonely Tristan da Cunha, all the way to the shores of South Africa. There Olo had turned north in the Benin current, and so to the Cape Verde Islands. Olo described the huge, almost silent, submarines that prowled now in the depths. Olo's dolphins had seen them firing sinister looking torpedoes, which swam for many miles at high speed and then sank to the bottom.

"A new game that Man plays," said Olo. "Before, in time of sinking ships and many dead men, metal fish hit other big ships . . . loud explosions killed many dolphins all over the seas . . . and destroyed hearing of millions of us."

"Practice for another wartime of destruction," Aka informed him. "Periodically men kill each other—sink other men's ships."

"Why?" an eavesdropping young female asked. "Why does Man do it?"

Aka said, "Man has always done so, even in days of Sea Kings. Even then there were savages on shores and pirates on seas. It is Man's custom," he concluded sadly. "It is Man's way."

Olo agreed, for as his tribe remembered, they too were descendents of the ancient dolphins of the Homeland. "Yes, and Sea Kings trained killer whales to accompany dolphins and Sea Kings' fleets and attack pirates' boats . . ."

"But never to kill . . . Man," observed Aka. "The killer whales used to ram pirate vessels, then grab . . . pirates' bow stemposts in jaws and rip bow away from boat, just enough so that pirates, if careful, could reach shore without sinking."

As the whirling riot of play went on around them, the Wise Ones "talked" of monstrous tankers, ten, twenty times bigger than the blue whale, which spewed black muck into the ocean as they barged along, a black muck that trailed for a hundred miles astern of them and smothered and killed everything on the surface of the sea, and that, after many months, coagulated into little balls of tar, which ignorant young dolphins swallowed, and which brought a lingering, agonizing death to them within a few hours, as their heartbroken mothers squealed in agonies of sorrow and often died of grief.

Then Olo reported seeing the fat-looking ships with murderous harpoon guns on their bows. His tribe, he said, had seen and avoided four of them in the southern waters of the Atlantic Ocean, and on one occasion some of his scouts' long-range receivers had been almost shattered with the pain of a sperm whale's agony as he sounded again and again, a great three-foot-long steel harpoon with six barbs on it and a defective explosive charge lodged deep in his body, until finally, after three hours, the dolphins, watching from six miles away, had heard the last, low mortal moans of the dying gentle giant pleading for the mercy of swift death, fade away.

Aka told Olo about the two young adults his tribe had lost in the nets; Olo in turn told Aka about the sixteen adults and three calves that his tribe had lost to fishing nets off the Cape of Good Hope, and of his three scouts whose hearing and acoustic-receiving domes had been completely ruined by an explosion in the water shortly after a fast ship had passed them. "A warship, with many guns and men on board," Olo added.

Aka then told Olo of the lone dolphin who had strayed into his tribe in the northern West Indies. This dolphin, he said, had told him that he had escaped from a place where Man was training dolphins to help him in war—to spy for him and to carry explosives on their backs and to sink ships. But the lone dolphin had realized finally that if he sank ships, then he might kill Man, and this was against the ancient pact that the Sea Kings and the dolphins had sworn to long ago in the Homeland of Atlantis. The lone dolphin had jumped over a twenty-foot-high barrier and escaped back into the sea. The loner had then searched for his tribe for many weeks. Aka had been able to direct him in its direction, for they had passed only days before, near the great rusty hulk of the half-sunken liner wrecked on a reef of one of the more southerly islands.

Also they told each other of the fish they had encountered, shoals of herring, cod, mackerel, whiting, bass, pompano, sailfish, pilchard, mullet, pollack, goby, grouper, tunny, tuna, sawfish, sharks and gar, bream and butterfish. Fish in all the Atlantic Ocean, from the northern edge of the Gulf Stream to a thousand miles south of Tristan da Cunha. Then they talked of the mammals—the narwhal and the rorqual, the grampus and the great blue whale, the humpback and the finback, and wandering off-track right-whales from the Arctic. Octopus, jellyfish and seals, walrus and mollusks. . . . Aka and Olo exchanged information so that nothing was, or would be, lost, until they met again near this same place a year hence. Between them, Aka and Olo, with their Wise Ones, transmitted and received, stored and retrieved in minutes as much information as would cause the Pentagon computer system to come to a shuddering overload shutdown and a permanent irremedial breakdown.

It was almost sunset when the two tribes of dolphins extricated themselves from one another and separated, to a welter of clicks, whistles, and sonar holograms, and swam on their separate courses for an hour, then gathered in sleeping groups to doze the night hours away.

The females all dozed on the surface, with their blowholes just above water level, slowly opening and closing them as they breathed. All the males slept slightly below the surface, waking every few minutes to rise to the air and breathe. If a male should forget to wake and breathe, or if a female calf fell fast asleep and started to sink, the circling night guards, quick as ever, swam under the sleeper and raked the sleeper's sexual organs with his or her dorsal fin. This did no damage, but it caused the sleeper's tail muscles to jerk the flukes upward violently, so forcing the offender up to the surface again. Then, if he or she did not wake, the guard butted the sleeper with his head gently and so woke him or her.

When Aka's tribe awoke the next day, first light was lilting in the eastern sky. They set out for the two-thousand-mile trek to their nursing grounds. They opened and closed formation as suited the circumstances: open formation if there was little life and few shoals of fish in the waters, and closed formation during the rarer periods when the fish were more numerous. The trek went on, day after day, with the tribe an entity in itself and yet composed of separate individuals all with his or her own characteristics of movement, of thought, of sound, of signals; some were better scouts than others, some more accurate navigators, some gentler nurses or tugs, some more precise depth-sounders, some more powerful surface jumpers, some more careful fish herders, some more intelligent, some more astute, some quicker, some more gentle; but all were under Aka's spell, and all followed his directions, and lent their assets of their whole beings to him, so that through Aka the tribe became something more than the sum total of its members, because the tribal cohesiveness and cooperative strength added protection from the sly sharks and the fierce swordfish, and an everlasting reciprocation of loyalty, love, affection, and comradeship.

On they ploughed and thrust, rose and dipped, on and on through the depths of the deepest parts of the Atlantic, almost as deep as earth's highest mountain. Day after day the tribe made their way along a track that would for a human be a desolate waste of unmarked waters, but that for them had been recorded and re-recorded every inch of the way by taste and the assuring twinkle of the guiding stars, from the very dawn of their history twenty million years before. Each day, at an hour that, traditionally, differed according to their position, Aka or one of the other three Wise Ones, recounted to all the others events that had occurred in that area, stories that had been handed down from adult to calf for the past thousand millennia and more, stories that time and time and time again drove into the dolphin psyche the message that they survived because they were tuned perfectly into their surroundings; that it was better by far to change position than to change the surroundings, that nature herself would soon enough do that—both to their surroundings and to themselves.

It was the fifteenth day of their ocean trek from Cape Verde. The tribe was now only one day's trek-distance to their nursing grounds around the lonely ocean rocks. Already the dolphins were feeling more and more at home as they recognized familiar traces in the ocean waters. They welcomed the subtle changes of color, salinity, and temperature, shades and nuances that informed them that once again, for the many millionth time, the tribe's peregrination right around the northern Atlantic was coming to an end, that once again they would be in their ancestral home for three whole months, until it was once again time to set off on the immemorially ancient trail of the tribe, back to the mating grounds away in the northeast. They had found an immense shoal of shrimp the previous day and were all well fed. Of a sudden, Aka received an urgent signal of a sonar "sighting." For two days there had been little on the surface but whales, some other dolphin tribes, a few barracuda and bonito, dorado and swordfish, and one large ship. When Aka caught up with the waiting scout he beamed the "sighting"—and immediately recognized the one-man boat the tribe had played with near the Island of the Whistling Men nineteen days before. Aka's great heart leaped. *A son of the Atlantean Sea Kings was coming home!* He sent a scout ahead of the main body to make sure that all was well, and upon his affirmative report that it was indeed, the tribe raced over to the boat.

Above the sea surface the day was sunny, without a cloud in the sky. The face of the waters was an undulating field of slightly ruffled blue, only a few shades lighter than the blue of the boat's hull. The sails of the boat were different from when the dolphins had last met her. Now only the large genoa was hoisted and hung baggily in the near calm, as empty as a sailor's pockets, the mainsail was draped over the deck, and the boom slatted noisily back and forth, back and forth, athwart the boat. The steering-gear rudder still wiggled and waggled just as it had done when it had last enchanted them. The only thing different about the hull was the green slime on the waterline—it was now half an inch longer. Again the dolphins crowded around the boat. Again they dived and leapt, whistled and clicked. Again they flung themselves at where the bow-wave would have been, but now they squealed as they found it was not there. Disappointed, they swam at the boat's side, and under the boat, and ahead of the boat. They did this for a few minutes, until Aka, with a feeling that something was very different from the last time, "looked" into the boat with his sonar and saw that *the man was not there.*

Aka carefully checked again. There was no living being in the boat.

Chapter 14

Josephine rinsed and swam, wallowed and sailed.

After the gale had spent itself, the ocean wind stayed in the north or on the eastern side of the north. For a week it blew at a steady rate of about eighteen knots during the day and diminished to a gentle ten knots or so at night. Now and again for short spells the wind dropped completely, and *Josephine* wallowed as Conan rigged up the rain-catcher awning and a big black bag of a cloud crept up overhead and suddenly emptied itself straight onto her. So it went, day after day, sun, wind, chores, and water.

By now Conan and the ship were old friends. He did his routine jobs—he had made a mental list of seventy-two regular daily duties—cleaning, cooking, running the engine to charge his batteries, sail repair, restowing gear, engine maintenance, rigging checks, navigation, radio routines; and faithfully *Josephine* did her chore for him—sailed steady and true before the wind in a southerly direction at as fast a speed as she could manage, according to the wind.

Daily, as Conan bent over the chart and marked the noon position—each little pencil mark was another day forward, another little step further beyond the previous day's—and all the time, day and night, even when he was dozing, he always seemed to know the position of the ship. At all times, in his mind's eye he saw her moving across the chart. Slowly but surely the faint pencil line reached down south into the middle of the vast, almost empty spaces on the chart which depicted the equatorial Atlantic wastes of waters. Sometimes, as he idled away the night on the helm under a blaze of stars set in black velour, Conan considered the length of his track down the Atlantic Ocean, from Lisbon to Rio. He reflected to himself that maps and charts tend to make for a blasé view of the wide spaces of the earth to a navigator, so that he begins to think of an entire ocean as merely a few inches of printed lines and white space on a piece of stiff chart paper. After a while he saw three weeks of days and nights perfectly expert sailing as only a series of small dots on the paper, seemingly heading nowhere in particular, like the shiny trail of an absentminded snail over a rhubarb leaf. Like the snail, all that Conan thought of as regards the vast distance was getting across it.

As for the race, Conan did not let his mind think too much about the whole course of it, nor about the angry track ahead past the Cape of Good Hope, nor even the gentler eastward sweep from Rio to the cape, but he did consider, sometimes, the long reach off Brazil, down to the latitude of Rio; even more did he anticipate the awkward and fussy maneuverings, delays, sail changes, and patience that the belt of doldrums around the equator and that he was now entering would demand. He recalled the old sailor's saying about big jobs—softlee, softlee . . . catchee monkee!

Until the twenty-fifth of April, Conan kept at bay a growing curiosity as to the progress and positions of the other competitors. Then one night, with good radio reception conditions and a chatty operator in Dakar, he learned that *Josephine* was in fact doing much better than he had hoped. Only Joe Morgan, in the fifty-five-foot sloop *Sir John Falstaff,* was to the southwest of him—and not very far away—a mere six hundred miles. Conan grinned and told himself, "which means that Morgan will probably have to beat for a couple of days against the southeast trades and the South Equatorial Current to claw his way around Cape San Roque, the northeast bulge of Brazil, in order to clear the cape and head south. That'll delay him while I roll on south . . ."

Conan found that most of the other yachts in the race were to the northwest of his position, with the first group of two racing neck to neck about five hundred miles away from *Josephine.* These, he learned, were *Southern Star,* Paddy Hunt's fifty-three-foot sloop, and *Ocean Pacer,* John Tyler's fifty-three-foot yawl. They were trailed, a day's sailing astern, by *Sundance Kid* leading the Swedish boat. Conan was pleased— it sounded as if Jack Hanson had gotten his feet wet all right. The

American's boat was followed by the Swedish *Ocean Viking* and Peter the Pole's unpronounceable boat (the radio operator said it looked like a censored swear-word.) Then came a bombshell. The French *Etoile du Sud* had retired from the race very early, having sustained rudder damage when she ran at speed over a Taiwanese fishing boat's steel net somewhere west of the Canary Islands. "One down—eight to go," he said to himself.

"What about *Flagrante Delicto?*" Conan requested the operator.

"Yes, she's around five degrees north, thirty degrees west, and everything okay. Miss Chatterton had a sail blow out on the twenty-third, but she's okay and going well."

Conan started to ask what Mary's course was, but he remembered that it was against the rules. Conan now knew that Mary Chatterton was hot in his tracks. She was only about one good day's sail north of *Josephine* and, like his own craft, well out in the center of the ocean, with plenty of sea room for clearing Cape San Roque. He thought to himself aloud, "So it's *Falstaff* first, *Josephine*, and Mary Chatterton at least as far as the latitude of Rio . . ." He shut down the radio and again spoke aloud, "So the woman did trail me. . . . She must have kept a close radio watch," and only now, three weeks later, was he sure that it was Mary Chatterton's craft that he had seen on the morning of his first night out, bright white sails on the horizon, stark against the black clouds in the offing of Lisbon.

This night, in the wide-open central ocean, it was as if Mary Chatterton were breathing down his neck. He grinned to himself and eased a little more the sheet rope of the huge genoa sail, and laid *Josephine* another fraction of a degree east of south, so as to have the southeast trade wind more on *Josephine*'s beam when the time came for him to encounter the South Atlantic—and that time was coming fast.

For day after day Conan saw little else but the boat, the sea, the sky, and a few leaping creatures. A change in the shape of the faraway clouds on the horizon was a cause of interest. A shooting meteor, ramming its way through the night sky, was an event of note. Opening a day's food pack, anticipating, guessing its contents, was a diurnal matter of gravity. By each Friday the "Sunday special" was looked forward to with increasing gusto. The fishing line was brought in a little more eagerly each evening; a catch he greeted a little more enthusiastically each time there was a struggling, bug-eyed dorado or bonito for him to welcome, and the empty line cast back in the sea astern a little more patiently, as each day joined all the others that had passed, until they all seemed like one, in every superficial respect, except for small differences—a change in sea, a change in the cast of light, the sun a little higher in the north each day—which Conan's sailor's eyes saw in all their grand import. The only change a landsman would have noticed in this week after the storm was the addition each day of another small dot on the chart, a half inch or so further down the white paper-space than the last.

On the first of May *Josephine* was becalmed. The northeast trade day wind simply did not show up for work that morning. By mid-forenoon the night wind had packed up and gone home. Only the sea and *Josephine* still labored. The sea, a limitless heaving blue field, breathed heavily and sighed like a prospective mother-in-law as *Josephine* shook and wallowed and cried like an abandoned bride for her errant groom, the wind. She rolled and she pitched under the climbing, blazing hot sun. The main boom clattered as Conan glowered at it. Finally, bleary eyed after hours of coaxing the boat forward in a feebling night breeze over a never-ending series of watery obstacles rising for ever and ever through all the dawn and early morning, and impatient for sleep, he angrily grabbed the mainsail halyard, threw it off its cleat, and let the sail clatter down onto the coach roof. He left it where it had dropped. Not in laziness, but so that the nylon sail would afford some extra insulation to the cabin from the suffocating heat of the sun. Then he sweatily made his way into the forward cabin, tugged and heaved at the sail bags, uncovered the cockpit awning, climbed back through the cabin again and up the ladder, threw the awning over the boom, raised the boom with the topping lift, and, cursing to himself as one of his toes stubbed a ringbolt, opened the three small ventilator hatches. Wearily he went below again and, almost immediately, still cursing the calm, threw himself on the berth. There, for three hours, his body resisted the sometimes gentle, sometimes violent, rolling, pitching, and wallowing, and his ears tried to shut out the creaking of blocks, the slopping of the steering-gear vane, the sloshing of water on the sides, and the chinking and clinking of utensils, pots, pans, pencils, and, it seemed, every other loose object on board.

When Conan bestirred himself and clambered aloft to take the noon sight, *Josephine*'s masthead scribed across almost all the upturned, hot blue bowl of the sky. She writhed on the undulating, heaving surface of an almost glassy sea like a drunken porpoise.

Conan jammed himself into a secure position in the cockpit, and held himself steady with one knee against a rising and falling wheel column and with the other knee resisted the jerks of the cockpit seat. He lifted the sextant and did his best to capture a wildly excited sun which chased all over the sea and sky.

Conan's platform was so unsteady and the readings of the sextant arc so remote from each other at first that he took a dozen shots and later, when his stomach had rejoined his brain, worked out the average, which gave him a latitude of three degrees north, as accurate as the sum of a dozen wild shots could make it. This latitude, with an assumed longitude of thirty degrees ten minutes west of Greenwich, put *Josephine* at approximately 120 miles north of St. Paul's Rocks. Then, to bolster his confidence in his own accuracy, Conan, for the first time since he had joined *Josephine*, switched on the $3,000 electronic loran receiver. Immediately the dark screen of the loran set gave him a set of time differences. He pushed another button and the figures on the screen changed to latitude and longitude. He peered at it silently and grinned—it read three degrees eight minutes north, thirty degrees twelve minutes west. If the electronic set was correct, he was only a matter of a couple of miles out on his own reckoning. It was typical of Conan not to use the loran each day. It could not be used in the deep reaches of the Southern Ocean, and so he kept his celestial navigation finely honed and refused to abandon it and become subject, perhaps, to the failure of an electronic gadget.

Conan carefully dotted the noon position on the chart on the heaving table, and made his way topsides again for fresh air, to try to lock his eyes onto the only reasonably steady thing in his world—the horizon. With his stomach still queasy, and his nerves rattled by the thousand squeaks and groans all around him, Conan shifted the awning and lay down on the cockpit seat. But in a few seconds he was up again—the ship had turned and the hot sun was burning his chest through his cotton shirt. Cursing, he clambered down below again and found restless, hot shelter on the drunken berth for another four hours.

By two hours after the swift tropical nightfall, the sea had eased to a gentle heave. *Josephine* rolled only ten degrees either way instead of the noontime thirty-five. Conan, feeling better now by far, made himself a meal of cold bacon, cut from the good innards of the otherwise fast-rotting side which Shaughnessy had brought from Ireland, and a pound of the bonito he had caught three days before, raw, cut in cubes, soaked in lime juice, salt water, and onion, until the outside of the meat was bleached white. It was delicious, not at all "fishy," and it saved raiding his supply of canned meat. With the bacon and bonito he ate the last of the fresh potatoes, mashed. With his meal he broke his rule and opened a bottle of French Chablis, to help him sleep away the evening until midnight. Then he climbed out of the stuffy cabin, hot from the stove-burner heat, and slept, for once a deep sleep, in the cockpit, until, in the early hours of the second of May, the almost complete silence around him woke him with a start.

For the first time in almost a month, there was no noise of the sea rushing and swishing past the hull, no chant of the breeze in the rigging wires, no clicking from the steering-wheel cables, no tapping and clinking from the galley. Except for the slight squeal of an anonymous block somewhere near him, and the almost inaudible sound of rippling water from the waterline, there was complete and utter silence. It was as if its spirit had left the ocean on the breeze's last, hot, dying breath.

As he lay there, Conan opened his eyes and gazed at first in astonishment, then in wonder, at the stars in the east melting after the dark purple forerunner of the dawn passed them, and they were overtaken by turquoise, violet, calamine, cerulean, hyacinth, azure, pink, rose, peach, orange, and blazing red. Then, quite suddenly, the sun pulled in his belt and flexed his muscles; the sky was all steely blue, and it looked so finely tempered and eggshell thin that Conan imagined if he threw a hammer at the sky it would shatter, splinter, and fall into the ocean in hot sharp pieces.

Conan stood up, crouched under the boom, and gazed around to smell for any sign of a breeze. There was none. The whole horizon, all around was, he thought, as empty as a Scotsman's sporran on Charity Day.

The meeting line of the sea and the sky was now, for the first time since he had left Lisbon, absolutely clear, defined, unmistakable, a dark blue-black line all around him, except in the east, under the sun, where it was yet silvery blue with glimmers of gold. Conan's horizon all around him was three and a half miles distant when he was in the cockpit, and five miles if he stood on the side deck by the shrouds, and it was empty, deserted, voided, abandoned. It was as if there were nothing in the world but the sea and the sky. It was as if land and life had never risen from the waters. It was, he concluded sadly, like the second day of creation. With a sigh, Conan decided to clean through the bilges under the cabin.

His breakfast was simple—porridge oats, eaten from the pan, and molasses, eaten from and with a hard biscuit, and all washed down with double-strong Earl Grey breakfast tea, which left Conan smacking his lips and rubbing his hands as he planned the day's work ahead.

Josephine's bilges were dry, except under the engine. Conan worked as fast as he could, while the cabin was still fairly cool. He swept out all the dust he could see and reach, and worked the little chain that passed through the limber holes to keep them free, and soon the cabin bilges were clean and clear. Then he moved aft and reached under the engine to clean out the tiny amount of oil and water that had leaked into the drip tray, practically all of it during filling operations.

When he finished that chore it was almost too hot to work below.

Conan, in his cotton shirt and shorts, moved topsides. He remembered the long steering-gear safety trip-line which he had trailed astern of the boat all the way from Lisbon—a safety measure Houghton had insisted upon, in case he accidentally fell overboard. He went onto the fantail and saw that it was hanging straight down into the depths. He intended to start the engine and test the propellor a little later, when he had dropped the genoa. He hauled the line on board so there would be no chance of it fouling the propellor when it started to turn. He would replace the line over the stern as soon as the engine test was completed. The log-line he left in the sea. It was led to the starboard quarter, and dangled well clear of the propellor. Feeling scorched by the sun, he returned to the cockpit. He crouched again under the main boom for a minute or two, then went forward to drop the great genoa, which was hanging slack, as if it were in despair at ever again feeling the wind. Conan started to go forward—and saw the turtle.

It was a big green turtle, almost five feet from flipper end to flipper end, and it pushed itself forward toward *Josephine*'s stern slowly and patiently, its head thrust forward indignantly. It reminded Conan of an old, old man trying to get out of a hoodlum-crowded cinema showing a rock-and-roll movie. Its expression was one of resigned panic. It made Conan think, for some reason, of an Anglo-Catholic author he had read of recently.

Then, as he gazed for a minute at the turtle Conan saw in his mind's eye great red chunks of raw turtle steak, and one in the frying pan sizzling away, with light blue smoke carrying from it the delicious aroma of fresh beef. He could even tie the turtle on a lanyard astern, until the wind rose, and slaughter it then. . . . He dashed aft, as quietly as he could, and dragged out a boathook from the nethermost corner of the quarter-berth. He quickly lashed a small snatch-block to the end of the pole, and through it reaved a good sturdy length of marlin. In the loose end he swiftly made a lasso to which he lashed with fine string, as bait, some potato tendrils, and above that he tied a small bolt for a sinker. Then he was ready to catch the turtle.

Conan hesitated for a moment, as he remembered the genoa still hanging loose, but he said aloud, as he climbed the ladder, "First things first, lad . . ." The genoa would be there in an hour's time—the turtle might not . . .

There followed a long, quiet, crafty wait, as silently, like a figure in a mad mimic's show, Conan waited for the turtle to come close to the ship. After half an hour he stalked it on his belly, up on the hot side deck. After another fifteen minutes he reached out with the pole now and then to test for distance and to tempt in the turtle by softly and gently jerking the potato tendrils in front of the turtle's face.

Still the reptile sniffed the hot, still air only five yards from the boat. As it moved its flippers, unhurried, resignedly, in the calm, cool sea, the turtle gazed intently, sometimes at the boat, sometimes at its own flippers, sometimes seemingly at nothing. All the while Conan stalked it, murmuring, "Now come on, old chap . . . just a wee bit closer now . . ."

All of a sudden there was a swirl of water around the turtle, and as Conan watched with a sense of loss, it turned around and started to swim away from the boat. When the turtle was ten yards off, Conan stood up, feeling almost baked by the sun on his back. "Damn and blast," he quietly said aloud.

As if the turtle had heard him, it turned again and swam toward *Josephine*'s side. Conan, as soon as he saw the animal turn, dropped down again on the skin-blistering deck. Again he waited, watching the turtle the whole time. Again the turtle looked as if it were wondering where the toilet was, for a good fifteen minutes, again it turned around and swam away slowly. Again Conan stood and cursed.

After the third approach and retreat of the turtle, Conan was about to lose the sailor's first necessity in the matter of human qualities: he was about to lose his patience, about to abandon the whole thing and attend to the genoa. Then, as he watched, the turtle started to swim slowly toward the stern, its curiosity evidently aroused by the trim-tab of the steering gear, which very slowly waggled silently from side to side.

Quietly excited and roused to the chase, Conan moved silently aft under the cockpit awning and waited a few minutes in the cool relief of the awning shade as the turtle, at an agonizingly slow pace, swam closer and closer to *Josephine*'s stern. Still Conan waited, in the shadows of the awning. He heard a slight bump as the turtle's shell knocked the counter. He jumped for the fantail, holding the boathook out in front of him. As he did this he took care not to snag the lasso in cleats and all the other bits and pieces that stick out on board a boat. Also Conan felt the first stir of a light air on his face.

At the stern rail, Conan peeped over. The turtle was even bigger than he had thought. It was a *real* biggie, almost six feet from the tip of its nose to the end of its back flippers. A whopper, Conan thought to himself. Too big, really, with no fridge on board. But meat's meat. Conan slowly, silently, dangled the lasso down until the bait was floating on the water. As he peered down, with the hot sun on the back of his neck, Conan saw that the turtle seemed to take no notice at all of the bait. Carefully Conan drew the lasso nearer and nearer to the turtle. Suddenly the turtle gave a slight start, and with a ponderous stroke of his front flippers he moved out, three feet. Another lazy stroke took him out another two feet. Conan decided to take a gamble and try to lasso the turtle. The light airs were breathing a little more now, almost enough to move the boat . . .

Conan lunged over the after rail of the boat just as the airs lifted the genoa slightly. He missed the turtle's flipper. He lunged again as the genoa filled a little more. He missed again. He tried yet again as the steering-gear vane lazily pivoted and found the light breeze. Again Conan missed. He determined to make one more try. He climbed over the after rail and reached out as far as he could, holding on to the rail with one hand, and on to the outstretched boathook and its dangling noose with the other. He leaned out as far as he could toward the turtle in the now slight swirl of an awakening wake in the flat sea astern. This time he caught the flipper.

Conan's heart leapt in triumph a split second before the turtle, with a great jerk of the flipper, dragged the pole, and Conan with it, down into the ocean.

After a seeming eternity of white-green water all around him, Conan let go of the pole. He shot to the surface of the sea. He gasped for breath and glimpsed the log-line propellor slowly turning only three yards below him, as *Josephine*, with her genoa lazily bellying, slowly, gently, quietly sailed away from him.

Conan retched and spat the water out of his nasal passages. He had swallowed a great deal. Then he glanced in trepidation at the log-line spinner. Its revolutions increased slightly; it was now four yards ahead of him. His racing heart sank as he remembered that he had pulled the safety trip-line on board.

In a blind panic, he struck out in an Australian crawl, racing to catch up with the twirling spinner. He hardly looked up at the boat as his head turned in the water and his arms thrashed and pulled, thrashed and pulled, until, ten minutes later, he paused out of breath and realized in horror that the spinner was further away from him—much further away. Twenty yards away.

Conan's breath sobbed and gasped for air as, terror-stricken, he saw the genoa sail, now fully filled with breeze, pulling away at the vessel. Frantically he swam on, alternating the crawl with a breaststroke, but hopelessly, as each long, gentle swell lifted him and showed his terrified stare the full genoa and the gentle wind-seeking of the steering-gear vane as it dutifully, accurately, stupidly, guided *Josephine* further and further away from him. Thirty yards . . . fifty yards . . . a hundred . . .

For another hour Conan swam in despair, pausing for a second when-

ever a swell lifted him, to desperately watch the boat, pleading and pray-
ing, sometimes aloud, sometimes in a low mumble, for the breeze to
drop.

Soon the boat was too far away for Conan to see her details clearly
through his salt-blinded, crying eyes. He reckoned and counted, as he
swam frenziedly after the boat, every inch that the sun moved on its arc-
ing track down to the horizon, and each inch the sun moved increased
his agony.

Another hour later, flagging now, Conan knew that the new wind
was not a fluke, not a solitary cat's-paw. He knew it would blow at least
until the dawn. He also knew that he was now all alone, a mere speck
in the vastness of the ocean, and that the nearest land was five miles
away, straight down. He knew that unless a miracle occurred before
dark, he was a condemned man.

All the late afternoon Conan swam, getting weaker and weaker, as the
sun dropped. He kept his longing, pleading eyes on the boat every time
a swell lifted him; he kept his eyes chained to the boat as long as he
could, and willed her to somehow wait for him. Sometimes he prayed.
Sometimes he cursed. Sometimes he pleaded, but still *Josephine* sailed on
away from him, until her sails were a mere pink blob bobbing in the low
rays of the sun as it sank into the twilight.

As darkness fell, Conan finally lost sight of *Josephine*. As he rose and
fell in the relentless, slow heaving waters, a million unhearing, heedless
stars gazed down at him coldly, and he wept like a lone child lost in the
dark, appalling reaches of infinity.

Part 3: Encounter

"The evidence presented by the ancient maps appears to suggest the existence in remote times, before the rise of any known cultures, of a true civilization, of an advanced kind, which either was localized in one area but had worldwide commerce, or was, in a real sense, a *worldwide* culture. This culture, at least in some respects, was far more advanced than the civilizations of Greece and Rome. In geodesy, in nautical science and mapmaking, it was more advanced than any known culture before the eighteenth century of the Christian Era. It was only in the eighteenth century that we first developed a practical means of finding longitude. It was in the eighteenth century that we first accurately measured the circumference of the earth. Not until the nineteenth century did we begin to send out ships for exploration into the Arctic and Antarctic Seas and only then did we begin the exploration of the bottom of the Atlantic. The maps indicate that *some ancient people did all these things*" (author's italics).

PROFESSOR CHARLES H. HAPGOOD,
Maps of the Ancient Sea Kings

"We are such stuff as dreams are made of . . ."

WILLIAM SHAKESPEARE,
from *The Tempest*

Chapter 15

ALL THE WHILE AKA SWAM slowly round and round the boat he focused his high frequency sonar into and through the hull. As most of his tribe circled the boat time and again, he raked the vessel with his powerful beam from stem to stern, but he found no signs of life. He was somewhat puzzled. He thought once or twice, while he circled the boat, that he heard some low acoustic signals coming from inside the vessel, but after he strained his acoustic receiver for a minute he decided that it must be the voice of the boat itself. He also decided to ignore it because it was far too low for him to be able to understand it, and the tones of the voice seemed to rise and fall somewhat like a neurotic porpoise's. To make absolutely sure that no one was on board he requested Huk and the other Wise Ones to do the same. They, too, after many minutes of probing the boat, signalled "no life."

Four young dolphins started to gambol ahead of the boat's bow, but Aka ordered them to stop. One of them took no notice. Huk raced over and butted the offender, not too gently but hard enough to stop him in his tracks. The youngsters now swam round and round him, sedately, with all the rest.

With his low frequency acoustic pulses Aka "addressed" the whole tribe of dolphins, with the exception of the outsiders who kept guard on a periphery five miles out from them.

"Aka's dolphins know," he said, ". . . no shore . . . coast within many day's journey . . . except . . . rocks of . . . nursing ground. Maybe man-from-boat going Atlantis. Dolphins . . . see . . . boat . . . rope-from . . . sail hangs over . . . side. This . . . not . . . way man sail. Accident. Man fallen from boat. Dolphins must try find man-from-boat. Men not live long in sea, like dolphin. Men not find food . . . water in sea like dolphin. Man not defend man from predators . . . like dolphin. Dolphins . . . find . . . man-from-boat . . . try save man."

"Why?" demanded Huk. In the tradition of the dolphins, it was the next senior Wise One's duty and privilege to challenge the leader.

"Dolphins' Laws . . . man-from-boat good man." Aka paddled gently with both his flippers.

Huk argued, "Man now dolphin's enemies . . . enemy all sea creatures. Kills young dolphins . . . cruel nets . . . underwater explosions . . . shatter . . . wound . . . ruin hearing, seeing . . . every living thing many miles around. Spews chemical . . . great ships . . . cities . . . poisons waters . . . dolphins cannot swim in many traditional, ancient haunts . . . Men kill young dolphins slowly, painfully, black muck gushes out great ships . . . deadly little balls goo floating in ocean . . . shoots dolphins with bullets from ships . . . baits cruel hooks . . . catches dolphins . . . sport . . . dolphin caught . . . men taunt . . . dolphin dies . . . Men throws back in sea. Dolphins mentally scarred rest of life." Huk flicked his own scarred tail, then he continued. "Not only dolphins . . . whales too. Man one million years history thinks dolphin after twenty million years physical, mental, psychic evolution, no know . . . past twenty-five years Man murdered eighty thousand finbacks. Man thinks dolphins too stupid reckon how long will take Man slaughter remaining thirty thousand. Man thinks dolphins not know only two thousand blue whales left all oceans of world. Only two thousand biggest, brainiest, gentlest creature ever lived. Only three thousand humpbacks. What Man think dolphin are? *What men think men are?*" Huk's signals were now becoming sharp and raspy. Some of the young dolphins became nervous and afraid. Aka ordered them to be calm.

Huk continued. "Man causes only fear . . . death . . . pain. Dolphins know all Men do on sea, in sea, under sea, over sea. Dolphins know when finback dying . . . agony . . . steel harpoons . . . blood reddens ocean miles around . . . finback's struggles . . . signals . . . screams . . . agony . . . pain . . . despair heard . . . every other mammal in sea . . . five hundred miles! Man not know dolphins know Man turned waters of world bloody slaughterground. Dolphins know Man turn sea . . . muck dumps . . . twenty-five years more . . . nothing left for mammals . . . slow . . . painful death . . . poisons! Let man-from-boat drown."

There were a hundred signals of agreement and assent for Huk, until Aka, in the age-old fashion of the dolphins, replied, addressing them all. "Huk speaks true. But man-from-boat not hunt . . . kill . . . except to eat . . . like dolphins. See boat; no nets; no harpoon gun; no black muck; man not fire bullets at dolphins when dolphins meet boat near Island of the Whistling Men. Man-from-boat make signals . . . Aka received . . . low baby frequency . . . good will . . . compassion. Same signals Sea Kings sent dolphins . . . ancient times . . . dolphin legends tell us. Dolphins must find man-from boat . . . rescue man."

Now Kweela joined in the debate. "Aka speaks true, Kweela . . . Om . . . swimming . . . Om suffering pain . . . man-from-boat feel for Om and Kweela."

Huk replied, "Boat only one boat . . . man-from-boat only one man. Man kill Man . . . Man maim Man . . . Man destroy Man. Man think dolphins not record giant explosions . . . great cloud in sky . . . number creatures Man maims . . . destroy. Man think dolphins not see . . . record . . . rockets . . . spacecraft . . . satellites; Man not know dolphins calculate angle, azimuth . . . five stars . . . less than one second. Man think dolphin not know Man takes death . . . destruction everywhere Man go—even they will soon take among stars . . . among creatures on other planets outside system . . . dolphin's sun. Man think because dolphins not greedy, because dolphins not covet any *thing* dolphins stupid. Man . . . greedy . . . covetous . . . neurotic about *possessions.* . . . Man depend on *things* outside Man . . . not develop Man's *senses* as dolphins over twenty million years. Man neglect Man's legends, Man's myths, not learn, like dolphins, from history! Man stupid . . . not dolphins. Dolphins know . . . memories handed down only two generations . . . dolphin's parents see thousand ships destroyed, thousands men blown up . . . burned . . . crippled . . . roasted alive in oil fires all over world's oceans for five years . . . dolphin's parents see fast warships rush over silent submarines below . . . drop explosives in sea . . . hammerings . . . tappings from trapped men in submarines on ocean floor . . . sometimes for days . . . until noise dies. Man sent planes out of sky . . . spewed fire at men from destroyed ships . . . submarine men picked up men from sunk ships . . . talked with men from sunk ships . . . shot men . . . threw back in sea . . . Aka told Olo of lone dolphin . . . escaped from place where men train dolphins for war . . ."

Aka interjected, "Other places men keep dolphins, study dolphins . . . make friends with dolphins. Some men trying speak dolphin language . . . train dolphins speak Man's language . . . understand each other. Later trained dolphins . . . interpreters . . . speak with ocean dolphins of Man's needs . . . dolphin teach Man . . ."

Huk exploded, "Train?" Huk thrashed his tail. "Man . . . short history
. . . culture . . . tradition . . . *train dolphins?* Who men think men are?"
Huk pointed his snout at *Josephine* as she lay wallowing only yards away.
"Only one boat . . . only one man. One man maybe harmless to dolphins
. . . but when man is with other men . . . Man enemy. Leave man-from-
boat to drown. Let all men drown!"

Aka responded, "Dolphins' ancient allies, Sea Kings of Atlantis made
war against pirates and savages."

"True," admitted Huk, "but Sea Kings destroyed only ships . . . Sea
Kings sent killer whales and trained swordfish . . . rip out pirate bows
. . . hole ships in hull . . . but Sea Kings always admonished dolphins . . .
all life sacred . . . sent dolphins . . . rescue men from sinking ships . . .
carry them . . . shore. Modern Man care little for life . . . modern Man
have nothing sacred . . . Modern Man stupid . . . Sea Kings ancient
friends of dolphins . . . wise, as dolphins legends say."

"Perhaps," suggested Aka, as all the tribe listened carefully, "not Man
not care about life . . . survival of life . . . perhaps Man just not think
about life. Perhaps Man have many other problems . . . on land . . .
which dolphins not know, which dolphins have no idea? Huk spoke true
. . . black poison. Dolphins puzzled why Man carry murderous muck
long distances . . . great ships . . . Aka maybe have answer. When dolphins left Islands of Western Ocean when sun last furthest north, when
dolphins entered warm Gulf Stream, . . . dolphins see long, long, bridge
. . . things moving . . . many colors . . . many different colors . . . with
men inside them . . . speeding along fast?"

There were several signals of assent from the dolphins close to Aka.
"Aka thinks black muck food for land boats which move faster than dolphins swim. Dolphins know Man use same poison in men's little sea
boats . . . noisy like land boats . . . sea boats leave rainbow-colored stain
on water like black muck from big ships leaves rainbow-colored stain on
sea. Black muck makes men move fast on land . . . black muck very important to Man. If Man not have black muck not able move about land."

"Man has legs," observed Huk. "Like dolphin's ancestors . . . as dolphins legends tell . . ."

Aka replied, "Aka means move about *fast,* as dolphins chasing shoal
of fish."

"Are men always chasing shoals?"

"Maybe men are. Maybe whatever Man chase on land when move
about so fast . . . Man need to survive. If black muck help Man move
about . . . if black muck only thing can help Man move about fast . . .
Man must have black muck to survive," Aka explained.

"At dolphin's expense? At cost of ruining all oceans . . . all seas? At expense ... misery ... pain ... senseless death ... dolphins see ... dolphins know ... dolphins discuss every time ... meet other dolphins? Five-eighths ... world's surface sacrificed so Man can chase shoals of whatever Man chases? Great oceans becoming noxious watery deserts empty of life so Man can swim faster about land chasing Man's mysterious shoals?"

Aka replied, "Man need to move ... like dolphins need to move. Man always carried *things* in ships—even Sea Kings carried things in ships."

Huk admitted, "Aka speaks true." Then his signal blasted, "But Sea Kings not use black muck like modern Man, to swim on land or sea. Sea King's cities and ships not have blowholes belching evil-smelling fumes into sky. Sea Kings used sun ... wind ... water of seas, like dolphins. Yet Sea Kings carried beautiful *things* to and from lands from around every ocean in ... whole world ... Sea Kings sent ships ... explore all world's oceans ... Sea Kings killed nothing but fish to eat."

Aka gave a signal-cry of triumph. "Exactly!" he exclaimed. "Huk speaks true ... everything Huk speaks ... true. As Sea Kings lived, so lives man-from-boat. Man-from-boat maybe descendent of Sea Kings come back ... see remnants of ancient home of Atlantis. If dolphins save man-from-boat ... man-from-boat return home of brothers ... tell other descendents of Sea Kings of Atlantis ... dolphins have not forgotten promises to Sea Kings ... dolphins have not betràyed pact with Sea Kings made twelve thousand years ago. Dolphins must save man-from-boat so ... man can be dolphin's messenger to Man of land, so Man of land will remember Sea King's pact with dolphins and again keep faith with Laws of Sea. *Aka orders dolphins save man-from-boat if man still alive!*" It was a command, a statement that there would be no more discussion on the matter of finding the man. The whole debate had taken forty-five seconds.

The dolphins all swam in silence for a moment, then Huk demanded, "How?"

"Wait." Aka swam around the boat once more. Again he studied every detail of the hull, from the forefoot, down past the keel, to the main rudder and the gently wiggling auxiliary rudder on the wind-vane steering gear. Slowly he swam around the boat, several times. He swam around it and under it, all the while observing, ingesting, rejecting, calculating, while the other dolphins, themselves swimming in a circle around the hull as it slowly lifted and descended in the long, calm ocean swell, watched him.

Huk, swimming close to Aka's tail, suggested, "We make a 'net' in line ... search ... surface that way ... ?"

Aka replied, almost absentmindedly as he calculated, "Would take too

long ... boat may have drifted ... days ... surface currents around here
... so devious ..." He did not finish what he was signalling.

All of a sudden an idea hit Aka. He turned his head toward the hull
and gently swam until his beak was only a fraction of an inch from it.
He stayed there, his tongue pressed slightly out from his beak, for a matter of a minute. "That's it!" he signalled. "Boat underwater ... covered,
as dolphins see, with red stuff. Stuff ... oozing out minute traces of
some kind of ... tastes like metal ... Sea Kings used for nails. Traces
so slight ... Aka ... only just taste."

Aka flung himself over gently on his back slowly, twisted as he
turned, and swam at a slow speed toward the stern of the boat and beyond it. He moved his head this way and that, swimming at a funereal
pace, calmly, so as not to disturb the water just below the surface of the
sea. The other dolphins waited, circling around the boat. After Aka had
reached a spot about half a mile astern in the boat's drift, he turned
again and swam back to the curious, waiting Wise Ones, Huk among
them.

"It's there," he said. "Very slight trace ... metal. Dolphins must ...
Aka must follow ... trace back until dolphins come to ... place where
man-from-boat, if man ... still alive ... and dolphins must move right
away. If ... sea starts ... move before ... wind, dolphins lose ... spoor,
although further away ... trace ... probably sunk ... some distance, so
... spoor ... more firm ... certain."

Huk declared, "Aka must lead ... Aka ... most sensitive of all
dolphins."

Aka agreed, "Yes ... Huk must stay with boat. Boat ... drifting south
toward ... Homeland rocks. Huk must accompany boat ... take half ...
males ... pregnant females ... nursing mothers ... calves with Huk.
Huk guard ... boat until Aka ... finds man-from-boat ... bring man
back, or until Aka returns to Huk without man ... Aka takes ... weaned
calves ... odd males ... other sixty adults with Aka ... form ... net, in
case Aka loses metal trace."

Upon receipt of Aka's signal the scouts came in, and the tribe divided
just as Aka had ordained. Then, as Aka admonished his search companions to be careful not to disturb the water close to him, they started
away, to spread out in a line, the calves interspersed among the adults—
ninety-one dolphins—and fanned out fast to take up positions 4 miles
apart, until they covered with their searching VHF beams the whole of
the sea surface in an area 372 miles wide, 12 miles fore and aft, and 6
miles deep. With Aka in the center of the line, as it spread out, slowly
they moved forward, all keeping time with their neighbor. Aka all the

while tasted his way along a spoor of chemical so fine and dispersed that the most modern instrument that man has yet produced would hardly be able to detect it. Aka moved forward at three knots all day until the chemical trace was down to ten feet below the surface. He signalled the dolphins close to him to relay the order to shorten the "net line" by half its width, and for the outriders to move ahead of the line and search the whole surface of the sea at speed, up to twenty miles north of him. Then, with the chemical trace too deep to be affected by surface current movements, Aka increased his speed slowly, to five knots . . . six knots . . . seven knots . . . and the whole dolphin search system moved forward with him.

When Aka moved off with the search party, Huk took command of the boat escort. He sent scouts out to guard a five-mile periphery and search for fish, while the remainder of his party, Kweela and Om among them, stayed close to the drifting boat. Some of the boat-escort now and then dived down to the black depths of the sea—right down to the very bottom two miles below—to search for squid with their sonar. Then, when the prey had been consumed they relieved the boat escort, so that they, in their turn, could search for fish and squid.

Three hours after Aka's party left the boat, a slight air lifted the genoa sail. Shortly after, as the dolphins watched, the boat started to move forward, very slowly at first, then she picked up speed. As the boat sent out a tiny rippling bow-wave the wind vane sought the wind, and it was soon in command of the boat, steering her south-southwest, across the track of the gentle breeze coming from east-northeast. The dolphins watched with their quick eyes, fascinated, as the genoa lifted, reluctantly at first, then bellied out, collapsed again, and bellied out again, and at last stayed filled with the light airs.

All afternoon long the boat sailed gently forward, with the dolphins all around it and playing in its bow-wave. All afternoon the boat slowly picked up speed, until she was making two and a half knots, holding her own against the half-knot northwesterly-going current, and moving due south, toward St. Paul's Rocks, which were slightly to the west of her true course, and by dusk, only forty miles away.

At dusk the gentle breeze died. The genoa collapsed and hung, sadly drooped again. The boat stopped dead in the water, and once again the current moved her slowly northwestward. All around, the dolphins dozed in groups in the gentle swells that raised and lowered the boat.

The night was calm and quiet, almost soundless, except for the low thudding of the genoa as it moved with the boat, the thin squeak of the mainsheet block as the main boom silently swayed to and fro, the lonesome clink of one tea mug against another as they swayed on their hooks over the galley sink, the lapping of the slight ruffles of water under the stern overhang, and the low, low tones of Noel Coward coming from the turned-down tape recorder . . . *"Don't put your daughter on the stage, Mrs. Worthington,"* the muted music rose through the still air, up toward the million shining stars suspended in the black, black night. But the dolphins could scarcely discern the pitch of the notes, so alien were they to their range of hearing. Those that did manage to hear something imagined that it was the boat talking or singing to herself, though they thought it strange that the boat should sing when she had no calf of her own, "And no man to sing to," said Huk.

The light airs rose again, this time from the northeast, two hours before the sun's first light purpled the eastern horizon. The dolphins were already awake. As they circled the boat slowly, making dark trails in the phosphorescent glow all about them, they amused themselves watching the genoa fill again, the boat start to move, the wind vane again take charge, and the boat steer herself. They swam at the same speed as the boat while they were near her, but sometimes a young one would feel frisky and head out into the distance, still within the ten-mile-wide circle protected by the scouts, and he or she sped out at high velocity, leaping and diving for a half hour at a time, but always returning to the escort grouped around the boat.

At the time the sun was about to peep over the horizon, one of the mature males, speeding out to relieve a scout, leapt in his joy at being free from the boat-escort, and at a height of ten feet in the air, sighted the rocks of his home far in the distance. Excited, he fell back into the sea with a great splash, sending a signal to Huk as he descended, all in a great flash and splatter. *"Atlantis ahead!"*

Within seconds twenty other mature dolphins and calves turned away smoothly from the boat, so as not to disturb the water around it, then, when they were a dozen yards away from the boat, they speeded off, leaping the while, to see the rocks of their nursing grounds, and sent back and to each other wild spasms of joy.

Soon Huk himself decided to take a look at the landfall. He gave a long look around the boat, dived down to about fifty feet, then swam fast, level, and straight, away from the spot under the moving vessel. He rose to the surface after a minute and made a mighty leap fifteen feet up above the sea surface, on top of a long swell. In a split second his eyes had directed themselves at the correct azimuth angle from magnetic north in the direction of where the rocks should be—and there they were, two low humps in the sea, shining brown in the low rays of the rising sun. Huk leapt again and again, whistling cries of greetings and delight, until he sensed the wind rising. He raced back to the now more quickly moving vessel.

The genoa sheet rope, as Huk watched it, tautened, and the genoa strained more and more as it drew the boat's hull forward faster and faster . . . and as she moved and increased speed, so did the dolphins, until soon they were thrusting and humping and pushing their tails at a rate of three knots . . . three and a half . . . four . . .

The boat heeled over to starboard and the wind vane worked more and more, keeping the boat steady on a broad reach from the wind, course now south-southeast. As the bow-wave worked up over the forefoot of the vessel, the dolphins, delighted, rushed for it, trying to move forward in it even before it was yet big enough to move their weight. Then they sank down, levelled out, and raced astern, rose to the surface and sped for the bows again and again, until at last the wave was big enough for them to play in it as they had done before, near the Island of the Whistling Men. Up and down the playing dolphins rolled, over and over, squeaking and whistling, until finally Huk himself gave in to the temptation and joined them in their frolics.

All the morning the boat sailed on, all the noontime, all the early afternoon, until the sun was almost down on the western horizon.

By the time the first faint shades of dusk were low in the western sky the boat had sailed herself almost forty miles since the first airs of the early morning and now, with the genoa billowing and the dolphins playing in the wave under the plunging, rearing bow, she raced ahead at four knots, *straight for the jagged teeth of the rocks of St. Paul,* directly ahead on the boat's course, only three miles away . . .

As dusk fell 118 miles to the north of St. Paul's Rocks, Aka, now diving and rising a half mile deep to follow the faint copper spoor, received a blurred high frequency sonar signal from the furthermost scout ahead. At first he could not make it out. He signalled again and again for the scout to repeat the message. Then it came back, still fuzzy, but clear enough to be understood—it was a holograph of a dozen sinister shadows, long and streamlined, with pointed noses and jaws that sometimes yawned wide open, and the shadows all circled another shape, even more fuzzy, but to Aka it was very like that of a man lying on his back on the face of the moving waters . . .

Chapter 16

THERE IS A POINT IN TIME and perception that is far beyond the realms of concern, anxiety, worry, fear, despair, anguish, or panic. It is even beyond the oft-anticipated but rarely encountered "moment of truth." It is the *point of purity,* and it is probably best known to small-craft solo sailors and lone mountaineers, some of whom have been on it for quite long periods of time. It is also a point known to various others, but usually they do not know it for very long: the crews and passengers of plummeting airliners, the bow-lookouts of two big ships in imminent headlong collision or a sky diver when his chute fails to open. It is the point at which it is realized that what can be done to resolve the problems resulting from a series of phenomena has been done, that there is no more that can be done, and that the situation is now in the hands of fate, destiny, or chance. Some call it being "in the hands of God." Others, who diligently seek the point in less adventurous, some might even say less dangerous, ways, might call it Nirvana. Many imagine that it is a state of bliss. More often it is a state of shocked paralysis.

Those who know the point of purity, those who have been on it, know that it is not a state of grace. They know that is the moment of realization of pure truth, that one is definitely alone in an infinite universe, and that one has no longer the comforting company of the choice of answering the first question raised in Hamlet's soliloquy.

Conan reached the point of purity about an hour after dusk, when he no longer even imagined that he saw *Josephine*'s pale sail, a taunting sprite on an unseeable horizon.

Conan had experienced the point of purity several times during his career at sea, and was no more enamored of it now than he had been the first time he had reached it, thirty-nine years before, off the North Cape of Norway. Therefore Conan did what would be bluntly expressed by his older, still rather Victorian, countrymen as "coming to his senses." He did it the only way that it can be done by a lone person: he placed all the blame for his predicament squarely where it belonged—on himself. This, over the ages, has been found to be as good a start to the solutions of personal problems as any other yet discovered. Conan figured it out simplistically—but when a man is alone, floating in mid-ocean, it is best to be simplistic.

"What a way to go!" Conan raved aloud at himself and the unanswering stars. "What a stupid, God-awful, insane, daft way to go—trying to catch a bloody old turtle in a dead-flat calm!"

That was the moment Conan came to his senses. Unbelievably even to himself, he laughed loud and long at the thought of his own carelessness.

When he stopped spluttering with bitter laughter, he reflected that the solutions to his problems were, as they always had been, three in number and simply expressed. First, he could change himself, but, except that he determined to keep his head, this did not in these circumstances apply. Second, he could change the nature of his situation; this was impossible. Third, he could remove himself from his situation; and this was the crux of the whole matter. He could remove himself, or he could be removed. He could remove himself only by suicide. That was against everything that Conan was or ever had been or ever would be, no matter how short his future. So he would have to encounter some force, circumstance, or phenomenon that *could* remove him. It was straightforward—either thirst and madness or another human being, either death or life.

He recalled the afternoon in the Red Lion pub in Sheridan Square. What was it Griffith Evans had said? If anyone knew about the basics of survival, Griffith did. He said the one thing he'd learned was the validity of somebody's—Heisen?—Heisenburg's Principles of Uncertainty. That was it. How did it go? "If three things might happen, one of them probably will. If it doesn't, then one of the other two might. But if not even this one does, then it's all on the last one. In the event of the last one not happening, which it might not, the experiment is best abandoned."

He lay for a while on his back, until the sun scorched him. "So that's it," he said aloud. "So that's it . . . life's an experiment. That's what Griffith was trying to tell me! But to prove what?" He thought again, staring at the steely sky over the vast humps of moving water. Then he murmured quietly, "That God has the privilege of telling us to mind our own bloody business, and get on with it, anyway."

He trod water, slowly. He dismissed the thought of the miles of water below him—the gloomy mystery—from his mind. He thought back over the events of the past few hours, trying to recall every little detail: the cold, appalling shock of his fall; the initial panic as he had realized that the boat was moving; the insane horror which had lent extra strength, at first, to his flailing arms; his mortification as the spinner tantalized and taunted him only yards ahead at first, then pulled away faster and faster; his despair at his own flagging strength as the image of the boat shimmered in the afternoon heat further and further away from him— a little bit further away every time he had raised his head to look at her; and his anguish as the dusk had finally veiled her, as if in kindness, or cruelty, he knew not which, as if to ease the pain of his fewer and fewer sights of her, or to turn the screw on his pain as she, now a wraith in the evening twilight, faded, then was gone, and he had fallen into utter despair at her abandonment of him to the careless sea.

Conan lay back to rest on the surface of the black, sparkling waters, his head thrown well back. He stared, fascinated, at the trails of brilliant phosphorescence all around him and below him; a billion minute constellations moving slowly on the undulating surface of the gleaming sea. He stared at the unblinking, unfeeling stars crowded in the eternal depths of the night sky. As he gazed he did what every reasonably intelligent distressed mariner has done throughout the millennia of human navigation at sea. He coldly counted his assets and carefully reckoned his chances. He did not do this suddenly—it took a good hour for the confusion in his mind to clear. Conan realized that his first asset was the comparative warmth of the water in which he was floating. If this had been the Southern Ocean he would have been dead hours before. Then he wondered if this was an asset or a liability. It might have been better . . . but he dismissed the dangerous thought and reckoned his situation.

Conan had a good idea of his approximate position. He knew that he had fallen overboard somewhere around 118 miles due north of the tiny, barren pair of islets right in the middle of the central South Atlantic named St. Peter and St. Paul, but commonly known as St. Paul's Rocks. He started to do a mental calculation of the possibilities of swimming for the rocks, but he soon abandoned it. Even if he could keep up a speed of one knot for five days (which he would need to), the current would sweep him, during the same five days, 118 miles or so to the west. St. Paul's Rocks were out.

Conan calculated his next best chance. Somewhere to the north of him, say half a day's sail, Mary Chatterton was steering *Flagrante Delicto* hard on what she probably imagined were Conan's heels. There was a slight—*wee* was the word that passed through Conan's mind—a wee possibility, one chance in a thousand or so, that Mary would pass close enough to Conan to see him and pick him up. But Conan was only too aware that what reduced the chances of rescue by Mary Chatterton to one in fifty thousand was whether or not she would be on deck as she passed him. What further reduced the chances of her rescuing him to one in a million was whether, even if she were on deck, she would be close enough to notice him.

Conan knew from his own experience at sea-searching for survivors of accidents—during the war and afterward, during yacht races especially—how difficult, how extraordinarily difficult it is to perceive the head of a human floating in the moving waters of the sea, even in a calm. The ocean is never dead-flat calm. There are always, even after weeks of windless days, moving hills and valleys of water. A human head is not much bigger than a fishing net float, and he himself rarely saw those until his boat was almost on top of them, and even then he saw them only momentarily, when they were on the breast or the crest of a wave.

Conan passed on to his next chance, even remoter than the first. Radio Dakar would report his silence to Lloyd's. Lloyd's might not take alarm for some days, though. They might consider that his radio on board *Josephine* was perhaps defective. Only after they had not heard from him for several days might they alert . . . what? The Brazilian air force? Perhaps the U.S. Air Force on Ascension Island, thirteen hundred miles to the southeast? Aircraft might locate *Josephine*, with some luck, in a matter of a few day's diligent searching of the ocean. It might be several more days before anyone was able to board her from a passing ship, or perhaps from a naval helicopter—with this Middle East nonsense there were more American and NATO naval movements now, not to mention the Soviets—around the shipping lanes to the Cape of Good Hope. But Conan dismissed the vision of Red Navy sailors hauling him on board their warship. By the time they had found *Josephine* and had searched the ocean to the north of her, he'd be long gone from thirst or madness, or both. Typically, and incredibly even to himself as the thought went through his mind, Conan wondered how long it would be before there was a satellite sensitive enough to pick up the temperature difference between the ocean water and the top of a human head.

Conan recalled again, as he slowly raised his head and trod water slowly, how he had, as usual when the wind was dead, not bothered his head about wearing a safety harness. He chastised himself over and over at the recollection of how he had hauled the steering gear-trip and safety line on board and had left it there. He cursed himself roundly for having been such a fool as to let the heat of the turtle hunt entice him into climbing over the stern rail. He even wondered if his return to a comparative sanity from the mad panic of the hopeless chase in the water during the day was a blessing or not. Perhaps it would have been better to have drowned right away? To have abandoned the experiment?

Even as the cold numbness crept over him and he started to shiver, Conan mentally seized the murmur of self-pity that was surfacing from somewhere deep within him, put a round turn and two half hitches on it, dragged it up onto the deck of his consciousness, heard it, judged it, hated it, and ditched it overboard. He realized now that self-pity had done nothing to subdue his anguish since the disaster, neither had it eased his own anger with himself for his stupidity in getting into this situation, and he told himself, as he had done a thousand times before in his life, that it would do nothing to solve his problem.

It had always been a tenet of Conan's faith—the rivets in his ship's sides—that there were far more profitable and worthwhile exercises to do than wallow in self-pity, so Conan reckoned his assets. First there was the fat he had gained from the good food and comparative lack of exercise since the start of *Josephine*'s voyage. That, he reckoned, would last him a fair forty-eight hours. Fresh water was the main problem, as always at sea. He had swallowed quite a bit of salt water when he fell overboard and as he swam after the boat in his panic. He would, he told himself, have to be very careful not to drink any seawater for as long as he could hold out, and after that to drink only a couple of palms a day, just enough so he did not consume more salt than his kidneys could deal with. In that way he might last out three days even, until he fell unconscious and drowned himself, fat and all. He thanked the fates that he was probably too far from land to be located and attacked by sea birds diving down from high above with their sharp, hungry beaks trying to tear chunks out of his head and shoulders, as happened often to castaways nearer land.

In any case, the end would not be too grim, he reflected, if only he could keep his head while there was still a chance that the night breeze might drop and that he might again see *Josephine* becalmed on the horizon in the daylight, or until he might be sighted by Mary Chatterton, or even by some other vessel, but he knew that the chances of that were highly unlikely in such a remote area of the ocean, so far from regular shipping lanes. One thing was absolutely certain, if none of these things happened, the increasing coldness as his body temperature lowered would eventually render him unconscious.

Conan trod water again, a steady, slow paddle. For some reason which he could not fathom, he was pleased that he had his waterproof Omega still on his wrist, and that he had given up smoking a year before. These two facts were not in themselves important, he realized, but he knew that in his situation any consolation was something to savor and hang on to. The watch was hardly necessary; after a month of living with the night stars he could tell time, give or take half an hour, by merely looking up and gauging the angles of the constellations above the eastern horizon. His first impulse, when he remembered the watch, was to think of it as a link with everything that was safe and secure, but after a moment's reflection he knew that this was nonsense. Nothing was safe and secure that was outside of his own head, and even there it was only so as long as he made a conscious effort to keep it so. The cigarettes, he remembered, he had given up at Ruth's insistence . . . and he grinned—all the while as he shivered in spasms hardly believing that he was grinning—as he reckoned on just how far up on his list of priorities, at that moment, was lung cancer.

Conan thought about Ruth at odd moments. He could feel an intense regret that he would never again be with her. He saw her in his mind's eye. Then, at one particular vivid image of her, he said aloud to himself, "Why not?"

His mind went back to his assets. He had his shirt and shorts. He decided that when the sun rose he would remove his shirt from his body and tie it over his head so it would protect him from the burning rays of the sun. This would save a mite of perspiration, prevent him from blistering, and he would be ready to wave the shirt if and when Mary Chatterton's boat passed him. He would be ready to wave it if *Flagrante Delicto* came within three miles of him. It was a small thing, it was a puny chance, but of such is the will to live, and with such have men done far more than merely saved them*selves.*

Then, as he laid his head back again to rest on his back and stare at the constellations, Conan coldly and calculatingly decided to fight for his life, even if the chances of survival were less than a billion to one. He made the decision calmly. He mulled it over in his mind, over and over. It was not only the thoughts of Ruth. It was not courage, it was not fear of death that brought him to his decision, it was something in his bones, in his blood, in the very depths of his heart. He tried to figure out what it was, but after long silent minutes of racking his head, as the black ocean swells, all gleaming with starlight and moonbeams and the twinkling trails of a million mysteries, moved him slowly up and down, he gave up searching for a reason and knew only that he was the way he was . . . and soon the sweet doze-salves eased his ache and whiled away his night, until the first purpling of the dawn over the achingly lonely sea and the sky.

It was the first time Conan had been in a sinking warship. What surprised him most was the *naked* violence of the explosions all around, and the calmness of the men. Leading Seaman Conan, as he scrambled down the crazily tilted ladder from "Y" gundeck, caught glimpses, through the thick black smoke pouring from where the destroyer's after-funnel had been, of dirty gray-painted bulkheads, lines, and hoses strewn all over the heeling iron deck, and the bodies of some of his shipmates all around, dead and dying. One was sitting calmly against a guardrail, holding his lower intestines in his hands. One, half of one leg blown off, was trying bloodily to crawl over the lifelines. There was too much noise to hear screams or moans. All around Conan men were shouting. Even their voices were drowned in the roar of steam escaping from the boilers, as it blew full power out of the pipes on the one remaining funnel.

Conan reached the ship's starboard side just at the moment that she was hit by another torpedo, somewhere forward. The ship lurched over another twenty degrees to port. As he and a dozen others jumped for a Carley float he caught a glimpse of flames amid almost solid black smoke as the forward funnel toppled. Then Conan was in icy-cold water, rising to the surface. He bobbed up right beside the Carley float and grabbed the cork bulwark. He heaved himself on board the ten-foot-long raft and was sick over the gray-haired head of Petty Officer Wilkes, who had hit the float head-on and smashed in his skull. When Conan boarded the float the only other live occupant had been a torpedoman, lying on the canvas bottom of the raft with one arm broken and lying uselessly under him. Within a minute eight other men and boys, all in oil-soaked overalls, with oil-caked heads, and oil-streaked antiflash gear, scrambled somehow into the frail rope-lashed raft. One of the filthy, wet-through, shivering arrivals looked for signs of life in Wilkes, and finding none, ordered him heaved over the side. "Get rid of this one, God save his soul," was all he said.

Conan wanted to protest, but when he found himself looking into the bloodshot eyes in the oil-smeared, haggard face of the ship's gunnery officer, who himself was streaming blood from his left sleeve, he was silent as the body was rolled over the raft side to the dirge of rumbles and roars and the screaming of a hundred men trapped by the holocaust below in the slowly sinking destroyer.

He couldn't remember how the raft had been paddled out so far into the night from the sinking ship. All he remembered was the cold, cold wind, and looking around over his shoulder and seeing the flames shooting high in the sky from the ship's boilers and lighting up the ever-creeping thick dull film of oil as it spread over the sea all around them, and reflecting from the terror-stricken eyes of oil-covered heads that somehow managed to swim through the oily sea. Some of them sank quietly even as he watched them. A half dozen managed to catch hold of the raft. Soon there eighteen men and boys depending for their lives on the buoyancy of a ten-foot contraption of bits of wood and rope. Those on the raft paddled out, digging away with the short paddles for all they were worth into the mucky slime on top of the freezing Arctic Ocean. All five of the hangers-on, one by one silently let go and sank. Then they heard a loud rumble. They paddled even more furiously. A low roar. Another vast sheet of flame shot up from their ship in her agony. Then they heard a shout from the sea, quite close.

"Hold on, lads!" the gunnery officer ordered quietly. "There's someone else . . . over there . . . okay . . . head for him . . . give way together."

They reached the shouting voice which came from a black head, covered in thick oil fuel. The head spluttered and spurted oil out of its mouth, and it shook, from side to side, as if in refusal.

"Grab a hold, man!" shouted the gunnery officer.

The lump of shiny black oil with eyes shook again, violently.

"What the devil's wrong with him?" the officer shouted testily, as he gazed again over his shoulder. "We'll have to get a move on—she's about to blow up any minute! Mahoney . . ." the officer turned to an able seaman, one of his own men, next to him in the raft "for Christ's sake grab ahold of the silly sod and drag him aboard if you can. . . . The rest of you paddle away for your lives. If she blows now the sea will be a raging inferno before we know it . . ."

They had started to paddle. Mahoney tried to grab the oil-smothered man in the water. Again the oily lump had shaken its head. It tried to lift something into the raft. It was a small box, just as oil covered as its bearer. Mahoney tried to grab the box, but it slipped from his hand. The man in the water held on to it . . . and then the ship, in one loud, deafening bang, blew up. The blast had blown the Carley float, and the 10 men in it, yards away from the spot where the ship had died a split second earlier. They managed to escape the worst of the oil fire on the sea surface, but several of them were badly burned and two died soon after they were picked up by their sister destroyer an hour and a freezing eternity later. They were the only survivors of a crew of 128.

On board the rescuing sistership, much later, when the convoy was only a day out of Murmansk, Conan had sought out Able Seaman Mahoney to ask him about the man with the box.

"Oh, that bloke?" replied Mahoney. "A funny bugger, that one. It was the civilian canteen manager. He was carrying the canteen cash-takings . . . and wouldn't let go. He shouted something to me when I tried to grab it off him, about *responsibility* . . . and now the poor bastard's dead as a dodo, ain't 'e? Burnt to a friggin' cinder . . . and all the akkers is at the bottom of the bleedin' oggin, ain't it. . . . Makes yer wonder, dunnit?"

"He got mixed up," said Conan. "Understandable, of course."

"Watchamean, Bill?"

"He meant *duty* not responsibility."

"Oh . . ."

As Conan dozed on his back the light breeze steadily died, until an hour before dawn the only sounds that he could hear in all that vastness of moving, gently sloped ridges of water were tiny splashes around his ears. For the rest, the world was silent, dead. Soon he heard a low drone overhead as the sky in the east lightened, and knew it was a transatlantic jet plane. He guessed from the direction of the sound, as he stared intently into the now roseate sky, that is was flying from Europe to South America. He waited in rising expectancy, even though he knew full well that the chances were that the plane would be far too high for him to see it. Then, as the hum neared and echoed from overhead, he turned himself around slowly in the sea, imagining that he was facing the plane, somehow placing himself nearer to it, closer to the humanity in the plane. He tried to imagine how it was on the plane, how the passengers were waking from their dozing and watching the dawn color of the sky. It would be a much longer dawn for them than it was for him, he reflected. They were flying with the dawn from east to west across the ocean, on their way to . . . what? Holidays? Visits from school? Business trips? They would have no idea that there was a condemned soul in the sea far below them, of course. . . . Hungrily Conan wondered what the plane passengers had eaten for breakfast. He strained his ears to listen as the plane's hum died in the southwest. Then he was alone again, all alone with the silent, heaving seas, which made no more noise than did the swift-lightening dawn. Conan turned himself around, treading water, so that the dawn was past his right shoulder and he was facing about north. He set himself to watch, every time a sea swell lifted him, over the whole horizon to the north, for Mary Chatterton's *Flagrante Delicto*. He anxiously watched on the rises and patiently waited when the sea dropped him down into a valley completely surrounded by other seas on all sides. As he watched and waited, watched and waited, he realized suddenly that he could not recall even what the color of *Flagrante Delicto*'s hull had been, though he remembered she was a ketch. She was the only ketch in the race, just as Mary was the only woman in the race ... which set him to thinking again about Ruth. His main thought now was regret that he had not insisted that she stay in Lisbon until the start of the race. He found the loss of even three days that he could have had with Ruth, and that he had let slip away, unforgivable.

At ten o'clock, when the sun was a blazing presence high in the silent sky, Conan carefully removed his shirt from his back and tied the collar around his head. He was careful to cover his shoulders, too, as best he could.

At eleven-twenty, something—the sense of a presence—made Conan turn to look behind him, toward the south. He saw a giant jellyfish only yards away from him, on the downward slope of the next sea. Conan quickly pushed the shirt back a little more securely and swam several yards to the east, so that the undulating, colorless monster with its ten-foot-long sting tendrils could pass him as it drifted and swam along with the current. Then he turned again to screw up his eyes against the sun's glare reflecting from a million ruffles on the seas as they heaved up and down, with a wary glance around him every few minutes.

Conan *felt*—the sky, the world was so profoundly silent he imagined at times he could *hear*—the sun pass over the brazen blue dome of the sky at noon, which was also marked by his sighting of two Portuguese men-of-war, large, tubelike creatures with the saillike membrane that they hold aloft over the sea surface to catch the breeze. Conan knew that they, too, have stingrays, but shorter ones than the jellyfish. As the afternoon passed on, hot and silent, he saw the long wavy glides of a few flying fish, and once, far away, the silvery flash of a leaping wahoo or swordfish.

Toward two-thirty, straining and wincing his eyes against the increasingly brilliant sea glare, he thought he glimpsed a white movement on the northern horizon; a mere suspicion of a shimmer of white above the blue silver—the hard silver of the heaving seas under the steely blue of the sky horizon. Excited and anxious, he waited for what seemed to him a century as one sea lowered him gently down into yet another watery glade between the moving ocean-hills and then lifted him slowly as the water under him formed its own hill yet again and held him aloft for a moment—which seemed to Conan no longer than a midge's breath—while he screwed up his eyes against the stabbing shafts of sunlight reflected from the ocean and peered to the north.

His heart leaped. *It was a sail!* Tiny, indistinct, hazy, far, far away, but it was there! He could only see it when the boat and he were on top of a sea, but the waiting now was spiced with hope, and as it was, so was he. Conan estimated that the tiny white blob he could sometimes see was the top of a mainsail, which was mostly below the horizon. The boat must be about five miles from him, and probably had a slight breeze. He was tempted to swim toward it, but judged it better to save what little energy he had remaining for when the boat came closer.

Even as he anxiously gazed for the boat every time a sea lifted him, and fretted until he saw it again, cat's-paws of the breeze appeared wafting over the very tops of the water hills. He checked the direction of the zephyr as best he could, against the direction of the sun. It was blowing from southeast. It might even be the forerunner of the trade wind. Silently, Conan waited, now and then sucking the water from one shirt sleeve to relieve his worsening thirst and a thick, dry, salty tongue. By now the skin on his hands and feet was beginning to tighten up with the prolonged immersion. He did not yet feel very hungry.

At three o'clock the wind had risen a little more, and the sail was nearing. Conan's hopes rose with the breeze.

At three-thirty he estimated the sail was no more than three miles away. At four o'clock she was only two and a half miles, near enough for Conan to see as she rose on a swell that she was indeed a ketch and she had a white hull. At four-thirty Conan untied his shirt and started waving it slowly over his head whenever the boat and he were within sight of each other. Patiently and eagerly, Conan waved his shirt and a few times he even shouted "Over here!" when the swell raised him.

At five o'clock Conan was still shouting and waving, but with tears in his eyes and his voice a pitiful croak. The ketch had changed course when she was only a mile and a half from him. He had seen a tiny figure on the ketch's stern as she took up her new course. It only made sense for Mary Chatterton to steer southwest, so as to get full advantage of the slight breeze and to avoid St. Paul's Rocks, thought Conan, but why in the name of God hadn't she waited another half hour, until she had passed the spot where he was?

Disappointment is easier to bear when a person is alone. There is no one else to blame, no other shins to kick, but Conan was not alone any longer, and as the ketch changed course while he watched in anguish, Conan cried loudly and waved hysterically, all to no purpose. Conan felt as if he could murder Mary Chatterton. He shouted and waved until the ketch was about three miles away, then he fell bitterly silent. He watched it, tinier and tinier, as it disappeared over the horizon until, at last, it was gone, and all hope with it.

He was silent until the dusk shadows again darkened the western horizon and the blood red sun sank to the line. Then as the last light of day crept away and hid, he stared with bloodshot salt-stung, sore eyes in a blistered face as tiny fish started to bite at his legs while he ever more feebly kicked them away and in horror watched a half-dozen triangular fins slide through the calm waters nearby. Conan exclaimed quietly, "Oh my God . . . not yet!"

A gray fin approached. Terrified at first, Conan could see the long streamlined shadow in the water below it. He kicked the water fast with both feet. The fin slid away. Conan took heart. Another fin approached. He kicked another kick . . . another retreat. So the deadly game of tag went on over the dusk twilight time, in an eerie silence, broken only by the noise of Conan breathing as he splashed the water, kicked with his feet, and beat with his hands whenever a fin menaced him or whenever small fish nipped at his legs.

Conan spent the time until after dusk almost dead with fatigue and thirst. He heard and glimpsed quick, noisy commotions in the waters nearby, in several places.

After dead silence for another hour, and after two days of horror and a night of unimaginably terrible stress, Conan, his body skin now dead white and wrinkled like old soap, his head and shoulders burned almost black and covered with blister sores, passed again into a state of semiconsciousness, uncaring now if the fins came or went. Floating up and down he surrendered himself to the heaving fields of silver-streaked gleaming blackness, while the tiny fish nipped his feet as his instinctive jerks against them grew feebler and feebler.

Chapter 17

IT WAS KWEELA who first realized that the boat was on a collision course with the rocks. In their joy at having returned at last to their ancient home, all the other dolphins of the boat escort gamboled and played, rolled, tossed and leaped in the bow-wave, even when the rocks were only two miles ahead. The outriders, now they were back above a familiar sea bottom, raced about in all directions, rising and leaping, falling and diving in orgies of homecoming delight.

The boat danced and jiggled on, her genoa sail still pulling well, even in the diminishing after-dusk breeze. Her steering-gear wind vane monitored the wind direction and steered accurately the deadly course, straight for the rocks—low black humps, their tops worn smooth by the ocean winds and seas over the eons of time since the mid-ocean ridge had slowly capsized between shifting tectonic plates and the waters of the world had risen until the two tiny islets were all that was left of Atlantis.

It was Kweela who, still fending off a complaining Om, stayed apart from the merrymaking around the boat's bow and swam on the surface. It was she who saw the black shapes ahead on the lighter horizon, and it was Kweela who raised the alarm, and whose narrow high-frequency signal penetrated Huk's awareness and finally dragged him away from the fun of the bow-wave.

As Huk raced across to Kweela he spun his head around rapidly, and by the time he reached her his brain had calculated the problem. He "ordered" all the dolphins around the bow to push the boat away from its course, so that it would head southwest. This a group of adults tried to do by bearing with their snouts against the port bow, but even though the boat waivered a little off course, the strength of the genoa and the steering gear made her insist on returning to a course heading for the rocks. The area of the port bow that the dolphins could push was too small for their number.

Huk considered the problem for a matter of a second or so. He told the remaining adults and the calves to push against the starboard quarter of the boat, so that the two groups heaving against the boat's hull in different directions would make her tend to pivot on her own axis in the water. Immediately Huk transmitted the hologram picture of what he wanted them to do to twenty adults and fifteen of the older calves, who raced around the stern of the boat and swam at the quarter, as if to ram the hull. Om found himself on the very end of the line of speeding dolphins, heading directly for the silently, slowly wagging underwater trim-tab of the self-steering gear. In seconds the other dolphins had their shoulders and snouts hard against the boat's hull, pushing with their tails to shift the boat's stern around, and Om had collided with the trim-tab. Om's 180 pounds, speeding at twenty knots, collided with the tiny rudder, knocked it askew, bent the pintle which connected it to the rest of the gear, and put the steering gear right out of commission, seized up solid. As the dolphins heaved against the plunging hull, the boat swung around. Now there was no resistance to their efforts, no continual attempt by the boat to return to the southerly course. The dolphins worked against the bow and stern, in opposite directions, until Huk got a western star in line with the boat's heading. Then, under Huk's flashed signals, the two groups laid on and eased off, to keep the vessel heading southwest, until she was a hundred yards to the west of the rocks and in still waters, out of the current and out of danger of collision.

While Huk guided the boat-steerers, he calculated to himself that if the boat continued to move at this rate, they would all be heading southwest until the wind dropped. He had recognized that it was the sail that caused the forward movement, and he knew that the wind worked the sail. He rose and leapt to inspect the sail again, and as it heaved on its sheet Huk recognized how power was transmitted from the sail to the boat's hull. As soon as the boat was in the lee of the rocks, to the northwest of the black humps, he swam around to the starboard side of the hull and leapt for the genoa sheet rope. He did not need to leap far— only six feet above the surface of the sea. With his quick eyes he searched for the rope against the bright stars in the black sky, but it was his short-distance acoustic echo signal that found it—all in a millionth of a second. His beak, already open, snapped shut on the sheet line, the conical teeth bit through it, Huk let his weight drag the fag ends of the rope down with him, and knew that it was broken clean in two. The breeze flung out the genoa sail right away before it. The sail flapped and fluttered free in the wind, powerless, and within a matter of a minute the boat stopped dead in the water.

The dolphins set to, again under Huk's directions, to push the boat's hull closer and closer to St. Peter's Rock, the westernmost one of the two islets, to get her into even calmer, even more protected water. Soon, yards from the granite hump, only as high above the ocean as a house but half as deep as Everest below, the boat sat peaceful and still, guarded by the dolphins. She sat silently, except for the soft jiggle of the steel hanks on the forestay as the breeze gently breathed on the genoa and moved it, fluttering like a nervous ghost in the bright moonlight, against the mainmast, and the now slow, long-drawn notes rising from the tape deck as it drew the last electricity from a run-down battery—"Doooont . . . puuuut . . . yooouuur . . . daauuughter . . . oooonnn . . . thhheee . . . staage . . . Miissssuusss . . . Wwooorthhiiinnnnggtoonn . . ." The tones were in such a low acoustic range that now the dolphins could feel the vibrations of the sound waves as they passed through the boat's hull. Some of them thought that the boat was crooning to them. They laid their long lower jaws against the hull and groaned back at her some of their millions-of-years-old dolphin nursing-songs of care, affection, and love, and pressed their beaks at the hull bilges, and caressed the iron keel gently with their tender flippers to calm the boat's fears and soothe her loneliness.

One hundred and eighteen miles north of St. Paul's Rocks, Aka ordered the reporting scout to return to him. Then, relaying the signal through closer intermediaries, Aka commanded all the wide-flung search schools to swing to the southwest and hurry in a long wide arc around the prowling sharks, so that they could attack from upstream in the current, thus avoiding detection by the sharks' acute sense of smell until the last second.

Swiftly, in bursts of speed up to thirty knots, the dolphins swung to obey the command, while Aka and the now returned lone scout surfaced, took a tremendous gulp of air, and dived deep, deep. Then they passed at speed directly under the ring of prowlers and their intended victim. As they shot through the darkness under the tense scene above, Aka and his companion fixed the general location of every moving and living body above them, innocents, predators, and victim, with their low-frequency acoustic waves. Each body was located, and its speed, depth, and direction of movement was calculated. They moved their heads in the direction of each slowly gliding shark, and beamed its sinister shape with their high-frequency sonar to reckon accurately the size and weight of each one of the six prowlers. By the time they shot up at a shallow angle to surface, they were two miles upstream of the sharks.

Aka was satisfied for the time being. If the sharks detected their presence, they would think that they were only two, and not detect the other two dozen dolphins now speeding around them on the western flank.

Aka and the scout waited for a few minutes, carefully monitoring every move of the sharks as they slowly closed their prowling circle around the man, and watching as the man kicked the water each time a prowler approached him. As the sharks became more and more bold, each time approaching the prey a little closer, so Aka and his companion moved a little closer to the man, until they were but half a mile from him, with their narrow sonar beam directed continually upon him, while their all-direction, low-frequency acoustic "dome" kept watch on the sharks.

Soon the fastest of the flanking dolphins began to join them and as they arrived Aka grouped them off into parties of four, three adults and one calf to a party. With the fours all grouped together, as the remainder of the flankers streamed in at speed, Aka ordered them into backing-up pairs, each pair to watch over two attack groups and to assist whichever party needed them. He ordered the whole half of his tribe to the attack, with himself and his companion taking up the rear as the dolphins surfaced, gulped air, and shot off, all together, all no more than three inches from his or her neighbor as their flailing tails propelled them forward at high speed down at a sharp angle. When they reached two hundred feet, the attacking dolphins levelled off and glided along for an eighth of a mile, until they were, each group, directly below the shark that Aka had chosen for them.

Up they sped, up, up, straight at the yet unaware sharks still lurking just below the surface of the sea swells. Aka and his scout made for a spot only ten feet below the man, where they braked their ascent in a millisecond and hovered, swimming slowly, to guard him.

As each attack group of four dolphins, each perfectly synchronized in speed of approach with all the others, reached a distance only five feet from each sinister shape, all the attackers clamped shut their beaks hard

and with an extra-powerful downbeat of their tails, they rammed, all together, right into the soft underbelly of each shark, their beaks penetrating up to eight inches into the guts of the predators. They ruptured the
liver, spleen, and kidneys of the fishes and, in seconds, left them, all six
of them, dead in the water and upside down, slowly sinking to the black
bottom two miles below.

The classical dolphin shark-attack was all over in a matter of half a
minute, all in utter silence.

Soon the dolphins were themselves slowly swimming around the man
in a circle, about three hundred yards away from him. Aka and his lieutenant then rose to the face of the sparkling heaving sea, about a hundred yards away from the man, to circle him even closer and to form
the first of the series of night guards for him. The rest of the dolphins
formed dozing schools and their own guards to while away the night,
until the first suggestions of light tinted the black sky in the east, fore-
telling the blazes of colors that would shortly put the night sky and the
stars to hiding in shame.

At the first light of dawn Aka sent one of his three Wise Ones to look
closer at the man and to approach him without touching him. The Wise
One slowly swam toward the dozing man on the surface, while Aka and
all the other dolphins watched with their sonar from three hundred
yards away.

The hundred shades of the dawn on the horizon were reflected in a
million ripples on the slopes of the moving water-hills as the Wise One
slowly moved closer to the floating body, now in a vale, now atop a rise.
When the Wise One reached a spot only ten feet from the man, he
stopped, and nervously beamed the human with his short-range acous-
tics. He "saw" the now empty belly, he "saw" the thickened tongue, and
he "saw" the twitches and gasps in the man's brain. The Wise One
moved his hologram reception down, down, searching for the man's emanations. He moved it down to the average adult dolphin's range—there
was nothing. He moved it to the reasonably intelligent calf's range—still
a blank. The Wise One then tried the baby range—the level of a new-
born dolphin—and there he found something. He concentrated, his narrow sonar beam all the while directed at the man's brain. It was a fuzzy,
blurred movement. The Wise One changed his frequency down to below that of a born dolphin, to that, almost, of a month-old dolphin fe-
tus—and the picture cleared. As the holograms came to life in the Wise
One's brain, so he transmitted them back to Aka, on the Wise Ones'
wave length, about 150,000 hertz above that of a man.

Aka saw many, many people in a place like a cave, but with straight walls and a flat floor and a white top. The people were all sitting on strange pieces of wood, all looking at other people sitting on a raised section of the cave floor. In front of the sitting people other men had big boxes on legs, which cast a bright light on the people on the platform. Aka gazed closely at one of the men on the platform. It was the man-from-boat. He knew it was the man from the color of his beard and from the pattern of his brain waves. The other man's hair and face and body covering were all a different color. The other man's hair was a bluish white, his face was softer and ruddy pink, and his body covering was a blue gray. The two men were making noises with their mouths, which Aka knew was the way that men communicated with each other. Suddenly, as Aka watched, the people sitting on the pieces of wood and the men with the boxes all hit their hands together and made louder noises with all their mouths. The ruddy-faced man stood up, waved his arms, and the strong lights went out, as he walked off the platform at the end of the cave and disappeared behind something that moved rather like a fishing net, but it seemed to be solid.

As Aka, puzzled, watched, the man in the water stirred and the hologram before Aka changed into the sky above the surface of the sea. When the man opened his eyes the Wise One reduced his buoyancy and sank silently below the surface. Then he turned and swam back to Aka.

"Strange," said Aka, as the Wise One reached his side.

"It must be a tribal meeting he was at—perhaps he is one of their Wise Ones?" suggested the Wise One.

They had kept Conan in the green room until last. He had watched the closed-circuit television as he sipped another whiskey and soda. He had absent-mindedly gazed at the female singer, who was not bad at all, if only her song had a bit more sense in it. Then had he watched the doctor who talked about kidney transplants, and the French acrobat who spoke very bad English and was shy. Then there was the woman who had looked a heavily painted sixty in the green room and now, on the screen, appeared a glib, cynical, much-married thirty, and held, as far as Conan could see, the men in her life as objects of ridicule for the audience to gloat and chuckle over. And all the while he had watched the Interviewer, listened to his impertinent questions, watched his calculating eyes. Now it was Conan's turn.

"You'd better hurry, five minutes isn't long to promote two books. . . . " said the girl.

Suddenly he was being hustled out of the green room, through a curtain, with bright lights shining in his eyes, and climbing onto a low platform, where he found himself sitting in the inquisition chair.

"And now, folks we have real-life . . . er . . . a sailor . . . er . . . Bill Conan . . . er . . . he's written three books . . ."

Conan said, "Two," but the Interviewer took no notice.

". . . yeh . . . here they are . . . *Ocean Fever* an' . . . er, yeh . . . *The Flying Dutchman* . . . heh heh, well . . . now Bill, tell us about your worst moments at sea . . ." The Interviewer looked at him trenchantly, as a gourmet looks at a juicy sirloin steak.

"Well . . . I suppose when I've had to take my own teeth out at sea . . ."

For a moment the Interviewer was nonplussed, then delighted. He showed his teeth as if he were metaphorically rubbing his hands together. He leaned forward and asked in a treacly confidential tone, "Say, Bill how'dja happen to hear of my show?"

"Oh . . . that . . . ?" Conan replied poker faced, in an innocent voice. "Well, you see, I was sailing around New Guinea, and I met up with this Australian district commissioner and he invited me to a banyan party, see . . . ?"

The Interviewer's face lit up with expectancy as if a course of succulant trout were being laid before him. There was a hush so solid among the audience that Conan imagined if he reached out he would be able to touch it.

". . . and he took me into the jungle, up in the hills, and the locals laid on a big feast. They had bones in their noses and they had singing and all the girls and the blokes dancing . . . and then we all set to, eating. We had piles of fruit and yams and roast pork . . ."

"That was really something, eh?" the Interviewer showed his teeth.

"Yes, and then we set off back to the coast, and I thanked the Aussie bloke for taking me along . . . and he asked me how I enjoyed the food . . . and I said, 'Great . . . especially the roast pork, and the Aussie said, "That wasn't roast pork, cobber, that was *long pig* . . .' "

There was a slight expression of puzzlement on the Interviewer's face.

". . . that's what they call a cooked human. When they die they bury 'em and dig 'em up after three or four days . . . ." Conan explained.

The Interviewer's face frowned deep lines on his brow. Then his eyebrows shot up as if his taste buds had just encountered a dainty morsel. "Yeah . . . ?" He wiggled on his chair. "An' what happened . . . ?"

"I spewed up all over the jungle floor."

The teeth breathed in hard, then expelled breath. "YEAH . . . ?"

"Yes . . . and the Aussie turned to me, all sunburn and topee, and he said in his Queensland drawl . . ."

There was a silence in the studio that could have been carved into small pieces and sold throughout the length and breadth of the land of the free. Conan continued in a loud deliberate voice, ". . . he said, 'That's nothing, mate, if you think that was a cannibal feast, *you wait 'til you get onto the Geoff Muffin show!'* "

Conan had hardly gotten the last words out when the whole studio had broken into an uproar. There had been whooping, cheering, and clapping from all the audience and loud laughter from the cameramen, the electricians, and all the other "guests." Muffin had thrown his head back stiffly as his face turned purple, then he had stood up and waved his arms over his head. "STOP THE SHOW!" he had shouted. The lights faded out, and the studio dissolved and Conan, his mouth twitching as he tried to grin with his cracked lips, opened his eyes and again pleaded with the cold stars above him—but they had been merciful to him before the approaching torture of another day of heat and blinding glare on the sea. As he closed his eyes he knew it had been his last night alive.

The dolphins dozed until the late dawn, when the sun was already climbing toward his noonday perch. Again Aka sent the Wise One over to check the man. Again the Wise One found the man's wavelength and again he transmitted the hologram back to Aka. Again Aka saw another crowded room, but this time the people sat at white boxes and seemed to be eating with strange shiny things in their hands to pick up the food and put it in their mouths. There was another human with the man. It was a female human and there were wooden carvings on the wall which looked like boats' hulls to Aka, but they were very small. The woman was talking to the man in between eating her food and putting a white thing up to her mouth, which had vapor rising from it. After a few minutes the scene blanked out again and again the man stirred and opened his eyes and mouth. The Wise One did not know if he made a noise. His hearing range was concentrated on other sounds in the ocean, up to six miles away, as he sank and returned to report to Aka.

Conan glanced at his wristwatch. "Early." He reached for the parcel Ruth was carrying and put it beside his chair.

"Don't drop my skates, Conan." Her voice was husky and low. She kissed him.

"So what's happening?" Ruth, quietly. She placed a hand on Conan's arm. She wore a tailored suit, gray with green trimmings.

Conan passed the cable to her.

Ruth quickly donned a pair of fashionable oversize glasses and read it. "And you've accepted."

"There really wasn't time to discuss—I had to get a cable away fast, so that Houghton would get it in time . . ."

"How long's the race?"

"It's the *Sunday Globe* race. . . . There's a fifty-thousand-pound prize—"

Ruth, smiling. "What's that in real money?"

"A hundred and eighteen thousand dollars . . . that's the prize."

Ruth drummed her fingers on the table and stared at Conan. She said, "But what about your writing, Bill? You've written four books since you came to New York. . . . You're becoming better known. You can ask for much bigger advances now. . . . You can probably ask for a twenty-thousand-dollar advance on your next book. Why do you have to go on this stupid race? How long is it for, anyhow?"

Conan finished his beer. (He stirred in his coma and threshed his head from side to side, until the water in his nostrils steadied him again.) "It's round the world, nonstop, Lisbon to Lisbon."

Ruth opened her mouth slightly and stared at Conan. She winced. "Say that again, Conan . . . slowly. My adrenaline is getting in my ears."

"Round the—"

"Yes, come on, Bill."

"It's a tremendous chance for me to . . ."

"Prove yourself?" Ruth, quietly, sharply. "Jesus Christ, Conan, you're fifty-six years old. You've just about done everything. You've proved yourself time and again. All your life you've been proving yourself, all the way from—what was it?—ordinary seaman to lieutenant, Royal bloody Navy . . ."

"Please, Ruth."

"All that time at sea . . . in small sailing boats . . . how many years was it?"

"Twenty-two."

"And you still haven't had enough?"

"That was mostly delivery trips. . . . This race is something really special . . ."

"What about us, Conan?"

Conan laid down his knife and fork and took a swig of beer (his head threshed again, but weakly). Her eyes were beautiful. "It's only for a few short months, Ruth. . . . Just this one last time . . ." He looked briefly away from her. There were two males, both in their mid-thirties, one bearded, the other heavily mustachioed, both dressed in black leather caps and jackets, both heavily festooned with chains. He looked back at Ruth. Their eyes met again. She smiled. Conan looked away from her again, to three blank-eyed steers making their way to a table. Suddenly, one of the prime Texas beef steers noticed Conan watching him. The animal glared at him in sullen hostility.

"Is it the danger, Conan?"

"Partly . . . there's that, too. Have to be independent, Ruth. The way I was brought up. Just don't ever want to have to be in the situation of asking you for anything . . ."

"Earn good money writing?"

"Yes, but I *am* a hundred and fifty-six . . . never get a chance like this again, Ruth. . . . Not for a big race . . ."

"How long is this race, anyway?"

"Looks like it'll be around ten months."

"You're mad, Conan. You know that? Do you realize you're absolutely stark-raving sane? But I love you, you sane, off-the-wall bloody limey!"

"It's all right with you, then, Ruth? You can come to Lisbon with me?"

"No, it's not all right, Conan, and you goddamwell know it, and yes, I'll come . . . and I might *just* be here when you get back. Why do you do it, Conan? Don't you know, can't you get it into that stupid head of yours that the time for heroes is long gone? Why the hell couldn't you be a—a yacht club race-coordinator, for God's sake, or—or—a—a—a castle pheasant keeper? . . ."

Conan glanced at the old half-model hulls on the wall, their varnish now dulled with years of exposure to the steam and smoke of the restaurant. The vision of a blackboard flashed by . . . on it was chalked in big letters: . . . *the subtlety, the flexibility, the mystery of sail—the infinite variety and the incalculable complexity of the forces that are harnessed to serve the sailor's purpose: the wayward wind that resists all mastery, the would-be bitch sea, the frail, fierce phantom which is the ship herself, and which is always something more than the sum of her myriad parts. Her power, at the same time restraining and urgent—the sleek, reluctant beauty of her hull under the dominion of the mute sails she wears* as she sails away from you, further and further . . . and further away from you . . .

Conan returned to semiconsciousness, and again he tried to part his cracked lips, as the sun commenced to slowly crucify him.

Aka said to all his dolphins. "Dolphins must save man . . . like Sea Kings rescued dolphin's ancestor Aye-ee. Prepare carry man. Lift man out of the water to warm and feed man first . . . not too much digested fish juice . . . Aka will taste dolphin's way back to boat . . ." The maturer of the adult dolphins started to move in the man's direction slowly, but Aka called them back. "Be gentle with man," he ordered. "Not swim too fast. Warm man in sun at intervals. Treat man as dolphins would one of dolphin's own wounded. Wise One swim ahead of man . . . make best slip-stream . . . one under man's back. One at each side. Hold man so man faces forward . . . upward all time, and dolphins must keep man's head above water."

Obediently, the dolphins all moved toward the man, and as they did so they remembered their ancient friends, the Sea Kings of Atlantis, and how the Sea Kings had rescued Aye-ee, the common ancestor of them all.

Chapter 18

CONAN SAW THE PURPLE SAILS just as the sun slowed over his meridian. When he first sighted them he thought they were Chinese junk sails. They had almost the same odd look about them, the obcordate shape of a leaf with its root and tip chopped off. All had a symbol on them—a circle around a cross. When he could see the hulls, however, Conan realized that the ships were not anything like Chinese junks below the sails. The hulls were long and finely cut by the bows as they cleaved toward him at an amazing speed, considering the little amount of wind. These hulls had more the shape of a tea clipper than a junk, and they were making at least ten knots.

As the purple sails and white hulls of the three ships drew closer and closer to him, Conan heard the music of trumpets. He looked the ships over with his sailor's eyes. All three vessels seemed to be constructed exactly alike, except that one was slightly larger than the other two, whose waterlines he reckoned at two hundred feet length. He followed the graceful sheer of the deck line from the bow, clear of all protuberances such as bowsprits and forestays, and inspected it as it swept back aft in a lovely flowing curve all the way to the finely rounded, slightly overhung stern. He could see three long deckhouses on each vessel, one on the stern, one a little forward of the after house, and one amidships. The three masts on each vessel were very thick—he immediately assumed they must be hollow—and shorter than the masts a square-sailed brig of the same length would carry. Also, he noted with surprise, they were completely unstayed. Just as on a Chinese junk rig, there were none of the forest of wires and cables that a Western ship would carry to support the masts.

One of the smaller ships sailed on toward him, leaving the other two to stand off. As Conan stared at the two stopped ships, he wondered at their purple sails. Instead of hauling them up to the yards, or dropping them onto the boom, as all the ships he knew did, these sails opened up in horizontal panels so that the breeze blew through them instead of against them. Each sail had, he counted, twelve panels, and each panel opened and closed exactly like the slats of a venetian blind.

Conan returned his gaze to the small vessel which was heading to him. She was steering from much more downwind toward him than he would have done. She was almost a mile away from him, to his northwest. Conan calculated that she was much too far from him and she would have to make another tack to reach him, but to his amazement the craft, when she was directly downwind from him turned on her axis and sailed *directly into* the wind, with the leading edges of her sail panels, which Conan could now clearly see were airfoil shaped, continually changing their attitude to the breeze. It reminded Conan of the flap-working of a plane on landing or takeoff.

As the vessel sailed directly to him, right into the eye of the wind, Conan listened for the sound of an engine. There was none. There was the music of harps and trumpets coming from somewhere on deck, and he heard voices in the far distance.

Conan watched the ship creep closer and closer. His eye caught the varied colors of flowers on the tops of the deckhouses. He saw the waving fronds of trees around them. He noticed that the ships had birds of brilliant plumage flying over them, and that the ship was accompanied by many dolphins and porpoises, who kept orderly ranks as they swam slowly round and round the hull. Then, for a moment terrified, he saw the black and white shapes of two killer-whales just ahead of the boat and to each side of her bows. But his concern soon faded when he saw that the killers were gently moving among the other dolphins in the sea all around. He looked up, wearily, at the brightly colored pennants flying from the mastheads of all three masts, and saw that they were gold and blue. Blue and gold—the Atlantic colors.

For a moment or two, as a sling hovered—magically it seemed to Conan—over him, he submerged. In the clear waters he saw the bottom of the ship, all the way from stempost to stern. He saw that there was no rudder—that these ships were steered by two large fins which projected out of the hull on each side, amidships. Along the sides of the hull, deep below, around the bilge, were long panels of crystal, which looked like underwater windows, and there were underwater doors in the hull, which as he watched, opened and admitted a dolphin and a swordfish into the ship, then closed again. Conan, out of breath and dozy, surfaced again.

By this time Conan was too weak to lift his head to gaze up at the high bows of the ship, which had stopped only feet away from him, but he guessed that the airfoil sails were holding the vessel as steady as a rock on one geographical point, just as surely as if she had been anchored. He was almost too exhausted to lift his head when the net-sling from the ship's foredeck surrounded him gently as he lay in the water and slowly started to hoist him on deck. As the sling rose, Conan's head and legs did not droop down. Conan was dozily aware that this was strange . . . and that he had landed on the ship's deck, that there were people around him, that they seemed to move and speak very, very slowly, that they were speaking in a strange language which seemed to be mostly vowels—then everything went hazy white again and he lost consciousness.

The first thing that Conan saw when he woke was a surface made of very fine fibers. He looked at it again. He moved his legs and the blurred deckhead above him swayed. He was, he found, in a hammock. He tried to raise his head to look over the hammock sides, but he was still too weak. He lay back and listened to the softly playing music, which reminded him a little of old Inca music he had heard a Peruvian Indian band playing once, long before in Callao. It sounded as if there were three flutes and two or three stringed instruments, and the music had the haunting quality of traditional Indian music of South and Central America, yet it had very little of its sadness. As he listened vaguely to the music something puzzled Conan. He still seemed to be in water. The hammock seemed to be suspended in water. The water was over his head. It was, he thought, the water that was causing his weakness, that prevented him from lifting his head on his neck. He turned his eyes downward . . . and saw the two flukes of his tail twitch slightly against the end of his tank, and felt the soreness on the inside of his flippers and realized why the people on deck had seemed to move so slowly. Conan blacked out again.

The people came to look at the wounded dolphin often. They were tall men and women with sunburned faces, and most of the men sported long, thin beards. Some of them, who seemed to be deferred to by the others, were dressed in silver suits of a sheer texture, over which they wore long black cloaks down to their sandaled heels, and tall conical hats over their long hair.

These men and women at first slowly, so slowly, prodded and probed Conan's flipper pits and other external organs, then fed him warm fish stew through long, clear tubes that were neither plastic nor glass, but that looked very like the stems of sea kelp, in some way strengthened, but still flexible and rubbery.

Other men and women wore round hats with flat tops, a little like those that college faculties and graduates wear on special occasions, and brilliantly colored long-tailed shirts over dark knee-length pants. They wore their hair shorter than the people who wore conical hats, but it was yet well over their ears. Some of them wore earrings and a few had tattoos. These were obviously sailors, and their hard-muscled arms and shoulders—even of some of the women—attested to their active, healthy lives. These people came by the tank and made a fuss of Conan, cooing to him in their strange consonantless language, while he tried to count the number of accents they had to each vowel they uttered, but got to five and gave up.

There were many women on board the ship. They were not treated by the men with any deference it seemed, except for their position in the ship's hierarchy. Sometimes the women brought children to see Conan as he lay in his tank, now rapidly recuperating from his exhaustion, and he twiggled his tail a little to the children's delighted laughter.

As the afternoon wore on and the shadows of dusk crept over the sky that Conan could see through wide, open portholes, lights lit up on board the ship. They were not oil, nor electric. They seemed to be some kind of very bright phosphorescent liquid which ran through transparent pipes all around the deckhouse bulkheads. Two men and a woman gazed down into his tank. Conan stuck his furry ears above water level to listen to them as they spoke with each other.

"O ah ah ee oo?" From the rising tone it was obviously a question.

"Ah oh ah ah ah ..." The reply. It sounded like a music scale.

Conan listened for a while, then settled down again halfway under water, breathing softly through the blowhole in his head, and wiggling his tail, glad to feel again the strength returning to his body. Now and then he blew a little geyser into the air, but most of the time he dozed in the swaying hammock in the huge fibrous water tank.

The following morning, after dawn lit up the sky and the tubes of liquid light had been darkened, Conan felt much better. He stirred and tried to swim in the hammock, but it was too constricting. He looked again, rather proudly, at his tail, seven feet away from his eyes, and chortled at a young woman who was looking down at him. She slowly touched his beak, he stuck his head right out of the water and rubbed it against her hand. As he did this he suddenly saw inside his head the *inside of her skull*!

He turned his head down, following the woman's spine and her ribs all the way down to her stomach, and saw that her appendix was inflamed. It was causing tension in her stomach. He tried to talk to the woman, but all that issued were some high-pitched squeaks from his blow hole. He pushed urgently against her hand, time and time again. Then she said something to him in vowels, and took her hand away, and left him.

Moments later she was back with one of the conical-hatted men. He whistled at Conan. At first it made no sense to him, but then he knew that the man was asking him what was the matter.

Conan tried to talk. It all came out as a very high pitched whistle.

The man smiled at him and nodded as if he understood. Then he whistled back to Conan. "It's all right, we know about Ehe-ehe's appendix—old Ah-uoh is our ship's diagnostician. You mustn't try to take over his job . . . you're too young still!" The man was silent for a moment as he smiled gently at Conan. Then he whistled, "It's all right, don't fret; she's to have it attended to as soon as we reach Atlantis—there's no hurry, another day won't hurt. You'll be better then and go back into the sea to rejoin your tribe. . . ."

The dolphin knew that there was something he desperately wanted to tell the man in the conical hat, but try as he might he couldn't quite think what it was. He instead told the man, "My flippers feel much better now." Again the man smiled at him and made the dolphin feel good, even though it was strange to have forgotten his own name . . . but he forgot even that when the woman caressed him again. She looked like . . . someone he knew. . .

That afternoon the elderly man in the conical hat, who seemed to be the ship's doctor, came again by Conan's tank. To his relief, he now recalled who he was. Gently, the doctor felt his flippers and prodded his stomach. Then he whistled, "Much better now. We're going to transfer you to the recuperation tank along with all your friends. When we get into harbor we'll open the doors and off you go . . . but mind you, only to the dolphin harbor, until your flippers are properly mended."

Conan moved in reply, signalling pleasure, and the old man called up four strong young men to carry him. In the carrying sling Conan found that his dolphin head and tail were extended fore and aft, so as they moved him carefully through the ship he could look around. They carried him head first, and Conan saw, as they passed through the first doorway into the ship's human living quarters, a well-lighted space fitted with furniture made of what seemed at first to be ivory, until his dolphin senses told him it was the bones of whales who had died of old age in the depths of the ocean and whose bones had been brought to the Sea Kings by his brother dolphins for the past thousand years.

Conan then noticed that the carpets on the floors were very fine, and similar to Persian carpets, with designs much the same, except that some of the rugs had depictions of the same kind of ships as the one he was now in, while others showed dolphins, whales, and other sea mammals. He noticed humans, whom he took to be stewards, young men and women, setting out long tables on each side of the crew's cabin, with black shiny plates and eating utensils. He stared at the tableware hard as he passed, with his dolphin eyes, and realized that it was all made of dark, glassy volcanic rock—probably obsidian.

As his carriers, all handsome young fellows, waited for the hatch to the deck below to be opened, Conan stared in wonder at the huge copper plate which extended over twenty feet square over the forward bulkhead, quite close to where his head now was. He stared at it. He gasped. *A large map of the world had been beaten into it.* At first it was very strange, at first some of the coastlines were almost unrecognizable, but Conan the navigator soon recognized it for what it was. It was an *azimuthal equidistant projection of the world* centered on St. Paul's Rocks, and, strangest of all, not only were the coasts of North and South America, Europe, Asia, and Africa depicted with what appeared to him to be reasonable accuracy, but also the shapes of Greenland and Antarctica as they had recently been found to be *under their respective ice caps!*

He stared at the world map, devouring as much of the detail of it as a dolphin's mind can in a mere minute and a half, and especially he stared at the group of islands and islets in the very center of the projection. It extended over a great area of the central Atlantic, and was about five degrees—300 miles—wide from west to east, and three degrees—180 miles—wide from north to south. He saw that the main island was roughly a round shape, and that on the northeast side was a long inlet, curving down almost as far as the middle of the island. To the south of the inlet, the very finely worked relief map showed a high conical mountain culminating in two sharp peaks, and instinctively Conan knew that he was looking at an ancient, a very, very ancient, relief map of the world, and that *those two paps were the rocks of St. Peter and*

St. Paul. As he still stared at the copper map, and was carried down the hatchway to the deck below, he realized that what he had seen was one of the ancestors of the portolano maps in the Lisbon Maritime Museum.

Conan was carried through a series of compartments, each one brilliantly lit by the tubes of liquid light, some decorated with more copper plaques and plates, some with figures molded in gold and silver, others with statues and carvings of animals and fish, in obsidian, amber, and whalebone, some with crystal tanks that were alive with fish of different types, and some that were plant nurseries, in which many varieties of young trees and vegetables grew in long troughs bathed by another form of golden liquid light, like sunlight. They passed through a dozen of these "inside greenhouses" and then through compartments that, although they contained many different kinds of animals, some free, some of the wilder ones in cages, were nevertheless kept spotlessly clean by their chimpanzee attendants, all of whom saluted Conan as he was carried past them in his sling.

The youths carried him down through yet another deck hatch to the lowest spaces in the ship. Even there all was light and clean. They passed along gangways which projected above tanks full of edible fish in water a dozen feet deep, they passed cod and mackerel and herring . . . and finally through a door that led to the mammals' tank. There his four attendants all softly patted Conan on the head and gently slid him into the water.

Conan soon found that the tank contained eight bottle-nosed dolphins, like him, three porpoises, and eight Weddel seals who had, the other dolphins told him, been with the ship since she had visited the Antarctic some months before.

"Ship in far south?" Conan whistled.

"Usual thing men do on Man's vessels . . . exploring . . . trading with Ee-en men . . . finding fish shoals, mapping coasts, finding good anchorages . . ." an old dolphin replied.

"Why?" Conan asked, rather precociously the old dolphin thought.

"Has nobody told Aye-ee? . . . Sea Kings already know Atlantis . . . soon slide into sea . . . gravity experiment . . . misfired. Soon waters rise again."

"Sailing to south, north, all over world?" asked Conan of the old dolphin, as he cynically wondered to himself in his Scottish way if any of the kind, smiling men and women on board had been involved in the experiment that had led to the coming world-shaking catastrophe.

"Men look for new home."

"Where Sea Kings new home?" Conan whistled.

"Sea Kings decided on inland sea away in northeast from Atlantis far eastern end; big island, much copper. Sea Kings move everything that Sea Kings can in next few months, before ridge under Atlantis slides under next ocean bottom-plate and whole land sinks to bottom of sea."

"Atlantis?"

"Of course Atlantis . . . where Aye-ee think Aye-ee is . . . Ee-en?"

Conan was silent for a few seconds while his brain digested the information just passed to it. Then he signalled, "But . . . but why Sea Kings carry different birds . . . fishes . . . mammals?"

The old dolphin looked at him as if to give a deep sigh. "Sea Kings collect different life specimens wherever Sea Kings go, and bring back to Atlantis . . . find out all about creatures . . . decide which of creatures shall go to Sea Kings' new home in Island of Copper in inland sea."

"We go to Island of Copper, too?"

"Where has Aye-ee been that Aye-ee asks such silly questions!" exclaimed the old dolphin testily. Then repenting, he explained. "Of course, Aye-ee had an accident. No, dolphins escort Sea Kings only to western end of inland sea . . . dolphins go no further, lest dolphins presence upset natural balance of life around those waters. But Sea Kings make promise, that if dolphins keep treaty of friendship, assistance with Sea Kings, Sea Kings will erect temple to Eer-ee, dolphin god, in Sea Kings' new home."

"Where is ship going?" asked Conan, looking around him.

"Ship on way Atlantis with two others Aye-ee saw, from voyage to land of rivers on western side of North Atlantic. Sea Kings traded fish, clothing, flint . . . obsidian tools with red men who live . . . hunt . . . fish in that land. Ship has been far upstream in mighty rivers, and has sailed through five big fresh water lakes . . . down big river of rains, all way back to salt water sea in . . . south."

"Men in land of rivers?"

"Many, men sang . . . danced . . . so did Sea Kings . . . they loved each other, like brothers . . . like dolphins."

"No war . . . no fighting?"

"The three ships . . . attacked by fierce men in southern salt sea, Oo-ee-ah sent killer whales . . . rip out bows of war canoes, and dolphins carried savages back to shore, to reflect on savages' lesson . . . but whether good or not dolphins not know. Attacks regular in those waters . . . in many men, not their nature to absorb good lesson . . . and if Man does, his children forget it . . . except for Sea Kings."

"Of course."

"Sea Kings . . . let Aye-ee out of tank," continued the old dolphin "whenever Aye-ee wishes, but best if Aye-ee stays until light signal tells ships land . . . sighted. Aye-ee might even stay in tank a little longer . . . in case Aye-ee's flippers not healed well. No point in Aye-ee getting out in sea . . . signalling for help again almost immediately."

"Aye-ee supposes not."

"Anyway, nothing to see but ships, and Aye-ee must have seen ships many times before."

"Yes."

The old dolphin suddenly spun round to face the doorway. The doorway slid open to reveal a water lock, inside which were crammed a whole half of a shoal of bonito. "Dinnertime," said the old dolphin. Then he said to Conan, "Get in fast and eat, before those greedy porpoise and killer whales are among fish." Almost immediately, like a bullet, the old dolphin was across the tank and among the bonito, grabbing, crushing, and swallowing for all he was worth, and Conan followed him, just as hungrily, just as quickly, and just as casually, and ate his fill of raw fish before the lights dimmed to tell them it was nighttime.

Conan slept that night in the tank with the other Cetacea and the seals, and took his turn as night guard along with the rest. But the other sea mammals were too old, too experienced, not to be always conscious of their breathing, and the only one who had his sex organs delicately scratched to make his tail flail violently downward and send him to the surface was Conan, and that about a half-dozen times.

The lights slowly brightened as dawn occurred outside the ship, and after a breakfast of raw shrimp, the lights suddenly flickered.

The old dolphin turned to Conan. "The guess was good. An hour after daybreak—ship's in sight of Atlantis! Wait a while before Aye-ee leaves the tank. It will save Aye-ee much energy if Aye-ee waits until ship's a few miles from port inlet . . . you youngsters always frisky and eager, but Aye-ee remember Aye-ee's flippers . . . not good strain them too much yet."

So Conan impatiently waited an hour, then, unable to restrain himself any longer, he swam over to the tank door and tapped it sharply with his beak. Silently, the water lock opened, admitting him to a compartment along the ship's side about twenty feet long and ten feet wide, at the far end of which was another door, this one leading to the undersea world outside the hull of the ship. Conan waited until the door behind his tail closed and the door in front of him opened. Then he thrust himself out into the green world of water rushing past the ship, twisted, and hurtled at twenty knots for the top of the sea and the open air.

Conan's hurl projected him ten feet above the sea, and, before he splashed down again, his quick dolphin eyes took in all the scene around him, all 360 degrees around him. He saw the ship's white sides, her spotless wooden decks, her flower-decorated deckhouses, the palms and beeches, firs and oaks which grew along her decks. He saw brightly clad crewmen, the women graceful and lithe, the young men strong and of pleasant demeanor, the older men husky, bearded, and kindly looking, all working to the sweet music of harps, flutes, and drums as the wind played on the purple panels of the sails and made itself sweet music as it passed through them. And Conan looked over at the other ships, both with their sails turned toward the wind, both with their airfoils quivering as they grabbed the breeze and passed it over their surfaces, both with lilting music drifting over from their decks, in time to the tune played in the biggest ship, and both with brave, long pennants of blue and gold streaming out from the tops of their masts.

The green sea below him when he dived was, he saw, alive with tropical fish of radiant hues: yellow jack, golden goatfish, scarlet and gold butterfly fish, blood-red and blue gobies, duck-egg-blue parrot fish, deep bronze cobia and batfish, green and black spotted flying gurnard, scarlet hogfish, ocher and green cowfish, deep blue trunkfish, and thousands upon thousands of darting rainbow-colored angelfish.

When Conan reached the shallower water nearer the coast, where daylight penetrated down to the seabed, he now saw the colors of the shapes he had previously only beamed with his sonar; deep bronze tethiya, ivory aphrocallistes, golden *Grantia*, a hundred different colored zoophytes, and red, gold, and white corals, *Corallium*, astrangia, *Millepora*, and organ pipelike extroprocts waving in the currents; *Bugula*, a delicate fountain of fronds, and *Tubulipora*.

The seabed was the display table, too, of a hundred different kinds of shells: razor clam, long-horned Scaphopoda, azure sea snails—delicately spotted olive shells, golden-green chitons, spirally wentletraps, great golden cowries up to two feet long, leopard-color volutes, deep black abalones, thorny oysters, and the lovely yellow-to-gold-to-brown purple tellin bivalves.

There were fragile-looking beige gulfweed, the dark green, broad, heavy fronds of laminaria, brilliant emerald sea lettuce, red, gold, and amber fucus and algae weed, beautiful orange carrageen, puce Ceylon moss, and rich bladder kelp. There were seaweeds from every clime. The whole of the Atlantis sea bottom was one great glorious garden of color everywhere.

In the blue sky there glided great black and white hooked-beaked birds which Conan at first did not recognize—until he realized they were long-extinct great auks. There were also black guillemots, double-crested cormorants, gray shearwaters, terns, eider ducks, mallard with their emerald-sheened heads, garnets and gulls, and frigate birds—stark white crucifixes hovering as if pinned to the azure field of heaven, and above all of them, high, high in the azure field of heavens, gliding motionlessly, the wide-wing-spreaded albatross, monarch of the ocean skies.

Conan, as he leapt in between swift dives, glanced fleetingly ahead . . . and flicked his tail flukes in involuntary wonder as a beautiful green, blue, brown, gold, and silver land rose before him steeply from the shining ceruleum of the heaving, breathing ocean and an elegant pearl ivory line of clean sandy beaches.

As he flailed and thrust, rose and hurtled, leapt and rolled, dived and twisted, the handsome land before him rose up, up, through the beryl green of palm-tree glades and the bice-emerald of tropical plantations, up, up through meadows and pastures of celadon and chartreuse, up, up through the off-white citron and gold of cotton and cornfields, on up past the almonds, ochers, sables, and cobalts of high barren rocks, on up and up to two exquisitely tiny pinnacles atop an ivory white snow-covered peak reflecting shining silver from the noonday sun into the cobalt blue of the sky which hung above all, a silent benediction.

Conan raced toward the myrtle hills at thirty knots, with all his power. After ten minutes of full-speed flailing, he remembered his sore flippers, and slowed down. As he did so, he looked again at the coast of the lovely land, and a beauteous white-gleaming city of tall, shining buildings, as lovely as a bride, stepped out from that fair green shore to meet his longing eyes.

Conan, with some other younger dolphins, raced on and on ahead of the fleet, straight into the harbor entrance, which was dominated by a five-hundred-foot-high bronze monument of two leaping dolphins, each with its chest on the other's shoulder. Between the two great bronze tails was space and height more than enough for four ships together to sail into and out of the harbor. The sea walls were of light-colored stone, and the whole two-mile lengths of each arm curving out into the sea were carved with high-relief images of leaping and diving dolphins.

Inside the harbor, the city-quay was almost two miles long and was also carved with dolphins, but in low relief. Against this long quay was moored a whole fleet of ships, all very similar to the one that had housed Conan for two days. Conan as he swam swiftly across the harbor with the other dolphins, all of them leaping and diving as they shot through the clear blue harbor water, counted with his fast dolphin's eyes and brain six hundred masts, all with purple sails on them, all with the sails at the same angle to the wind, all with their slats wide open.

The two hundred ocean ships were moored three deep, and through the spaces between their bows Conan could see the quay was crowded with people, all with boxes and bales of belongings, and he could see that many people had already boarded some of the ships and were chanting songs of farewell as their ships slowly moved away from the quay. Conan saw that all the wide streets and avenues of white, golden-roofed villas leading up the slopes of the mountain from the seafront were empty of traffic and people, and he realized that he was watching part of an epic—the evacuation of Atlantis.

After they had made three swift circuits of the harbor, the young dolphins, with Conan among them, raced out again through the older dolphins at the entrance, past the slowly moving ships crowded with sadly singing people. They sped round the headland north of the city and into an inlet with an entrance as narrow, it seemed to him, as a dolphin's throat. They rounded the bend—and there was the blue sailboat with her flapping genoa sail and the sheet-line in the water, dangling over the side . . . most unseamanlike . . .

Conan raced and thrust his tail at full speed to leap right over the boat.

Conan landed with a thump, yet gently, on top of the heaped folds of mainsail in the cockpit well and came to for a few seconds, then with a great sigh, fell asleep again.

Conan woke in the shade of the awning on the morning of Tuesday, May fifth. At first he was too groggy and thirsty to look around him, to see how the awning always shaded him. His eyes were too sore and blinded by the almost three days of glare and salt to see clearly the smooth dome of rock only yards away from *Josephine.* He was too tired, too weary, too utterly drained by his dolphin dream of Atlantis to worry about a small thing like a steering-gear pintle. He was almost too desiccated, weak, and exhausted to crawl down the companionway ladder and work the freshwater pump, and almost too thirsty to remember not to drink too much at a time—only one tin mug every ten minutes.

He stared through swollen eyes at his berth, slouched over to it, and threw himself down on it.

He slept for many hours until he woke and told himself he would repair the genoa jib sheet and the steering-gear pintle the next day, or when he could see better. Then he would set off again, with a fresh breeze, and catch up with the woman and the man ahead of her and be first around Good Hope . . . and win the bloody race for Ruth. . . . He fell asleep again.

Soon the only sounds were Conan's light snoring, the jiggle of the steel hanks on the forestay wires, the soft squeak of the mainsheet block, and the lapping of the waters around *Josephine*'s waterline and around the backs of the twenty dolphins who still faithfully guarded their charge.

The tape player had finally stopped only moments before three dolphins, one of them with a great white scar on his head, had leaped all together right across the boat and dropped Conan into the cockpit, but gently, onto the piled folds of the mainsail.

The only damage to Conan, after three days of rest, food, and fresh water had done their work, were severe sunburn, some blisters, a bruised rib, and very sore armpits, rubbed red and raw from being supported for almost forty hours by two thin, hard, but sensitive flippers, one under each arm.

Conan mailed his long letter to the writer of this tale with the rest of his mail—mainly to Ruth Fleming—by helicopter hoist at a point three-hundred miles east of Rio de Janeiro, in late May 1981. *Josephine* was then leading the whole race fleet.

Joe Morgan, in *Sir John Falstaff,* had retired from the race with a hernia a week before Conan posted the letter. *Ocean Pacer* and *Southern Star* had retired from the race days before that, when both vessels collided at a combined speed of twenty knots off Recife. The vessels sank, but their skipper-crews, John Tyler and Paddy Hunt, were both rescued by the Brazilian navy. After their rescue, John Tyler had to be restrained from attacking Hunt.

It is presumed that *Ocean Viking*'s radio has broken down. She has been sighted several times by different ships at different positions in the South Atlantic off the coast of Brazil, but she is lagging so far behind all the rest of the field that it is also presumed that Sven Larsen will retire from the race and put into Rio.

Now, as I write in early June 1981, *Josephine* leads Mary Chatterton's *Flagrante Delicto* by two hundred miles, having passed her during a northerly gale as both vessels crossed the Tropic of Capricorn five days before Conan posted his letter.

The closest competitor astern of Mary Chatterton was Jack Hanson on board *Sundance Kid,* three hundred miles astern of *Flagrante Delicto,* and he in turn was closely trailed by Peter the Pole in *Blytskwtska.*

All four of the remaining race competitors are now, as I write, running before the steady, strong winds of the roaring forties, eastering for the Cape of Good Hope, which, Conan wrote, he hopes to clear by the end of June. He anticipates sailing the 17,000 miles from Good Hope to Cape Horn and around that notorious islet, by the end of November this year, and returning to Lisbon by the end of February 1982. Then, he writes, he will "swallow the hook" and head for the Philippine hills.

Conan wrote in his letter to me that he had just completed the careful mounting on a mahogany plaque of a highly polished obsidian knife which had mysteriously found its way into *Josephine*'s cockpit somewhere near St. Paul's Rocks, and a Polaroid picture of a huge bottlenosed dolphin with a livid white scar on his head, leaping and laughing, a merry twinkle in his eye, close to *Josephine*'s bow.

Epilog

They that go down to the sea in ships,
That do business in great waters;
These see the works of the Lord,
And his wonders of the deep.
For he commandeth, and raises the stormy wind,
Which lifteth up the waves thereof . . .

. . . He maketh the storm a calm,
So that the waves thereof are still.
Then they are glad because they be quiet;
So he brings them unto their desired haven.

From *Psalm 107*

Also available from Sheridan House

A Sea Vagabond's World by Bernard Moitessier

An authoritative guide to living the life of a Robinson Crusoe, written by a legendary sailor and ecologist. Explains clearly and concisely how to prepare for an extensive cruise, make the passage and attain self-sufficiency on a deserted atoll.

Titanic Survivor by Violet Jessop

The newly-discovered memoirs of a stewardess who survived both the *Titanic* and *Britannic* disasters. **"Many books on the subject are being published, but few can match this survivor's firsthand account in imparting a sense of immediacy....An important contribution to the growing body of Titanic literature."** *ALA Booklist*

Travellers on a Trade Wind by Marcia Pirie

The engaging true adventures of a couple who abandon their careers and sail off around the world in their home-built ketch, *Moongazer*. **"Whether you intend to sail across the Pacific or not, read this book. It is about faraway places and interesting characters, unexpected adventure and fabulous landfalls....perceptive and entertaining."** *Cruising*

Unlikely People by Reese Palley

A witty, irreverent tribute to the unique brand of people that gives up the shore and takes to the sea. From Tristan Jones to The Dumbest Sailor in the World, Palley has met them all and tells their stories with humor, charm and inimitable style.

Wanderer by Sterling Hayden

The inspiring autobiography of a Hollywood star who turned his back on society and set sail with his four children for the South Seas. **"His writing about the sea evokes echoes of Conrad and McFee, of London and Galsworthy....Beautifully done."** *Los Angeles Times*

www.sheridanhouse.com